SUDDEN

FICTION

LATINO

SUDDEN
FICTION
LATINO

Short-Short Stories from
the United States and Latin America

EDITED BY

Robert Shapard
James Thomas
and Ray Gonzalez

INTRODUCTION BY Luisa Valenzuela

W. W. NORTON & COMPANY   NEW YORK LONDON

Copyright © 2010 by Robert Shapard, James Thomas, and Ray Gonzalez
Introduction copyright © 2010 by Luisa Valenzuela

For information about special discounts for bulk purchases, please contact
W. W. Norton Special Sales at specialsales@wwnorton.com or 800-233-4830

Manufacturing by Lakeside Book Company
Book design by Brooke Koven
Production manager: Devon Zahn

Library of Congress Cataloging-in-Publication Data

Sudden fiction Latino : short-short stories from the United States
and Latin America / edited by Robert Shapard, James Thomas,
and Ray Gonzalez ; introduction by Luisa Valenzuela. — 1st ed.
p. cm.
Includes bibliographical references.
ISBN 978-0-393-33645-0 (pbk.)
1. Hispanic Americans—Literary collections.
2. American literature—Hispanic American authors.
3. Short stories, Latin American. 4. Short stories, American.
I. Shapard, Robert, date. II. Thomas, James, date. III. Gonzalez, Ray.
PS508.H57S844 2009
813'.0108868073—dc22

2009037087

W. W. Norton & Company, Inc.
500 Fifth Avenue, New York, N.Y. 10110
www.wwnorton.com

W. W. Norton & Company Ltd.
15 Carlisle Street, London W1D 3BS

1 2 3 4 5 6 7 8 9 0

CONTENTS

CONTENTS

7

CONTENTS

EDITORS' NOTE

For years we loved Latin American short-short stories. We found them almost by accident in books and journals where we were seeking American stories for our *Sudden Fiction* and *Flash Fiction* anthologies. Thanks to the excellence of the translators, we were learning that great short-short stories can come from any part of the world, and that nowhere in the world are they more brilliant or popular than in Latin America. Naturally, we wanted to bring some of this writing to our readers as soon as we could. Because of our success with an earlier volume, *Sudden Fiction International*, which brought U.S. stories together with translations, we decided to use the format again; it also seemed a good idea, this time, to make the U.S. side Latino, because we had seen the work of so many wonderful veteran and young Latino writers on the rise here.

However, we worried that the focus might be too wide, too epic. After all, it spanned not only all of the United States but all of Spanish-speaking Latin America. We asked Ray Gonzalez what he thought of the idea. He said it had never been done. Yet he was enthusiastic, so we were encouraged to try, if he would agree to join us.

Together we plotted a search: we would seek the best stories, regardless of type or topic, would favor recent works, leaving room for a few modern classics, and, of course, most important of all, would look for stories that were very short. But exactly *how short?* As short-short fiction has continued to grow in popularity world-wide, its categories have proliferated. *Micros* (stories sometimes less than one hundred words long) are popular in Latin America, but so are great stories of a more traditional *short-short story* length (several pages long). Would such different sizes work in the same book? The in-between length, *flash fiction,* popular in the United States, is considered by some to be its own category, therefore more properly consigned to its own book. We debated. We reread. And we decided not to worry about sub-subgenres. We liked them all. We chose *Sudden Fiction* for a title because the first books in that series were wide umbrellas covering anything (as long as it was very short).

Then we embarked on a yearlong search through bookstores, libraries, blogs, and zines. We circulated discoveries among our-selves, argued merits, and made selections. The stack indeed grew widely various. Would it hold together? Ray Gonzalez considered what it all meant: "This is a historic gathering of writers, because the U.S. Latinos are writers who have never forgotten their ancestral roots. By placing them alongside Latin Americans, we are showing how the short-short form transcends borders and that Latin Ameri-can literature's influence continues, even as Latinos create their own literary traditions."

We also thought these short-short stories, as a group—whether Latin American or just plain American—were the best we had ever collected.

Finally we had enough stories to send to Luisa Valenzuela, in our eyes the best person in the world to write an introduction, as one of Latin America's foremost authors in not only the novel but every length of story, including micros. Where Ray Gonzalez found connections between Latino and Latin American writings, she found oppositions. For her the mix was surprising, in terms of lengths, language, and images of the world. Yet she glimpsed among the paradoxes of the collection a common narrative line, and was inspired—or rather challenged—by Julio Ortega's story "Migrations" to write her introduction in English, rather than Spanish to be translated.

"Migrations" deals with translation, memory, suffering, and triumph, and the discovery of a new language that is "not simply a mix of Spanish and English but . . . the language of the first inhabitants of our new century." We could think of no more appropriate story to serve as a comment on the collection, and to honor, by placing it as an epilogue.

WE ARE grateful for the help, above all, of the late Carol Houck Smith, who nurtured this *Sudden Fiction* and *Flash Fiction* series; and Amy Cherry, at W. W. Norton, for guiding us through this book with Denise Scarfi; Nat Sobel, our steadfast agent; Revé Shapard, as always an editor's editor; Margaret Bentley, who read with such insight and good judgment; and Mercedes Fernández Beschtedt, who invited us to address the V Congreso Internacional de Minificción 2008, in Argentina, where we learned that the Spanish-speaking world leads the way with literary and theoretical discourse in micro and mini fiction.

Luisa Valenzuela

INTRODUCTION:
A SMUGGLER'S SACK

I have before my eyes a twenty-year-old newspaper clipping from San Diego, California. The photo, taken on the beach at the frontier, shows a priest with his feet practically in the water blessing a marriage across the link fence. She is American and stands on her side of the fence, dressed as a perfect bride; he is Mexican, on his side, also in white. All three are barefooted, of course, and when the ceremony is over the couple will kiss precisely at the border. It is a real wedding, a performance, a statement, and it is a short-short story that I associate directly with the present anthology. Now, standing between the United States and Mexico, there is a wall, which we hope will come down as soon as possible, and this volume represents, for starters, one way of breaching the separation.

The bride in the photo is Emily Hicks, author of *Border Writ-*

ing: The Multidimensional Text; the groom is Guillermo Gómez-Peña, a well-known artist dedicated to the theme of the frontier. Their marriage is over but the symbol remains. As is usual in any good short-short story, what is left out of the scene is what counts, what will reverberate in the mind of the reader.

You have in your hands a selection of very special short-short stories, both Latin American and Latino. What a name, *Latino*!: the taxonomy of the U.S.A. absorbing and at the same time rejecting its immigrants, as if they belong to Nowhereland; the perfect contraction of language, suggesting the pride of those who insist on being called so and their implicit exclusion by those who use the term as a label. *Chicanos, Nuyoricans*, now *Latinos*. "Cultural smugglers," Emily Hicks calls the whole lot of us, those who in the north are catalogued as *Hispanics*. Which is good, of course. What else would a writer choose to be?

We have here a sackful of smuggled pieces, written either in Spanish (Latin American stories) or in English by authors of Latin American descent (Latino stories). The unusual, vital, surprising mix in many ways abolishes the wall of separation without totally blending, maintaining each group's idiosyncratic personality.

That's why now, in Argentina, I choose to write this piece in English, crossing borders, meeting Julio Ortega's challenge of writing in a language one wasn't born to. Why not, if in many communities in southern parts of the United States the American national anthem is sung in Spanish? Ortega's story, eloquently titled "Migrations," a blend in which reflections on translation and poetry come together, appears to me as an emblem of the collection.

At the other end of the spectrum we have a classic piece by Borges, his "Book of Sand," which likewise mirrors this or any other good anthology, virtually a *summa* of much that has been written, a précis not responding in this case to the horror of the incommensurable but to the joys of variety. The stories in this volume are so short that anywhere you choose to open it you stumble upon a new image of the world. It is like a basket full of delicious food, enticing. Some of these images are hot as chili peppers, others are sweet and sour, or decidedly acid, with a humor of their own.

You have to carry a light weight to be able to cross borders, real or symbolic. That's what the short-short story is all about, light and at the same time very rich in connotations, reverberations, implications, suggestions. All that and more. These are notions that were carefully taken into consideration by Robert Shapard, James Thomas, and Ray Gonzalez in their choice of stories. "First we want to find the most entertaining, meaningful, well-written, challenging intellectually and emotionally, and memorable ones," as they told me in a letter. "Second, we want variety, in kinds of stories and writers and sources. Third, we look at themes or topics, but only to make sure we are not unbalanced." The question of length was also given serious thought, and the decision was finally made to choose chiefly what the editors call the "longer" pieces, "of 2-3-4 pages rather than the ½ page that one might find in Monterroso or Galeano." That is to say, a concept more akin to traditional short-shorts than to our Hispanic notion of *microrrelato*, which is now considered a genre in its own right.

It is surprising, though, that the *extremely* short-short stories (one line, as in Monterroso's classic "El dinosaurio," or even no word at all, just a blank page, as in Guillermo Samperio's "Fantasma"), of which we have here bright examples by Ana María Shua, are paradoxically being cultivated mainly by authors who speak Spanish—such a baroque language as opposed to spartan English. It may be true that it was Hemingway who first established the modality of the six-word story with one he was very proud of: "For sale: baby shoes, never worn." (I, personally, would have written it in the singular: "baby *shoe* never worn," but of course there is always the choice of how eerie you want the implications to be.)

Following that trend, in November 2006 the journal *Wired* invited thirty distinguished English-language authors to follow Hemingway's path and concoct six-word stories, getting excellent results, but this success hasn't led to a new genre, as nanofiction became in our latitudes.

In any case, in the broader category of short-short fiction, the limits are very flexible. These same anthologists organized their *Flash Fiction* books with stories of 750 words max.

I USUALLY compare the novel to a mammal, be it wild as a tiger or tame as a cow; the short story to a bird or a fish; the microstory to an insect (iridescent in the best cases). So here we have a rich assortment of goodies like a shoal of fish with some flies thrown in for a better catch. And it is interesting to match the specimens of the north with those of the south (of the border). Proper Latino writers usually have their hearts in their old or their parents' old homeland, in that other language which they more or less abandoned by choice or by force. They have a distinct approach to fiction, made of nostalgia. Sandra Cisnero's *"Pilón"* is exemplary in this sense, for she speaks of her homesickness for a country "that doesn't exist anymore. That never existed. A country I invented. Like all emigrants caught between here and there."

An invented country, like Alicia Rodríguez's "Bisbee," a place that "is not there." Vignettes of melancholy, *costumbrismo*, stories with soul, such are most of the stories written in English by authors of Hispanic origin.

They arise from a sense of obliterating differences, for example in the first paragraph of Fernando Benavidez, Jr.'s "Montezuma, My Revolver," where it is "as if there was no border between us and them, no fence or armed guards, no difference between the U.S. and Mexico."

The transition is made in Carmen Naranjo's poetic story,

"When New Flowers Bloomed." From a tranquil town lost in the mountains "young people emigrated in search of work and a different life. They were drowning in the ravine and the slimness of the mountain." Then the miracle happens, and two newcomers, thanks to the love that grows between them, turn the town into a dream that will forever be missed once it is lost, a town where the inhabitants remain "inextricably bound by the haunting of a place they can never return to," says Antonio Farias in his own story, "Red Serpent Ceviche."

THIS ANTHOLOGY offers us the diverse faces of the moon, both visible and invisible, often opposed. So we may find both magic realism (García Márquez) and anti–magic realism (Rey Rosa). It comes as a surprise to discover that most Latin American writers in this book seem to dream less than the Latinos. Crude reality can hit them hard, as is the case with Brother Bartolomé Arrazola in Monterroso's "The Eclipse." And love can be devastating (see Bolaño) or it can spring from the most horrible and painful shared secret (Allende).

One way or the other, a common narrative line seems to surface in the reading of these very dissimilar short shorts—like the curves of a giant anaconda emerging from deep waters—perhaps because many of them have to do with books or writing (Borges, Díaz, Jaramillo Levi, Ortega, Shua's "Respect for Genres"), as well as oral tales (Leis, Saenz, Villanueva—and even tagging—Urrea). I would have liked to write a story myself responding to the energy derived from this collection, but one challenge is enough for the day. So I leave it to you, the reader, our accomplice. Short-short fiction allows for the joy of playing the elating game of estrangement and familiarity and creativity while we navigate worlds that will be enriched by our understanding.

SUDDEN FICTION LATINO

Luis Alberto Urrea

THE WHITE GIRL

2 Short was a tagger from down around 24th St. He hung
with the Locos de Veinte set, though he freelanced as much as he
banged. His tag was a cloudy blue/silver goth "II-SHT" and it went
out on freight trains and trucks all over the fucking place. His tag
was, like, sailing through Nebraska or some shit like that. Out
there, famous, large.

2 Short lived with his pops in that rundown house on W 20th.
That one with the black iron spears for a fence. The old timer feeds
shorties sometimes when they don't have anywhere to go—kids
like Lil Wino and Jetson. 2 Short's pops is a *veterano*. Been in jail
a few times, been on the street, knows what it's like. He'd like 2
Short to stay in school, but hey, what you gonna do? The *vatos* do
what they got to do.

2 Short sometimes hangs in the backyard. He's not some nature pussy or nothing, but he likes the yard. Likes the old orange tree. The nopal cactus his pops cuts up and fries with eggs. 2 Short studies shit like birds and butterflies, tries to get their shapes and their colors in his tag book. Hummingbirds.

Out behind their yard is that little scrapyard on 23rd. That one that takes up a block one way and about two blocks the other. Old, too. Cars in there been rusting out since '68. Gutiérrez, the old dude runs the place, he's been scrapping the same hulks forever. Chasing kids out of there with a BB gun. Ping! Right in the ass!

2 Short always had too much imagination. He was scared to death of Gutiérrez's little kingdom behind the fence. All's you could see was the big tractor G used to drag wrecks around. The black oily crane stuck up like the stinger of the monsters in the sci-fi movies on channel 10. *The Black Scorpion* and shit.

The fence was ten feet tall, slats. Had some discolored rubber stuff woven in, like pieces of lawn furniture or something. So 2 Short could only see little bits of the scary wrecks in there if he pressed his eye to the fence and squinted.

One day he just ran into the fence with his bike and one of those rotten old slats fell out and there it was—a passageway into the yard. He looked around, made sure Pops wasn't watching, listened to make sure G wasn't over there, and he slipped through.

Damn. There were wrecked cars piled on top of each other. It was eerie. Crumpled metal. Torn-off doors. Busted glass. He could see stars in the windshields where the heads had hit. Oh man—peeps died in here, Homes.

2 Short crept into musty dead cars and twisted the steering wheels.

He came to a crunched '71 Charger. The seats were twisted and the dash was ripped out. Was that blood on the old seat? Oh man. He ran his hand over the faded stain. BLOOD.

He found her bracelet under the seat. Her wrist must have been slender. It was a little gold chain with a little blue stone heart. He held it in his palm. Chick must have croaked right here.

He stared at the starred windshield. The way it was pushed out around the terrible cracks. Still brown. More blood. And then the hair.

Oh shit—there was hair in strands still stuck to the brown stains and the glass. Long blonde strands of hair. They moved in the breeze. He touched them. He pulled them free. He wrapped them around his finger.

That night, he rubbed the hairs over his lips. He couldn't sleep. He kept thinking of the white girl. She was dead. How was that possible? How could she be dead?

He held the bracelet against his face. He lay with the hair against his cheek.

When he went out to tag two nights later, 2 Short aborted his own name. Die Hard and Arab said, "Yo, what's wrong with you?"

But he only said, "The white girl."

"What white girl? Yo?"

But he stayed silent. He uncapped the blue. He stood in front of the train car. THE WHITE GIRL. He wrote. It went out to New York. He sent it out to Mexico, to Japan on a container ship. THE WHITE GIRL.

He wrote it and wrote it. He sent it out to the world. He prayed with his can. He could not stop.

THE WHITE GIRL.

THE WHITE GIRL.

THE WHITE GIRL.

Josefina Estrada

THE EXTRAVAGANT BEHAVIOR
OF THE NAKED WOMAN

The woman who walks naked through the streets of Santa María provokes astonishment in the children, delight in the men, and incredulity and anger in the women. She sits down at the corner of Sor Juana Inés de la Cruz and Sabino, next to the bicycle repair shop. The children come out of the two adjacent slums and cross the street to watch her as she sniffs glue from a bag, her only possession. She doesn't seem to care that she's naked, yet neither could you say that she'd made a conscious decision to display her dark, abundant flesh.

Even when she's sitting down you can tell she's a woman of vast stature. At shoulder level, her hair is a mass of tangles that contains balls of chewing gum, bits of earth, dust and fluff. The applause and whistles of the onlookers grow louder when she opens her legs and begins to scratch herself hard in the most impenetrable part of her being. At this point, the young men, who are always hanging around, can't suppress their laughter. Instinctively, as if fearing that at any moment they too might reveal their mysteries, they finger the flies of their trousers.

And when the woman lies down and turns her back on them, the onlookers begin throwing things at her. She takes a while to react, but they all know that as soon as she sits up, she'll get to her feet and chase her attackers. And the children will then be able to see that her breasts are not, in fact, stuck fast to her ample abdomen. Some of the smaller children go and tell their mothers that "the woman who wears no underpants or anything" is on the loose again. And their mothers forbid them to go back outside.

There was a period when she was seen by several women near where Aldama crosses Mina. Then for two years she prowled up and down Avenida Guerrero. She would go to sleep surrounded by a pile of clothes donated by well-meaning people, and which served her as both pillow and mattress. When she grew tired of her bundle of clothes, she would burn it using the same solvent she inhaled.

The huge, dark woman goes into building sites to wash. The glee of the workers reaches its height when she bends over to drink from the tap. They're beside themselves with excitement when she picks up handfuls of lime and powders her armpits. Any man bold enough to approach her has always been repelled by the ferocity of her insults. The women who live around Calle Sor Juana complain not about the exhibition she makes of herself but about the fact that she's freer than the men. Instead of putting an end to the extravagant behavior of this woman—which arouses lewd thoughts even in the most saintly of men—the police, they say, spend all their time arresting drunks.

Translated by Margaret Jull Costa

Andrea Saenz

EVERYONE'S ABUELO CAN'T HAVE RIDDEN WITH PANCHO VILLA

Mexicans are always making things up, Grandma Jefa told us the week before she died. Don't ever believe these family legends people have. It's like how white people like to say their great-grandmother was a Cherokee princess, but worse. Isn't that funny, she cackled, getting sidetracked. A Cherokee princess, *que menso*.

We were at El Dorado Park in Long Beach for a family party like always, the area with the barbecue pits and the good covered picnic tables that Aunt Silvia had paid a cousin $10 to sit on since 10:00 a.m. so another family wouldn't take them. It was someone's birthday, Emma's baby's first, not that he understood any of it. All the cousins were sitting drinking Sprites and eyeing the cake while Grandma Jefa held forth on the storytelling abilities of Mexicans. I was home for spring break and feeling pleasantly sleepy in the heat, my belly full of Aunt Marta's chili beans.

You take this old guy, Grandma Jefa says, waving a hand at Grandpa Lalo sitting in the sun. He rolls his eyes at her and tugs his cap down. Can't keep a story straight to save his life. When we were young he used to say that the Aguilars were 100 percent Spanish, Basque even, that's where we got the skinny nose and the long ears. Being from Spain was high-class back then, you know, *se creen la muy muy*. Then twenty years later everyone's saying Chicano this and Raza that and it's better to be *indígena* so now he's saying the Aguilars are half Hopi and the whole tribe came down to Mesilla, New Mexico, to dance at his father's funeral. *Ridículo, ¿qué no?*

Grandpa Lalo cranes his head up. *Qué dices de mi*, Jefita? he yells. What are you saying about me?

Ay, nothing, nothing, she yells back, and he shrugs and closes his eyes to the April warmth. Grandma Jefa turns back to us, black eyes sparkling through the soft tan folds of her face.

It's not just your *abuelo*, she says. Everyone's family is like that. Everyone's grandmother drank with Diego and Frida. Everyone's *tíos* were at the March on Washington and struck with César Chávez. She's counting the lies on her hand now, pointing at each of her thick fingers. Everyone's *tías* acted in Teatro Campesino and saw Bobby Kennedy get shot, and everyone's grandfather rode with Pancho Villa. Everyone's *abuelo* can't have ridden with Pancho Villa, *mijos*. The Mexican army would have seen them coming ten miles away!

Dad almost saw Bobby Kennedy get shot, says Ricky, Uncle Beto's son, who is sitting with his bored-looking fiancée, a girl with hoop earrings as big as jar lids.

And praise Jesus that he didn't, says Grandma Jefa, clutching her heart. I had a terrible, terrible dream the night before, and I told Beto he could not go to that rally because something bad was going to happen, and he was just mad as a wet cat because he was on one of the student committees and he would have followed Bobby Kennedy right through that back kitchen where it happened. Grandma Jefa shakes her head in horror. I said no, or, like Beto used to say, *nel*, Manuel, and he sat there watching it on TV and not talking to me until all of a sudden the shooting happened. And now I bet he's happy he didn't go and catch a stray bullet, you just ask him. She sits back, triumphant. Most of us have heard this story before, and I wonder if the other cousins are thinking what I am, which is that there's no reason Grandma and even Uncle Beto aren't making this whole thing up too. Once I start thinking that family histories are nothing more than drunken boasts and *corridos* passed off as truth, there's no end to it. The mirrors in the maze. My Borges professor should get his hands on Grandma Jefa.

Emma's baby starts crying, and Grandma Jefa takes him off Emma's lap and clucks at him. So you see, *mijos*, she says over the baby's round head, you just be careful about all the *cuentos* these old Mexicans tell you. The only things you can really believe are the Holy Bible and what you see with your own eyes. The baby sticks out his small tongue at all of us, to underscore this last point, and grins. The cousins all grin back.

The next Thursday, when I was back at school, she died, quickly and quietly. Heart attack. Grandpa Lalo heard her call for him in Spanish from the backyard, and by the time the paramedics showed up, she was gone, her eyes closed, her head resting on the newly cut grass. Mom called to tell me that everyone would understand if I didn't come to the funeral, because tickets to fly back on short notice were too expensive for us. I felt terrible. My roommate helped me call the airlines anyway, and Mom was right. We didn't have the money. It's okay, my mother said several times. Grandma was old and she lived her life. She'll know you wanted to go.

So I don't see Grandma Jefa's funeral, and have to get the story secondhand from my mother and my cousin Lola, Emma's sister. They tell me Aunt Marta sang real pretty, like she always does, and Grandpa Lalo held up better than anyone expected, just leaning on his cane a little more than usual. And my mother says Lola did a perfect job of reading the note I had sent as a sort of apology to the family and Grandma Jefa.

The last time I saw her, Grandma Jefa told us we should only believe the Bible and what we see with our own eyes. But the Bible says, blessed are those who have not seen, but yet believe! I'm not sure what to do.

In the end, I think we should err on the side of too much faith in people and too much faith in the stories that make up our history. None of us grandkids saw Josefa Aguilar Perez raise five kids and run a business, but I choose to believe the story that she did it with more style than anyone in Eas' Los. And right now, you can't see me to know that I miss Grandma and I miss the Aguilars, but I hope you'll believe it anyway. Los quiero mucho.

It's one in the morning in New York when I finally get off the phone with my family. I'm sitting in the dark feeling sorry for myself, watching the silhouettes of midtown from out our southern window.

Tell me something funny, I say to Lola. I feel so depressed about all of this.

Lola thinks for a moment. You know what Pancho Villa's last words were? she says. My mom told me today.

What?

He said, Don't let it end like this. Tell them I said something.

No.

I swear, girl, says Lola, and then she has to go, and again I have to release the slender string that holds me to my family. I put down the receiver and it's just me, and the thought of Grandma Jefa, whose last words I don't know.

I look out at the lights of this island, and hear in the sweep of taxis and trash trucks and subway cars the sound of Los Dorados cresting the hill on horseback, ancient rifles at the ready, the army of a thousand grandfathers. If any of this story is true, and some of it is not, it's that Jefa had something to say. That much we saw with our own eyes.

Enrique Jaramillo Levi

THE BOOK
WITHOUT COVERS

For Miguel Angel Flores, a young Mexican poet

I had just sold that book I found discarded among the ruins. Actually, only the covers were burned off. Every page still had the words more or less intact.

The old man in the shop on the corner bought it from me; he had all kinds of things there, dismembered and repulsive. I explained to him that Gustavo, a friend at the university, had assured me this was a strange novel, full of ambiguous scenes that allowed for a great number of interpretations. Gustavo said its ideas had to do with problems of witchcraft and since they were so well written they did really keep your attention alive. "Haven't you read it?" the old man wanted to know. "Oh, no," I said. "I am majoring in math and those things don't interest me at all." The old skinflint offered me eighty centavos for it, which I had no recourse but to accept.

I should say, though later on Gustavo would refuse to accept this, that I was forced to notice that a kind of deep fascination had been coming over Gustavo as he went through the pages. I didn't want to interrupt him and decided to wait to read it myself until after he was finished. Actually, something like a fear of reading any farther got into him, and he even told me the damn thing wasn't any good and I'd better just throw it out. But he refused to go into any detail; the only thing he remarked on was what I later told the old man, about the alleged witchcraft, which, according to Gustavo, was the product of a morbid, deluded mind. However, I was too lazy to start reading it; the only thing I recall about it then is having noticed that the book lacked any indication of when and where it was printed, or who its author was.

The curious thing is that it wasn't burned up in the fire, as happened with all the other books in the library. Apparently they still haven't been able to determine the reason for the catastrophe. When I arrived, the rubble was still smoldering, but the body of the poor devil who took care of the place at night had already been carried away. Someone remarked to me not long back that they had found the fellow in a seated position, as if he had been relaxing. This is the first time that anything unusual has ever happened in this boring town.

They had scarcely let me know that the shop on the corner was in flames when I had a strange foreboding. Just as happened months before, the only thing able to be salvaged was that damned book. They found the old man in the rear, stretched out on what remained of a cot, charred to a cinder. They assume that it was the result of an accident, although so far they haven't determined the exact cause.

The firemen were still trying to put out the fire when I got there. One of them leafed through the book while the others were arranging the hoses back on the fire truck. I assumed he was the fire chief and offered to buy the book from him. "Take it," he said with a weary face. "You can have it, I don't understand a thing." It was then that I felt a great need to become familiar with its mysterious content. My hands were trembling and in spite of all I could do it was impossible for me to keep my attention on that devastated place where not a single other curious onlooker had come. I did notice that the book, though a bit more scorched than the first time, continued to be perfectly legible.

You who are taking a brief, curious look at these timeless confessions—I am reading now in the solitude of my own room—which you will soon take for a gratuitously imaginative creation, you must get accustomed to the fact (since it is not simply an esoteric idea, as is usually thought) that everything that is going on here has already happened, it continues happening, and inevitably it will be relived again in every experience that favors a rereading. Each page is a small variation of the same phenomenon, just as you in some way have always been an alternative of some other person. This tardy discovery of the multiplicity of lives enclosed within your existence never ceases to be normal, nor that of the knowledge you are now acquiring about the simultaneity of moments one lives without knowing it. You are the character who will not long delay being touched by his exploits, just the same as he participates in every one of your acts. You will be able to recognize yourself when you meet yourself, when another reality imposes itself upon you and confronts you with what has always been going on.

Afterwards the reader will be made to feel (at least it made me think so of myself right away) that it is he himself who is living every obscure and apparently inevitable anecdote, until other individuals surface who in different circumstances continue being the ones who are reading, as if everything were happening outside the text. And thus, interminably, many lives that coexist are lived without ceasing to be as independent among themselves as they are in this life in which I am still reading and in another life wherein someone (I'm not sure if it is you, he, or I) reads that the fire is all around the one reading the sentence which it is already becoming impossible to get out of, since the flames are devouring the scream you will probably have to utter when you feel my flesh roasting which you know is yours and about which, despite the fact that no one is reading anymore because all the moments have been fused together, the most likely thing is that it is someone else's even though it is in us where the pain continues to be felt.

Translated by Leland H. Chambers

Junot Díaz

ALMA

You have a girlfriend named Alma, who has a long tender horse neck and a big Dominican ass that seems to exist in a fourth dimension beyond jeans. An ass that could drag the moon out of orbit. An ass she never liked until she met you. Ain't a day that passes that you don't want to press your face against that ass or bite the delicate sliding tendons of her neck. You love how she shivers when you bite, how she fights you with those arms that are so skinny they belong on an after-school special.

Alma is a Mason Gross student, one of those Sonic Youth, comic-book-reading alternatinas without whom you might never have lost your virginity. Grew up in Hoboken, part of the Latino community that got its heart burned out in the eighties, tenements turning to flame. Spent nearly every teenage day on the Lower

East Side, thought it would always be home, but then NYU and Columbia both said *nyet,* and she ended up even farther from the city than before. She is in a painting phase, and the people she paints are all the color of mold, look like they've just been dredged from the bottom of a lake. Her last painting was of you, slouching against the front door: only your frowning I-had-a-lousy-Third-World-childhood-and-all-I-got-was-this-attitude eyes recognizable. She did give you one huge forearm. *I told you I'd get the muscles in.* The past couple of weeks, now that the warm is here, Alma has abandoned black, started wearing these nothing dresses made out of what feels like tissue paper; it wouldn't take more than a strong wind to undress her. She says she does it for you: *I'm reclaiming my Dominican heritage* (which ain't a complete lie—she's even taking Spanish to better minister to your mom), and when you see her on the street, flaunting, flaunting, you know exactly what every nigger that walks by is thinking. You met at the weekly Latin parties at the DownUnder in New Brunswick. She never went to those parties, was dragged there by her high-school best friend, Patricia, who still listened to TKA, and this was how you got the chance to strike while, as your boys put it, the pussy was hot.

Alma is slender as a reed, you a steroid-addicted block; Alma loves driving, you books; Alma owns a Saturn (bought for her by her carpenter father, who speaks only English in the house), you have no points on your license; Alma's nails are too dirty for cooking, your spaghetti con pollo is the best in the land. You are so very different—she rolls her eyes every time you turn on the news and says she can't "stand" politics. She won't even call herself Hispanic. She brags to her girls that you're a "radical" and a real Dominican (even though on the Plátano Index you wouldn't rank, Alma being only the third Latina you've ever really dated). You brag to your boys that she has more albums than any of them do, that she says terrible white-girl things while you fuck. She's more adventurous in bed than any girl you've had; on your first date she asked you if you wanted to come on her tits or her face, and maybe during boy training you didn't get one of the memos but you were, like, umm, neither. And at least once a week she will kneel on the mattress before you and, with one hand pulling at her dark nipples, will play with herself, not letting you touch at all, fingers whisking the soft of her and her face looking desperately, furiously happy. She loves to talk while she's being dirty, too, will whisper, You like watching me, don't you, you like listening to me come, and when she finishes lets out this long, demolished groan and only then will she allow you to pull her into an embrace as she wipes her gummy fingers on your chest. This is me, she says.

Yes—it's an opposites-attract sort of thing, it's a great-sex sort of thing, it's a no-thinking sort of thing. It's wonderful! Wonderful! Until one June day Alma discovers that you are also fucking this beautiful freshman girl named Laxmi, discovers the fucking of Laxmi because she, Alma, the girlfriend, opens your journal and reads. (Oh, she had her suspicions.) She waits for you on the stoop, and when you pull up in her Saturn and notice the journal in her hand your heart plunges through you like a fat bandit through a hangman's trap. You take your time turning off the car. You are overwhelmed by a pelagic sadness. Sadness at being caught, at the incontrovertible knowledge that she will never forgive you. You stare at her incredible legs and between them, to that even more incredible *pópola* you've loved so inconstantly these past eight months. Only when she starts walking over in anger do you finally step out. You dance across the lawn, powered by the last fumes of your outrageous *sinvergüernzería*. Hey, *muñeca*, you say, prevaricating to the end. When she starts shrieking, you ask her, Darling, whatever is the matter? She calls you:

a cocksucker
a punk motherfucker
a fake-ass Dominican.

She claims:

you have a little penis
no penis
and worst of all that you like curried pussy.

(Which really is unfair, you try to say, since Laxmi is technically from Guyana, but Alma isn't listening.)

Instead of lowering your head and copping to it like a man, you pick up the journal as one might hold a baby's beshatted diaper, as one might pinch a recently be-nutted condom. You glance at the offending passages. Then you look at her and smile a smile your dissembling face will remember until the day you die. Baby, you say, baby, this is part of my novel.

This is how you lose her.

Ana María Shua

3 MICROSTORIES

CANNIBALS AND EXPLORERS

The cannibals dance around the explorers. The cannibals light the fire. The cannibals have their faces painted in three colors. The cannibals prefer the heart and brain, disdaining the tender flesh of the thighs and the leftover intestines. The cannibals consume those parts of the body they believe will instill in them the virtues they admire in their victims. The cannibals partake of their ritual banquet without pleasure or mercy. The cannibals don the explorers' clothes. The cannibals, once in London, deliver scholarly lectures on cannibals.

RESPECT FOR GENRES

A man wakes up next to a woman he doesn't recognize. In a thriller, this could be the result of alcohol, drugs, or a blow to the head. In a science fiction story, the man would eventually understand that he exists in a parallel universe. In an existentialist novel, the lack of recognition could simply be due to a feeling of alienation, of absurdity. In an experimental text, the mystery would go unsolved and the situation would be handled with the turn of a phrase. The editors become more and more demanding, and the man knows, with a sense of desperation, that if he doesn't manage to fit himself into a genre soon, he runs the risk of remaining painfully and forever unpublished.

THEOLOGIAN

In the seventh century A.D., a group of Bavarian theologians debates the sex of angels. Obviously, no one admits that women are capable of discussing theological matters; after all, back then it was doubtful they even had a soul. Nevertheless, one of them is a cleverly disguised woman. She asserts emphatically that angels must only be male. She knows, but doesn't disclose, that among them there will be cleverly disguised women.

Translated by Rhonda Dahl Buchanan

Stephen D. Gutierrez

CLOWNPANTS MOLINA

Clownpants Molina begs now outside the store in town. A lean figure no longer in clown pants but worn jeans and a workman's shirt blood-spattered and frayed.

"Got some change, man, so I can eat?"

"Sure, Johnny," you start to say, reaching behind you, shaky. You jumped him one time, you remember, three or four dudes from the neighborhood when he first moved in, nothing serious, just a little initiation welcoming him, wrestling him down to the ground and smothering him.

Stood back triumphantly and let him up. Slapped his back for him but still. Fuck. Punks.

"Anytime." And you press a buck into his palm and go off on your own, into your car parked at the curb and down the street, catching him in the rearview mirror moving in front of the store again, begging.

Small store with a sign out front: L&M Handimart. Local store. You're in the neighborhood seeing your mother. Picking up a soda on the way out.

"Clownpants Molina, man," you think, and remember the time he wore clown pants to school. Pink things with wide pockets sewn on to the front, a brass zipper shiny bright, and black belt loops.

"Kmart shoppers, under the blue light," you mocked along with all the rest into his ear, cupping your hands into a megaphone and, seeing the wide grin spread across his face, feeling good after all. He liked this. He didn't mind.

Clownpants Molina was almost a TJ, almost a wetback. Moved in straight from the barrio for a little better life. Caught on real fast. Hanging on the edges of your set but in.

A middle-school dandy. Got rid of the clown pants. Levi's. And flaming gypsy shirts and sparkling white teeth. Clownpants Molina was good-looking, bright, raising his hand in class to stump the teacher, smartass, breaking into that smile of his.

Inimitable. Special. Clownpants. But he dropped out of school in the ninth grade, cold. Bragged he didn't need this shit anymore. He was cooler then, spoke more English—he was pretty shy still—and wore his hair slicked back, *cholo* style. "Man, fuck school," he said. "I ain't learning nothing." Proved his point by writing some figures in the dirt.

Basic algebra. "What? Rather be making money, dude." Broke the stick in two and walked off down the railroad tracks, leaving you hanging. You and the guys standing around with nothing but your own grins and an empty bottle of wine, Clownpants Molina wiping his mouth as a last gesture, down the tracks.

He was still Clownpants Molina. When you'd see him, "Hey, Molina," and afterwards, "I saw Clownpants down by the tracks with those other dudes he hangs out with, *cholos.*" You shook your head.

Your friends shook their heads. You rued his departure. You missed him. Clownpants Molina the clown always giving you laughs. Kicked out of his house.

Bad years for him, Clownpants Molina drifting from pad to pad in the mean part of town, on the other side of the tracks, staying on the bedroom floors of friends whose parents finally kicked him out, too. Getting a chick pregnant, knocking her up, a handsome *chola* with a beauty mark on her chin, Raquel, who didn't put up with too much shit. She kicked him out. Everybody kicked him out.

Your set watched and told him, "Man, Johnny, get it together." But he didn't listen. He was listing now, lazy, walking around town with a tattoo on his back, Christ in his agony, on the cross, looking up to the sky for help, his father, you realized, absent.

"Molina, why don't you get a job, man?"

"I'm on a mission," he'd say, gold-toothed now, for the one knocked out. And wink and not let you know what the hell was going on.

Clownpants Molina was living in the duplexes by the worst factories in town, the soap factory with the two big pipes blackening your sky and the chicken factory that stunk real bad and sent feathers floating into the air that dropped into the front yards of the wetbacks sitting on their porches resting after a hard day's work. "Whew, man, it stinks around here," you said when you bicycled over as a kid, checking out the factories, weaving in the big parking lots toward the action, where it happened, the setup. Diesel trucks lined up at the side of the killing place.

Men standing on tall ladders pulled chickens out of the cramped cages and hung them upside down on the conveyer belt taking them inside in a quick efficient line of death.

Stunk awful. Blood. "Man, let's get out of here."

Clownpants Molina was taken in by a group of wetbacks. "His own people," you said to yourself, quickly, not as if you meant it, but as an old reminder of when he first showed up in town, wearing those clown pants, speaking that clown talk, "Hey, man, how you a-doing?" grinning, and then no more.

And that's where he was now, living. Panhandling on the side and mopping up the bloodstained floor at night. Moving in with different people when he needed to, always the sight of Clownpants Molina at red-burning dusk watering the front lawn of whatever shabby rental he stayed in, cigarette in hand, skinny, wasted, waving to you if you happened to drive by, as if this was his real life, happily home, not begging in front of the fucking store you used to hang out at as *chavalos*. Kids.

Clownpants Molina had gone down fast. First the drinking, you heard, like his old man, a tall, sunken, withdrawn man always riding him, barking out orders when you picked him up at his house the years he hung out with you cool guys, asking you to meet him on the corner but when he was late, caught slaving at the side of his house, pulling weeds, his old man standing over him, ordering him in Spanish, meanly.

Do it right. What are you, a girl? You caught that much.

And then the needle. How many years later? Clownpants Molina slipping like a clown falling on the floor under the big top, hanging with the bad dudes now, you knew, hardcore *vatos* from East Los who picked him up in a lowered Chevy and scowled if you said anything, "Hey, what's happening?" or "How's it going, man?" sniffing almost with those upturned noses, watching for Clownpants to come stepping down the porch, a Pendleton shirt draped over his arm serving as a hanger, with an abrupt nod for you, the boys, goofy now as you passed in a pack on the way to the store to score a six-pack or just sit on the wall for a couple of hours talking shit under the moonlight.

Clownpants Molina didn't say much. But he was cool. Always a friend, just not tight anymore. Involved in his own set away from yours, doing things, you heard, that were crazy and stupid.

Smoking dust. Shooting up. Killing.

"Naw, man, not Clownpants, man."

"Yeah, Clownpants, man, he shanked some dude in Rosemead. He was cruising with the *vatos* from Los. Got into it down there, he said, at the burger joint where Sangra hangs out. You don't want to fuck with those dudes."

"You don't want to fuck with Clownpants."

"You ever call him that, to his face?"

"No."

Silence. Clownpants. Seventh-grader in pink pants with wide pockets sewn on to the front, a brass zipper shiny bright, and black belt loops.

"Clownpants!"

"Hey, Clownpants!"

Vato standing outside the store, hitting you up for money. Still got that grin on his face you thought was gone. Humbled.

"Got some change, man, so I can eat?"

"Sure, Johnny," you say. Reaching for your wallet.

"Anytime." Whip out a dollar and give it to him, folded, neatly in his palm, "Sorry, man, it's all I got."

49

Virgilio Piñera

INSOMNIA

The man goes to bed early but he cannot fall asleep. He turns and tosses. He twists the sheets. He lights a cigarette. He reads a bit. He puts out the light again. But he cannot sleep. At three in the morning he gets up. He calls on his friend next door and confides in him that he cannot sleep. He asks for advice. The friend suggests he take a walk and maybe he will tire himself out—then he should drink a cup of linden tea and turn out the light. He does all these things but he does not manage to fall asleep. Again he gets up. This time he goes to see the doctor. As usual the doctor talks a good deal but in the end the man still cannot manage to sleep. At six in the morning he loads a revolver and blows out his brains. The man is dead but still he is unable to sleep. Insomnia is a very persistent thing.

Translated by Alberto Manguel

Alma Luz Villanueva

PEOPLE OF THE DOG

To the children of Mexico City

The young man, with the wind god clinging to his back, runs ahead of me. His entire body is tattooed with snakes, birds, and circles. They are strangely wonderful. Beautiful. They crawl, fly and spin up his powerful legs, to his groin, to his chest and back, and the wind god is strapped to his back like a baby. Is he his mother, I wonder, chasing him, knowing I will never catch him. I laugh, thinking how a wind god would be born from a man: a fart. Why would a god want to be a baby? Why does he choose the young man with the beautiful tattoos? Maybe he's safer with a man, I think. Women are weak. My mother was weak. She could no longer feed me, protect me from the new man who fed us all. When he took my food, she cried. When he hit me with his fists till I bled, she cried. When he threatened to kill me, she cried. Go to the city, you'll survive there, my mother said, so I came. I'm almost a man, I'm almost ten. I sleep with four other boys, two younger. The older boys torment us, raped the youngest, made him whimper all night, now he's shy and will not speak.

The young man, with the wind god clinging to his back, climbs into a boat and, kneeling, begins to paddle. I feel the water at my feet and smile at the freshness. I haven't bathed since my mother's house. The baby wind god smiles at me, upside down, his head thrown back. It must be uncomfortable and stupid to be a baby and have someone take you wherever they want to go, however they want to take you. But the wind god does look happy, like he trusts the young man, like he wants him to be his mother and carry him everywhere, so I jump into a boat and begin to paddle, following the smile of the baby wind god. The young man never looks at me, as though he doesn't even know I'm chasing him. Just the baby wind god knows I'm chasing him. I paddle so hard and fast, changing sides of the boat to make me go straight, that I'm covered with the sweet lake water. I'm not tired at all. If I was ever hungry, I don't remember. If I was ever thirsty, I don't remember. If I was ever hurt, I don't remember. If I was ever afraid, I don't remember. The young man's tattoos begin to crawl, fly and spin faster and faster, his skin seems to be dancing and the baby wind god looks at me and laughs. A fart, a fart, he says in baby talk, but all I smell is the sweet lake water. If I was ever afraid, I don't remember.

The young man, with the wind god clinging to his back, glides under a half-circle rainbow and when I follow him I'm covered with all the colors, only I have no tattoos, but it's better to be lots of colors than just naked with nothing on. His snakes, birds, and circles dance with color, but the baby wind god, even though he has hands and feet and a head, is beginning to look like a cloud. When he opens his mouth a small jagged piece of lightning shoots out and drops into the water. It sizzles and turns into a glowing shell. I grab it and put *it into my mouth; it tastes like light, I laugh out loud. If I ever felt pain, I don't remember.*

The young man, with the wind god clinging to his back, raises the paddle over his head and yells with joy like a song. There's land and a beautiful city. There are strong and fearless Indians everywhere and their women smile, bathing their children and washing their own long, black hair in the morning sun without fear or shame. They look at the young man—his dancing snakes of red and purple, his birds of blue and green, his spinning circles of yellow and orange—and lower their eyes with respect. I look at the beautiful city and it feels familiar, like Mexico City when I first saw it, before I entered it, before it ate me up. But this city feels like a long time ago when there were Indians everywhere, people that looked like me and my mother, not the Mexican who wants to kill me. I look at the baby wind god and ask, "Is this Mexico City long ago?" The baby wind god opens his mouth and an eagle flies out and lands on a cactus, stretching his huge wings, and turns his head from side to side and shits. I want to laugh, but the young man turns, for the first time, and looks at me. Only his face is naked, except for one small tattoo on his forehead that looks like the moon or sun. Sometimes it's the moon, sometimes it's the sun. One side of his face is gentle, the other side is fierce. He turns away from me and steps onto the shore. The young man holds his fingers in a circle, his hand high in the air. There are drums beating and the sounds of women crying, as though someone has died. The men gash their arms and legs so that blood runs out. The cactus that the eagle rests on blooms, full of soft, feathery flowers, and a snake sleeps under the cactus in the warm sun. The snakes and birds on the young man's body are still, so are the circles. He looks like stone. Then the baby wind god becomes a thin white cloud and passes through the young man's circled fingers. The thin white cloud comes to me and I breathe him in. If I am dead, I don't

remember. Quickly, I leap from my boat and I know what I must do.
I leap and cling onto Quetzalcoatl's back and I remember peace,
a clear, wide peace as big as the sky, as far as I can see and even
farther. Now I know we will go together to look for her, she who isn't
weak, she who feeds and protects us. I will remember Quetzalcoatl,
I will remember the wind god clinging to his back, I will remember
the baby wind god.
   I will remember birth.

THE WOMAN bends over the child's body, pushing his thick, black
hair from his forehead. The blankets that cover him are filthy. She
notes that his shoes are still on, stuffed with rags against the cold. A
tube of glue lies next to him, uncapped. There is no sign of blood,
no sign of struggle. His face looks innocent, terrible with peace and
the stillness of death. His face is without pain and she imagines a
kind of light surrounding him, but she straightens herself immediately. The woman is Mexican, but the Indian in her blood has
claimed her features.

The boy who'd come to her office was one of the boys they
fed and clothed when they came to the shelter, when the funds
were there. He'd asked her to come with him because his friend
wouldn't wake up. He said his friend had gone with a man and he'd
paid his friend with money and some pills. He tells her a younger
boy is missing and that he thinks the older boys have killed him.

Sometimes, the woman sighs, I think the dead ones are better
off than the living. The sigh is a mixture of sadness and anger.
There are no parents to contact, no relatives, no one to mourn this
child, and the next one and the next. Now, I'll go call the police
and they'll come and take the body and dispose of it like a dog.

The woman doesn't know that the ancient one, Quetzalcoatl,
came from a clan called the Chichimecs. People of the Dog.

The boy quickly probes the dead boy's pockets and takes the remaining pesos. The woman sees it but says nothing. Like a dog, she thinks, covering the dead boy's face with the filthy blanket. The seven-month fetus within her moves, with a leap, making her sigh loudly, disturbing the room with her sudden wind.

Gabriel García Márquez

LIGHT IS LIKE WATER

At Christmas the boys asked again for a rowboat.

"Okay," said their papa, "we'll buy it when we get back to Cartagena."

Totó, who was nine years old, and Joel, who was seven, were more determined than their parents believed.

"No," they said in chorus. "We need it here and now."

"To begin with," said their mother, "the only navigable water here is what comes out of the shower."

She and her husband were both right. Their house in Cartagena de Indias had a yard with a dock on the bay, and a shed that could hold two large yachts. Here in Madrid, on the other hand, they were crowded into a fifth-floor apartment at 47 Paseo de la Castellana. But in the end neither of them could refuse, because they had promised the children a rowboat complete with sextant and compass if they won their class prizes in elementary school, and they had. And so their papa bought everything and said nothing to his wife, who was more reluctant than he to pay gambling debts. It was a beautiful aluminum boat with a gold stripe at the waterline.

"The boat's in the garage," their papa announced at lunch. "The problem is, there's no way to bring it up in the elevator or by the stairs, and there's no more space available in the garage."

On the following Saturday afternoon, however, the boys invited their classmates to help bring the boat up the stairs, and they managed to carry it as far as the maid's room.

"Congratulations," said their papa. "Now what?"

"Now nothing," said the boys. "All we wanted was to have the boat in the room, and now it's there."

On Wednesday night, as they did every Wednesday, the parents went to the movies. The boys, lords and masters of the house, closed the doors and windows and broke the glowing bulb in one of the living room lamps. A jet of golden light as cool as water began to pour out of the broken bulb, and they let it run to a depth of almost three feet. Then they turned off the electricity, took out the rowboat, and navigated at will among the islands in the house.

This fabulous adventure was the result of a frivolous remark I made while taking part in a seminar on the poetry of household objects. Totó asked me why the light went on with just the touch of a switch, and I did not have the courage to think about it twice.

"Light is like water," I answered. "You turn the tap and out it comes."

And so they continued sailing every Wednesday night, learning how to use the sextant and the compass, until their parents came home from the movies and found them sleeping like angels on dry land. Months later, longing to go farther, they asked for complete skin-diving outfits: masks, fins, tanks, and compressed-air rifles.

"It's bad enough you've put a rowboat you can't use in the

maid's room," said their father. "To make it even worse, now you want diving equipment too."

"What if we win the Gold Gardenia Prize for the first semester?" said Joel.

"No," said their mother in alarm. "That's enough."

Their father reproached her for being intransigent.

"These kids don't win so much as a nail when it comes to doing what they're supposed to," she said, "but to get what they want they're capable of taking it all, even the teacher's chair."

In the end the parents did not say yes or no. But in July, Totó and Joel each won a Gold Gardenia and the public recognition of the headmaster. That same afternoon, without having to ask again, they found the diving outfits in their original packing in their bedroom. And so the following Wednesday, while their parents were at the movies seeing *Last Tango in Paris*, they filled the apartment to a depth of two fathoms, dove like tame sharks under the furniture, including the beds, and salvaged from the bottom of the light things that had been lost in darkness for years.

At the end-of-the-year awards ceremony, the brothers were acclaimed as examples for the entire school and received certificates of excellence. This time they did not have to ask for anything, because their parents asked them what they wanted. They were so reasonable that all they wanted was a party at home as a treat for their classmates.

Their papa, when he was alone with his wife, was radiant.

"It's a proof of their maturity," he said.

"From your lips to God's ear," said their mother.

The following Wednesday, while their parents were watching *The Battle of Algiers*, people walking along the Paseo de la Castellana saw a cascade of light falling from an old building hidden among the trees. It spilled over the balconies, poured in torrents down the façade, and rushed along the great avenue in a golden flood that lit the city all the way to the Guadarrama.

In response to the emergency, firemen forced the door on the fifth floor and found the apartment brimming with light all the way to the ceiling. The sofa and easy chairs covered in leopard skin were floating at different levels in the living room, among the bottles from the bar and the grand piano with its Manila shawl that fluttered half submerged like a golden manta ray. Household objects, in the fullness of their poetry, flew with their own wings through the kitchen sky. The marching-band instruments that the children used for dancing drifted among the bright-colored fish freed from their mother's aquarium, which were the only creatures alive and happy in the vast illuminated marsh. Everyone's tooth-brush floated in the bathroom, along with Papa's condoms and Mama's jars of creams and her spare bridge, and the television set from the master bedroom floated on its side, still tuned to the final episode of the midnight movie for adults only.

At the end of the hall, moving with the current and clutching the oars, with his mask on and only enough air to reach port, Totó sat in the stern of the boat, searching for the lighthouse, and Joel, floating in the prow, still looked for the North Star with the sextant, and floating through the entire house were their thirty-seven class-mates, eternalized in the moment of peeing into the pot of gerani-ums, singing the school song with the words changed to make fun of the headmaster, sneaking a glass of brandy from Papa's bottle. For they had turned on so many lights at the same time that the apartment had flooded, and two entire classes at the elementary school of Saint Julian the Hospitaller drowned on the fifth floor of 47 Paseo de la Castellana. In Madrid, Spain, a remote city of burning summers and icy winds, with no ocean or river, whose landbound indigenous population had never mastered the science of navigating on light.

Translated by Edith Grossman

Antonio Farias

RED SERPENT CEVICHE

He searches their faces trying to find his own. More different than alike, he thinks, as he continues to scan their features, letting the steady rumble of the #7 train mesh with his thoughts. He spies his father sitting at the other end of the train, his thoughts off somewhere, inhabiting a place Simon can no longer afford to follow.

We eat different cheeses, drink different liquor, speak different tongues—I crave ceviche while you cherish cuy, pero somos una gente? *My people were fishermen, we harvested an ocean before it*

Ceviche—also spelled seviche, Latin American coastal dish consisting of mixed seafood that is "cooked" in lemon juice. Cuy—an animal resembling a guinea pig and considered a delicacy in the Sierra Mountain region of Ecuador. *Pero somos una gente?*—but are we the same kind of people?

was sold to gringos—did you know that gringos are now Japanese? Diversity isn't all it's cracked up to be, tú sabes.

Mi gente son galleros, mi gente macheteros, brujos *healing an ancient wound? I travel 3,000 miles south as my mind navigates through ancient stories to find you. I write countless words to make you mine; take your photographs hoping they'll solve the riddle that tumbles in my head—*quién somos?

In the end, the nostalgia that haunts my dreams belongs to my father. Mi gente *are here among me now,* en el corazón. Un pueblo salpicado *with salsa, burritos,* mofongo, *and barrio dreams—*un pueblo *waiting for its sons and daughters to embrace it, even as they leave behind a broken heart.*

There, mornings grew thick with comfortable smells. The kitchen upstairs, with its firestone oven, was where I learned to eat. Still I smell the moist yucca bread, and the hypnotizing smell of coffee.

La Cabuya exists on no map, yet its people are firmly rooted in the land. They have cemeteries to prove it. It exists in the hearts of those who call it home, those who left thinking they could forget. Those like me, who claim it, pull it out of the past and dust it off. We need cuentos *and images of our own if we're ever going to feel secure enough to let go and make the future ours.*

Simon catches the brief stare of a fellow passenger, who quickly looks away.

You see longing in my eyes as we ride the #7, red serpent carrying us from one millennium to the next—acknowledge me, your brother, hermano, father, Mámak *to those yet to come.*

Mi gente son galleros, mi gente macheteros, brujos—my people raise roosters, my people use machetes, my people are shamans. Quién somos?—who are we? En el corazón—in my heart. Un pueblo salpicado—a village flavored. Mofongo—a dish consisting of mashed plantains. La Cabuya—a rural area in Ecuador located north of Bahía de Caráquez. Cuentos—stories. Hermano—brother. Mámak—Quechua word meaning "mother, originator of life."

The train pulls into Queensboro Plaza, where the mass of crayon people line the platform.

In this city, signs abound, overloading the senses and making it impossible to read them accurately. Sometimes there are strong warnings, signs whose meanings people have forgotten, leaving behind a tremor that can be felt but not explained. There are still a few who can read the pig's liver, interpret the movement of the waters, and look into the souls of broken men.

The brujo *was my compadre, my friend, he rescued himself from a life in a Guayaquil sweatshop in order to arrive just in time to help a dying child,* mi hermano. *If you call him* Pacha, *he'll smile and take you for someone who knew him in a past life. He once cured a* traficante *of a common cold and was proclaimed a miracle worker.*

"You see, mijo," *Pacha once said, "the local priest believed that liberation for* los pobres *could be found in this world, so now he sleeps with a bullet in his head."*

In Brooklyn basements, Florida swamps, California deserts, they fight roosters and go to jail, their families going hungry, as animal rights advocates hurry back behind their suburban walls. Here and there they are men entering the ring with roosters who have none of their ego problems. Majestic animals, they live and die so their masters can release their frustrations, messengers to the ancient guardians that still inhabit the hills, the jungle, the erupting Cordillera of the condor. They leave this world carrying the poison of rage so that the workers' machetes can sleep another night.

Simon looks over and traces out his father's features, letting his hand absently follow along the contours of his own face, as he won-

Guayaquil—major coastal city in Ecuador. Pacha—Quechua word meaning "place-time, Earth." Traficante—dealer. Mijo—colloquial term for "my son." Los pobres—the poor. Cordillera—a mountain range that runs from Colombia to Bolivia, its peaks in places extending above 20,000 feet.

ders what made it possible for that man, whose blood beats through his veins, to have let go of a past long enough to let the future take root. He wonders if he can ever put an end to his perpetual wandering, in order to live here, in the urban heart of a new people.

Mi nueva gente, he thinks, letting the words tumble as the train veers around a corner, about to go underground.

Memories well up and gently crawl into a comfortable position next to him, his father, the last remnant of a world without bridges.

Simon gets up, offering his seat to a pregnant woman who could pass for the sister he never had. He walks over toward his father, sure to surprise him, thinking there will be fewer and fewer opportunities to meet up with him like this, two men riding the red serpent into an unknown future, inextricably bound by the haunting of a place they can never return to.

Mi nueva gente—My new people.

Aída Bortnik

CELESTE'S HEART

Celeste went to a school that had two yards. In the front yard they held official ceremonies. In the back yard the Teacher made them stand in line, one behind the other at arm's distance, keeping the arm stretched out straight in front, the body's weight on both legs, and in silence. One whole hour. Once for two whole hours. All right, not hours. But two breaks passed, and the bell rang four times before they were allowed back into the classroom. And the girls from the other classes, who played and laughed during the first break as if nothing had happened, stopped playing during the second break. They stood with their backs to the wall and watched them. They watched the straight line, one behind the other at arm's length, in the middle of the school yard. And no one laughed.

And when the Teacher clapped her hands to indicate that the punishment was over, Celeste was the only one who didn't stretch, who didn't complain, who didn't rub her arm, who didn't march smartly back into the classroom. When they sat down, she stared quietly at the Teacher. She stared at her in the same way she used to stare at the new words on the blackboard, the ones whose meaning she didn't know, whose exact purpose she ignored.

That evening, as she was putting her younger brother to bed, he asked once again: "When am I going to go to school?" But that evening she didn't laugh, and she didn't think up an answer. She sat down and hugged him for a while, as she used to do every time she realized how little he was, how little he knew. And she hugged him harder because she suddenly imagined him in the middle of the school yard, with his arm stretched out measuring the distance, the body tense, feeling cold and angry and afraid, in a line in which all the others were as small as he was.

And the next time the Teacher got mad at the class, Celeste knew what she had to do.

She didn't lift her arm.

The Teacher repeated the order, looking at her somewhat surprised. But Celeste wouldn't lift her arm. The Teacher came up to her and asked her, almost with concern, what was the matter. And Celeste told her. She told her that afterward the arm hurt. And that they were all cold and afraid. And that one didn't go to school to be hurt, cold, and afraid.

Celeste couldn't hear herself, but she could see her Teacher's face as she spoke. And it seemed like a strange face, a terribly strange face. And her friends told her afterwards that she had spoken in a very loud voice, not shouting, just a very loud voice. Like when one recited a poem full of big words, standing on a platform, in the school's front yard. Like when one knows one is taking part in a solemn ceremony and important things are spoken of, things that happened a long time ago, but things one remembers because they made the world a better place to live than it was before.

And almost every girl in the class put down her arm. And they walked back into the classroom. And the Teacher wrote a note in red ink in Celeste's exercise book. And when her father asked her what she had done, and she told him, her father stood there staring at her for a long while, but as if he couldn't see her, as if he were staring at something inside her or beyond her. And then he smiled and signed the book without saying anything. And while she blotted his signature with blotting paper, he patted her head, very gently, as if Celeste's head were something very very fragile that a heavy hand could break.

That night Celeste couldn't sleep because of an odd feeling inside her. A feeling that had started when she had refused to lift her arm, standing with the others in the line, a feeling of something growing inside her breast. It burned a bit, but it wasn't painful. And she thought that if one's arms and legs and other parts of one's body grew, the things inside had to grow too. And yet legs and arms grow without one being aware, evenly and bit by bit. But the heart probably grows like this: by jumps. And she thought it seemed like a logical thing: the heart grows when one does something one hasn't done before, when one learns something one didn't know before, when one feels something different and better for the first time. And the odd sensation felt good. And she promised herself that her heart would keep growing. And growing. And growing.

Translated by Alberto Manguel

Dagoberto Gilb

SHOUT

He beat on the screen door. "Will somebody open this?!" Unlike most men, he didn't leave his hard hat in his truck, took it inside his home, and he had it in his hand. His body was dry now, at least it wasn't like it was two hours ago at work, when he wrung his T-shirt of sweat, made it drool between the fingers of his fist, he and his partner making as much of a joke out of it as they could. That's how hot it was, how humid, and it'd been like this, in the nineties and hundreds, for two weeks, and it'd been hot enough before that. All he could think about was unlacing his dirty boots, then peeling off those stinky socks, then the rest. He'd take a cold one into the shower. The second one. He'd down the first one right at the refrigerator. "Come on!" Three and four were to be appreciated, five was mellow, and six let him nap before bed.

"I didn't hear you," his wife said.

"Didn't *hear* me? How *couldn't* you hear me? And why's it locked anyways? When I get here I don't feel like waiting to come in. Why can't you leave the thing unlocked?"

"Why do you think?"

"Well don't let the baby open it. I want this door open when I get home." He carried on in Spanish, *hijos de* and *putas* and *madres* and *chingadas*. This was the only Spanish he used at home. He tossed the hard hat near the door, relieved to be inside, even though it was probably hotter than outside, even though she was acting mad. He took it that she'd been that way all day already.

Their children, three boys, were seven, four, and almost two, and they were, as should be expected, battling over something.

"Everybody shut up and be quiet!" he yelled. Of course that worsened the situation, because when he got mad he scared the baby, who immediately started crying.

"I'm so tired," he muttered.

She glared at him, the baby in her arms.

"You know sometimes I wish you were a man cuz I wouldn't let you get away with looks like that. I wouldn't take half the shit I take from you." He fell back into the wooden chair nobody sat in except him when he laced the high-top boots on, or off, as he already had. "You know how hot it was today? A hundred and five. It's unbelievable." He looked at her closely, deeply, which he didn't often do, especially this month. She was trying to settle down the baby and turned the TV on to distract the other two.

"It's too hard to breathe," he said to her. He walked barefooted for the beer and took out two. They were in the door tray of the freezer and almost frozen.

"So nothing happened today?" she asked. Already she wasn't mad at him. It was how she was, why they could get along.

"Nothing else was said. Maybe nothing's gonna happen. God knows this heat's making everybody act unnatural. But tomorrow's check day. If he's gonna get me most likely it'll be tomorrow." He finished a beer leaning against the tile near the kitchen sink, enjoying a peace that had settled into the apartment. The baby was content, the TV was on, the Armenians living an arm's reach away were chattering steadily, there was a radio on from an apartment in a building across from them, Mexican TV upstairs, pigeons, a dog, traffic noise, the huge city out there groaning its sound—all this silence in the apartment.

"There's other jobs," he said. "All of 'em end no matter what anyways."

It was a job neither of them wanted to end too soon. This year he'd been laid up for months after he fell and messed up his shoulder and back. He'd been drunk—a happy one that started after work—but he did it right there at his own front door, playing around. At the same time the duplex apartment they'd been living in for years had been sold and they had to move here. It was all they could get, all they were offered, since so few landlords wanted three children, boys no less, at a monthly rent they could afford. They were lucky to find it and it wasn't bad as places went, but they didn't like it much. They felt like they were starting out again, and that did not seem right. They'd talked this over since they'd moved in until it degenerated into talk about separation. And otherwise, in other details, it also wasn't the best year of their lives.

He showered in warm water, gradually turning the hot water down until it came out as cold as the summer allowed, letting the iced beer do the rest.

She was struggling getting dinner together, the boys were loud and complaining about being hungry, and well into the fifth beer, as he sat near the bright color and ever-happy tingle of the TV set, his back stiffening up, he snapped.

69

"Everybody has to shut up! I can't stand this today! I gotta relax some!"

She came back at him screaming too. "I can't stand *you!*"

He leaped. "You don't talk to me like that!"

She came right up to him. "You gonna hit me?!" she dared him.

The seven-year-old ran to his bed but the other two froze up, waiting for the tension to ease enough before their tears squeezed out.

"Get away from me," he said trying to contain himself. "You better get away from me right now. You know, just go home, go to your mother's, just go."

"*You* go! *You* get out! We're gonna stay!"

He looked through her, then slapped a wall, rocking what seemed like the whole building. "You don't know how close you are."

He wouldn't leave. He walked into the bedroom, then walked out, sweating. He went into the empty kitchen—they were all in the children's room, where there was much crying—and he took a plate and filled it with what she'd made and went in front of the tube and he clicked on a ball game, told himself to calm himself and let it all pass at least tonight, at least while the weather was like it was and while these other things were still bothering both of them, and then he popped the sixth beer. He wasn't going to fall asleep on the couch tonight.

Eventually his family came out, one by one peeking around a corner to see what he looked like. Then they ate in a whisper, even cutting loose here and there with a little giggle or gripe. Eventually the sun did set, though that did nothing to wash off the glue of heat.

And eventually the older boys felt comfortable enough to complain about bedtime. Only the baby cried—he was tired and wanted to sleep but couldn't because a cold had clogged his nose. Still, they were all trying to maintain the truce when from outside, a new voice came in: SHUT THAT FUCKING KID UP YOU FUCKING PEOPLE! HEY! SHUT THAT FUCKING KID UP OVER THERE!

It was like an explosion except that he flew toward it. He shook the window screen with his voice. "You fuck yourself, asshole! You stupid asshole, you shut your mouth!" He ran out the other way, out the screen door and around and under the heated stars. "Come on out here, mouth! Come out and say that to my face!" He squinted at all the windows around him, no idea where it came from. "So come on! Say it right now!" There was no taker, and he turned away, his blood still bright red.

When he came back inside, the children had gone to bed and she was lying down with the baby, who'd fallen asleep. He went back to the chair. The game ended, she came out, half-closing the door behind her, and went straight to their bed. He followed.

"I dunno," he said after some time. He'd been wearing shorts and nothing else since his shower, and it shouldn't have taken him so long, yet he just sat there on the bed. Finally he turned on the fan and it whirred, ticking as it pivoted left and right. "It doesn't do any good, but it's worse without it." He looked at her like he did earlier. "I'm kinda glad nobody came out. Afterwards I imagined some nut just shooting me, or a few guys coming. I'm getting too old for that shit."

She wasn't talking.

"So what did they say?" he asked her. "At the clinic?"

"Yes."

"Yes what?"

"That I am."

They both listened to the fan and to the mix of music from the Armenians and that TV upstairs.

"I would've never thought it could happen," he said. "That one time, and it wasn't even good."

"Maybe for you. I knew it then."

"You did?"

She rolled on her side.

"I'm sorry about all the yelling," he said.

"I was happy you went after that man. I always wanna do stuff like that."

He rolled to her.

"I'm too sticky. It's too hot."

"I have to. We do. It's been too long, and now it doesn't matter."

"It does matter," she said. "I love you."

"I'm sorry," he said, reaching over to touch her breast. "You know I'm sorry."

He took another shower afterward. A cold shower. His breath sputtered and noises hopped from his throat. He crawled into the bed naked, onto the sheet that seemed as hot as ever, and listened to outside, to that mournful Armenian music mixing with Spanish, and to the fan, and it had stilled him. It was joy, and it was so strange. She'd fallen asleep and so he resisted kissing her, telling her. He thought he should hold on to this as long as he could, until he heard the pitch of the freeway climb, telling him that dawn was near and it was almost time to go back to work.

Marco Denevi

THE LORD OF THE FLIES

The flies imagined their god. It was also a fly. The lord of the flies was a fly, now green, now black and gold, now pink, now white, now purple, an inconceivable fly, a beautiful fly, a monstrous fly, a terrible fly, a benevolent fly, a vengeful fly, a just fly, a youthful fly, but always a fly. Some embellished his size so that he was compared to an ox, others imagined him to be so small that you couldn't see him. In some religions, he was missing wings ("He flies," they argued, "but he doesn't need wings"), while in others he had infinite wings. Here it was said he had antennae like horns, and there that he had eyes that surrounded his entire head. For some he buzzed constantly, and for others he was mute, but he could communicate just the same. And for everyone, when flies died, he took them up to paradise. Paradise was a hunk of rotten meat, stinking and putrid, that souls of the dead flies could gnaw on for an eternity without devouring it; yes, this heavenly scrap of refuse would be constantly reborn and regenerated under the swarm of flies. For the good flies. Because there were also bad flies, and for them there was a hell. The hell for condemned flies was a place without excrement, without waste, trash, stink, without anything of anything; a place sparkling with cleanliness and illuminated by a bright white light; in other words, an ungodly place.

Translated by José Chaves

DAY AH DALLAS MARE TOES

Luna Calderón

DAY AH DALLAS MARE TOES

To Phil with love

My name is Río. Kids always say, "Like the Rio Grande?" And then crack up. I don't get what's so funny about that. Río, like Río J. Olivares. That's it.

When I was born, my name was Río Jefferson. That sounds weird but that's the name my mom gave me. Someday when I meet her, I'll ask her why she named me Río. I don't know where the Jefferson came from, 'cause she's Mexican, my bio logic mom is. My birth certificate says, Father's name: unknown, Mother's name: Marta Pérez, Baby's name: Río Jefferson. So when my dad adopted me, I got his last name. Now my name is Río Jefferson Olivares.

Uncle Jeff is the white guy whose picture Daddy keeps on the mantle. I made up this story about him. It's not for real, but I like it.

It's that my bio logic mom used to know Uncle Jeff, and that he was my blood father. Maybe Jeff is short for Jefferson. I keep thinking that Uncle Jeff and me have to be blood related. Ever since I was little, like before kindergarten, I heard whispering like wind in my ear. I finally figured out it was Uncle Jeff. See, when I'd be falling asleep at night, I'd see his face smiling and floating around. I've had zillions of dreams about him. He tells me stories and funny things, like you're so cute, and let's eat chocolate. Also sometimes serious things. Like what to do when I have a problem. It's like my very own TV show.

There was the time when Doug Nelson kept sitting behind me in reading group and pulling my ponytail. I hate when people mess with my hair, so I was thinking about how to get him back. Then, in my dream that night, Uncle Jeff showed up and said, "Río, sweetie, Doug likes you. That's why he's acting like that." I listened to Uncle Jeff. Didn't do anything to Doug. He was right. On Valentimes, Doug Nelson put a big chocolate heart in my Valentimes box. He didn't give one to anybody else. I kept staring at him, remembering what Uncle Jeff had said. He kept looking at his shoes. Then I stopped looking at him and just ate my chocolate heart. It was the good kind—no junk in the middle.

NEXT WEEK I have an oral presentation for social studies. It's pretty much like show-and-tell, except we're too old to call it that. Miss Wilson said that we had to build an altar for a deceased relative because it's Día de los Muertos next week. 'Cept she said, "Day Ah Dallas Mare Toes." Cici Ramírez and I cracked up, but not loud. We both pretend like we don't speak Spanish. But we do, and the way Miss Wilson said it was hecka stupid. When I got home, I saw Uncle Jeff on the mantle. I knew I had to make an altar for him. The next day I told Miss Wilson I didn't have any blood relatives. Told her I was choosing Uncle Jeff.

"Oh yes, well, you have an alternative family," she said. "It's okay to bend the rules." I don't like social studies. I don't like Miss Wilson that much. I don't get it why she's so into Day Ah Dallas Mare Toes. She's not Mexican or Latin or nothing, I mean anything. When she was talking about it, the other kids in my class were rolling their eyes and going, "Ooooh, I don't want to give food to a dead person, that's weird." I rolled my eyes too, just so they wouldn't think I'm strange, but I know about this stuff.

Aunty T, that's my Daddy's best friend, he calls her his sister. She takes me to a Día de los Muertos thing every year. There's music and Aztec dancing and a lot of altars. Some of them are cool. I asked Aunty T what the altars were for. To honor and respect the dead, she said. You put up pictures of dead people. Next to 'em you put flowers, their favorite food, stuff like that. She has an altar at her house with a lot of dead people. Uncle Jeff is one of them. One day I told her that I talked to him. She said she did too, like it was no big deal.

"We're not using a Ouija board. Are we doing it wrong?"

"Nah," she shook her head, "there's a lot of ways to communicate with those on the other side." That's what she calls dead people.

"I'm supposed to make an altar for Día de los Muertos. It's for Miss Wilson."

"What a great idea!" She was all excited.

"I don't like Miss Wilson."

"Sometimes people we don't like have good ideas."

I told her I didn't know anything about Uncle Jeff. Didn't know what to put on his altar. She told me a bunch of stuff. He was from Canada. The priests sent him here to the States. Uncle Jeff was a priest and so was Daddy. I wanted to know were they priests together? They weren't. They met after they left the priesthood. They left it 'cause they wanted to be openly gay.

"Couldn't they be openly gay priests?" I asked Aunty T.

"That's a whole other story," she said, and never told me why.

AUNTY T couldn't finish the story 'cause she had an appointment to get her nails done. I interrupted Dad from his reading even though I'm not supposed to. I knew he wouldn't care 'cause I needed to ask about homework. After Uncle Jeff decided to be openly gay, he went to social work school, and that's where he met Daddy and Aunty T. During that time, Daddy and Uncle Jeff were best friends. They lived together for a year. Uncle Jeff loved to clean and he was really nice, but after a while he got on Daddy's nerves.

"Why don't you move out from me? I get on your nerves practically every day," I wanted to know.

"This is different, I'm your father." Daddy's eyes got all big like the time I asked him if adopted fathers love their kids as much as blood fathers. I asked him if I could have some ice cream. He said yes. We didn't talk about it anymore.

LATER I asked Aunty T why Uncle Jeff got on Daddy's nerves. She looked kind of embarrassed. "It's no use keeping secrets." She told me the rest.

Uncle Jeff was in love with my Daddy. Same way Daddy loves his boyfriend John, and Doug Nelson loves me. But Daddy wasn't in love with Uncle Jeff. Just like I'm not in love with Doug. The difference is that Daddy liked Uncle Jeff like a friend. I don't like Doug like anything. I asked Aunty T if Uncle Jeff ever found another boyfriend. He didn't. He was sad about that. He wanted a boyfriend that looked like James Dean. He was always going on diets to lose weight so he could look better. It was hard 'cause he liked food a lot. Especially peanut butter and chocolate. Aunty T said Uncle Jeff was one of the nicest people she had ever met. She told me that one day he was standing on the street and he met this guy named Stephen. Stephen didn't have a place to live, 'cause he had run away from his mom in New Jersey. Uncle Jeff told him to come and stay at his house. Aunty T said she and Daddy were really mad at Uncle Jeff. They told him he was too nice. He could put himself in danger by inviting strangers to his house. But he didn't care. He did it anyway. Stephen got a job at a pizza place and slept on the couch. Until Uncle Jeff died.

Jeffery Robert De Angelo, that was his full name. He got run over by a car. On a Saturday. After breakfast. He had come over for pancakes with Aunty T and Daddy, then he went to buy a bed. A blue car hit him. He was crossing the street to get to the mattress store. Aunty T got tears in her eyes when she was telling me that part. I kind of felt like crying too. There was a big memorial service. I've never been to one. It's when they say nice things about the dead person right after they die. The room was really full. A lot of people came from Uncle Jeff's job. The ones that got there late had to stand up. For two hours, people said nice things about Uncle Jeff. Aunty T said Uncle Jeff was probably thrilled about that, wherever he was.

Stephen-the-pizza-guy didn't stand up to say anything, but the memorial service and the burial couldn't have happened without him. He was the one who paid for it. Everybody was really worried about where the money was coming from. You need a lot of stuff when someone dies. A casket, a grave, food for the party. Stuff like that. Morticia was charging $8,000 even and nobody had that much money. Everyone was worried. Then, all of a sudden, Stephen-the-pizza-guy walked out of Uncle Jeff's kitchen with a garbage bag that he kept in the freezer. It had $8,219 in it. He paid the bills and only had $219 left. After that, he took a bus to L.A. Aunty T said no one ever heard from Stephen-the-pizza-guy again.

I STARTED my altar. I'm using the Thanksgiving tablecloth. Daddy said I could. He even gave me some stuff to put on it. A red toothbrush, some toothpaste, and Irish Spring soap because Uncle Jeff brushed his teeth and washed his face like twenty times a day. I got a bag of Reese's Peanut Butter Cups, a postcard of James Dean, and a little sticker of a Canada flag. Daddy's letting me take the picture from the mantle to school on November first, the day of the oral report. Aunty T gave me a pack of Marlboro cigarettes. She said Uncle Jeff smoked like a chimney. Everybody used to say it wasn't good for him. But she's glad he smoked. He really loved his cigarettes. Anyway, it didn't make any difference 'cause he got hit by a car. When it's your time, it's your time.

I'm also making Uncle Jeff a card. On the outside it has a big red heart. On the inside it says "Dear Uncle Jeff, Happy Day Ah Dallas Mare Toes. Ha-ha. I love you very Much. Love Río." My handwriting isn't so good, but I'm sure Uncle Jeff can read it. Dead people know everything anyways.

Augusto Monterroso

THE ECLIPSE

When Brother Bartolomé Arrazola felt that he was lost, he accepted the fact that now nothing could save him. The powerful jungle of Guatemala, implacable and final, had overwhelmed him. In the face of his topographical ignorance he sat down calmly to wait for death. He wanted to die there, without hope, alone, his thoughts fixed on distant Spain, particularly on the Convent of Los Abrojos, where Charles V had once condescended to come down from his eminence to tell him that he trusted in the religious zeal of his work of redemption.

When he awoke he found himself surrounded by a group of Indians with impassive faces who were preparing to sacrifice him before an altar, an altar that seemed to Bartolomé the bed on which he would finally rest from his fears, from his destiny, from himself.

Three years in the country had given him a passing knowledge of the native languages. He tried something. He spoke a few words that were understood.

Then there blossomed in him an idea that he considered worthy of his talent and his broad education and his profound knowledge of Aristotle. He remembered that a total eclipse of the sun was to take place that day. And he decided, in the deepest part of his being, to use that knowledge to deceive his oppressors and save his life.

"If you kill me," he said, "I can make the sun darken on high." The Indians stared at him and Bartolomé caught the disbelief in their eyes. He saw them consult with one another and he waited confidently, not without a certain contempt.

Two HOURS later the heart of Brother Bartolomé Arrazola spurted out its passionate blood on the sacrificing stone (brilliant in the opaque light of the eclipsed sun) while one of the Indians recited tonelessly, slowly, one by one, the infinite list of dates when solar and lunar eclipses would take place, which the astronomers of the Mayan community had predicted and registered in their codices without the estimable help of Aristotle.

Translated by Edith Grossman

Fernando Benavidez, Jr.

MONTEZUMA, MY REVOLVER

The first time I ever died, I was stabbed in the chest then set on fire by my friends on the bridge. It was late afternoon, and it seemed like the world was resisting the change of light, when everything looks the same peaceful gray, all one blurry shadow. As a kid, I thought, this is what heaven must took like—always dusk, just dark enough to fall asleep forever. The outlines of the American buildings merged seamlessly with the background of a flat Mexican landscape as if there were no border between us and them, no fence or armed guards, no difference between the United States and Mexico—at least, not at this time of day.

I remember thinking I was jealous of the old men and women making their way across the crowded bridge by foot, faster. They stared at us—three punks in a fancy black truck, practically standing still in the smog of the crossing. We inched forward one conversation at a time. The sun disappeared behind the edge of the world to my left, and to my right, *los viejitos* walking. The daylight was being swallowed by the stench that arose from the brownness of the Rio Grande in the summer, but I loved that smell.

Chuy was in the back seat and Bobby Loco in the front. These were my partners and best friends. Chuy got his name from his father, even though his mother called him Jesús, which he hated. And Bobby Loco, Roberto Garza to his mother, earned his name on the streets of Brownsville. We did almost everything together, even the dealing. Vicente Fernandez played loud as hell and the feeling of music pounded our chests. "El Rey" was like our anthem. We talked in raised voices about plans for that night. It always led to stupid shit that nineteen-year-olds talk about when they've got money and time—who we've fucked, who we wanted to fuck, who wanted to fuck us, and lies we told as truths. The trip across the bridge would be a slow one, and we knew it. But, it was finally Friday, and that's all that mattered.

Cano, our fat boss, sent us on a big delivery guaranteed to make us a lot of money. It was the reason we were still here, still doing this shit after high school. Chuy's cousin Carlos was border patrol and worked on Fridays except when his ugly wife, Mona La Llorona, needed him to take care of their baby. She was a nurse always on call or some bullshit like that, so Carlos had to be ready to go when she needed him. We had it all figured out, though, when a delivery had to be made. Carlos was just an added guarantee, the kind of security we were willing to pay for.

Bobby Loco was also the only real American citizen in my truck and it made us feel safe too. Chuy was a *mojado* like me, but we both pretended we weren't, for the girls mostly. I could speak English because I graduated from a high school in Brownsville, where I met Bobby, who barely talked at all. Chuy, I met in a

Mexican jail when we were just *chavalones*. I graduated for my father, who died the summer before ninth grade, shot by Cano. I know. I was too angry to feel anything at the time. So at the funeral, my mother cried enough for the both of us. I just stared at *el jefe*'s coffin even after everyone left. *Pinche* Cano pretended to be angry about my father's death, pretended he would seek revenge in his name, find out who did it, do what a son's supposed to do.

Cano was my *jefe*'s best friend—partners with him, like me, Bobby, and Chuy. He even took care of me after my father died, out of guilt, maybe fear. Of course, I loved my father, and that's why I went to work for Cano after the funeral, selling dime bags to middle schoolers for candy money. I did it because I knew it was him all along—*pinche* Cano.

Working for that fat fuck was how I'd get my revenge, and I couldn't wait for the day to come when I could get close enough to pull the trigger. It took me five years to decide to do it. By then, I was nineteen and big time—it was harder to do because of the money. I told myself, just one more big deal and then Cano's dead.

Sometimes, I couldn't hold his fat ass up when he'd lean in on me, breathing hot, sour words in my face, high on coke, smelling of tequila.

"*Yo quería a tu jefe, chingos, carnal.* I loved your *apá*," he'd confess repeatedly. "I loved him, *chingos*."

"I know, Cano," I would tell him, "I know."

Every night he got drunk like that, I thought I'd do it. Kill him.

We knew we were on the U.S. side already. A dirty plaque stuck to the railing on the right marked the line. We were so high by then. I always carried a .357 Magnum on my waist, and I wore a gold cross, blessed by Padre Buendía for protection. Chuy, in the back, always sucked on his stupid lollipop, a nasty habit we all hated but tolerated because of his connection at the checkpoint.

Bobby carried a big knife in his boot, usually. He liked starting shit for no reason. He was famous for it, even. They used to call him "Animal"—in high school before he dropped out—in part because of his size, part of it because of his temper. Known throughout middle school for losing an eyeball while playing with bottle rockets, by the time he was twenty, he was the most feared *vato* in Brownsville. His glass eye had a red pupil, scary, but stupid at the same time.

Yeah, Bobby was a killer, or at least was fucked up enough to kill. That's why Cano liked him. For about a month, the *chupacabra* was blamed for all Bobby's fine work in Brownsville. It was all over the *Brownsville Herald*—pictures of Bruno Cano's enemies, gutted—big dealers found dead in alleys, trying to hold on to their insides spilling from their bodies, eyes wide, open-mouthed, or just left thrown in their cars or the cornfields north of town. "The Chupacabra at Large," the paper would say. Bobby Loco always made it look like an animal did it. That was his talent.

Right before I had left the house that night, my mother gave me a revolver that belonged to my father. It was all he left me, she said. It was all I was packing. Back at my place, I'd forgotten my .357, so this was good because I hated being without protection. I had put my *jefe*'s revolver in my right boot, where he used to carry it, where it belonged. Mamá was proud to see me handle it the way she said *el jefe* would. He never called it a gun, but a revolver, and he named it Montezuma. He used to say that he only used it for "special occasions," like for revenge, mostly. One bullet at a time, for one target was his rule.

The fiery blue pearl grip fit perfectly in my hands.

I had my father's hands.

The gun was engraved with the original nickel plate finish from 1948, a strong weapon, fucking beautiful. Montezuma was my baby now, my revolver, and saving my own ass was always a "special occasion."

I stopped drinking as soon as the sun went down and told Chuy and Bobby to shut up. It never took us this long to cross, I thought. Something was wrong and I lowered the volume to listen to myself for a moment.

We were stuck behind a dirty rig with mud flaps that were decorated with shiny naked women. The mufflers growled every time it moved a foot. I couldn't see very good in either direction. Behind us, another rig blocked our view to Matamoros. *La migra* looked restless up ahead. Heads in uniforms moved in and out of car windows and made me nervous. Maybe Mona La Llorona had called Carlos to take care of the baby tonight.

"You think we're fucked?" Bobby asked me.

"I don't know, *vato*. Did Carlos tell you *qué no iba estar?*" I asked Chuy.

"No. *No me dijo nada,*" he said.

"You didn't talk to Carlos *o* La Llorona *tampoco?*"

"*¿Cuál llorona?*"

"Your cousin's wife, *baboso*—Mona La Llorona!"

"No. No. She didn't call," he insisted.

"Fuck!"

I saw two border patrol guys walking toward us, checking with their flashlights, hands on their shiny, government-issued Berettas, approaching everyone with caution.

This was no routine.

We'll shoot it out with them, was my first reaction. No. We'll make a run for it and do what Cano told us to do in a situation like this.

"We should burn the shit and run," I said.

No one said anything back.

Bobby started to get paranoid, sweating on my leather seats, hand on his knife. Chuy spit his candy out the window and finished the line of coke carefully balanced on his left hand. We always carried five gallons of gasoline behind the third seat of my truck just in case we needed it, and it looked like we might. Chuy struggled with the tank, to bring it over. He washed the seats behind me with gasoline as fast as he could before I realized what Bobby was doing with his big fucking knife.

U.S. Customs reported that their hunch about us was bad information on their part. They didn't ask me any questions because Chuy had emptied the drugs before we left Matamoros, and I didn't know it. Fucking Cano. *La migra* found no drugs in my smoldering truck, just me, pronounced dead at the scene, stabbed and burned alive by those fucking *putos*. Montezuma was found and returned to my mother, unharmed. She told the authorities at the hospital that it was a family heirloom.

The first time I died, I was stabbed in the chest then set on fire by my best friends on the bridge. I checked out of Brownsville Medical Center two weeks later, unrecognizable from the burns, ready to settle the score with Bobby Loco, Chuy, and, most of all, Bruno Cano—ready to hold Montezuma once again and kill in honor of my father.

Pedro Ponce

VICTIM

The victim is not deaf to the soundtrack. She is not blind to the audience leering over popcorn cartons. She knows. As she unlocks her door and steps into the darkened kitchen, as she turns on the lights and shuffles through the day's mail (mostly bills she will never have to pay), she knows. She's about to Get It. She sets down her purse and makes her way to the bedroom.

She sheds her clothes, ignoring the scattered whistles coming from the theater seats. She covers herself in a short silk robe. The flimsy material is too slight for the weather where she lives, but she knows the rules. A sudden scraping sound gives her an excuse to look out into the middle distance at the eyes watching her. She cannot let them see her look. Whatever fear she feels can register only briefly, for as long as it takes her to realize that the scraping is just a tree branch pressed against her window. Later, there will be the shadow behind the shower curtain, the thrust of a knife through the belly, the slow sinking to the tiled floor. For now, she must arrange herself into a blank, doe-eyed calm. She steps out to the living room for a cigarette.

The soundtrack swells with tortured strings and computerized shrieks. She must sit through it all, just another night at home on the sofa. Her friends at the office are home, too, with husbands or boyfriends, or else out at the bars. She desperately wants a beer. But there is no time. She looks over her shoulder and parts the curtains behind her. Beyond the frame, where the audience can't see, the paramedics have already arrived. A police car idles beside the ambulance. She sees the detective inside yawning as he waits for the screams that will signal his entrance.

She turns back to the dimly lit living room with what the audience takes to be a bemused stare. But she is actually looking squarely at the killer. He sullenly taps his watch while standing at the aquarium. The ridges of his clown mask are softened by the blue-green light of the tank. She takes one last drag on her cigarette and breathes it out in a narrow white funnel. Her satisfied smile is obscured as she vanishes down a darkened corridor.

Carmen Naranjo

WHEN NEW FLOWERS BLOOMED

It was and still is a round village making a circle in the hollow. The houses face the mountains, and seeing them one can predict the weather: it will be hot; it will rain; the wind tonight will be terrible; a calm day, perhaps sultry, around four o'clock the rain will start to fall; it will dawn drizzling; there may be a tremor today.

A town that grew and shrank according to the unsteadiness of the country, sometimes the leaders would think about agriculture, other times about industry, always about commerce, most of them about seeing that everything went along as it should, calmly, without worsening the poverty of so many poor. A town with eucalyptus, orange trees, cypresses, dusty streets, orchards, chayote plants, happy shouts from everyone who meets and greets you with jubilation, loquaciousness, nonsense, and a sky with convulsed clouds. The houses were built with whatever was at hand, some wood, a little brick, some zinc, unsheltered, wind, cold, heat, some decorated flower pot and primitive disorderly gardens where the chickens wander among the marigolds and the ducks among the lilies.

A tranquil town in which an old man dies between the details of the agony and the inventory of what he left: a yoke of century beginnings, a mortar in disuse, a rare sewing machine for sewing who knows what, some open-toed shoes, a razor completely rusted through. A peaceful town in which the birth of a child is communicated in a very loud voice from hallway to hallway, from alley to alley. It was a girl. Another one. Poor things, what's to become of so many? And the illness is combatted with medicine prescribed by the doctor and with herbs recommended by those who know about those things.

A town that always faces toward the mountain and admires, loves, and respects it, please God don't send it down on top of us, because then we wouldn't even be able to tell what happened. And the mountain, ever-changing, brings them news of events that their timid minds, as shut-ins, don't dare to consider. A new priest will arrive, don't take him too seriously, he is obsessed with sin, poor sinner, everything frightens him, don't be frightened. And in the summer two very young and ingenuous young people will come; however, you'll never have such an incredible opportunity to rely on such excellent teachers, who will teach you what had been forgotten a long time ago and it's necessary to remember so that new flowers can bloom.

It was an age in which the town almost became a village. The young people emigrated in search of work and a different life. They were drowning in the ravine and the slimness of the mountain. Some had stayed: the old ones, old grandparents and great-grandparents, a couple of great-great-grandmothers totally committed to God, and the parents who were aged prematurely and disconnectedly by the accelerated changes of the telegraph, the telephone, radio, and television.

She arrived first, one Sunday on the last of the four buses. She was going to take charge of the school and teach first to sixth grades of the diminished school-age population, which approached thirty children, ages seven to twelve years. Her name preceded her. Eugenia Maria de los Angeles Rivera Mancilla, born in a place known as the Cumbres de lo Alto for the Perfection of the Holy Birth. She looked very pale, too young for that rabble of sparrow hawks, but the mountain told them it is she, the awaited, the one who manipulates the winds and knows her letters, and behind those blue eyes resides the wisdom of life.

Eugenia Maria de los Angeles stopped on a corner, and ran her eyes over the row of houses. It required only a few seconds of investigation for her to know that she was at the ends of the earth. She raised her eyes to the majesty of the mountain to rapidly verify that she was at the beginning of the exposed beautiful things, which she knew were not given gratuitously or by chance but for legitimate merit, earned through will and that stubborn tenacity for overcoming any adverse situation.

Her first lesson was brilliant. She kept the kids awake, in spite of the fact that they had arisen before the mountain could become a profile, a black and threatening shadow, much less a grid of stray trees and weeds in the disorder of God, who was quite disorderly when it came to spontaneous natural growth. She simply showed maps and contrived to stimulate curiosity about the flat vision of the everyday.

The announced priest didn't arrive, as the decision to transfer Father Toño had been changed. With a certain inertia he had been doing good work; at least he hadn't provoked any complaints or unnecessary intrigues or problems with the tranquil and patient community.

The young man arrived eight days later, carrying his youth on his back and his enthusiasm for beginning his first professional job in the administration of a farm that had everything and was going to cultivate even more.

They met in front of the school with burning glances. He couldn't stand it and approached, reaching out his hand. José Luis Villacencio, at your service. She smiled in the most natural way imaginable, a smile that couldn't be extinguished or terminated.

From then on they were inseparable during their free time. They went to the plaza, walking tirelessly down all the paths of the town. For them the birds were singing, the flowers open, the eucalyptus perfumed, and the day and the night began, the clouds filmed a chalky white, the twilights lengthened.

No one in the village made any comment; it seemed very natural to them, they were so perfectly matched, so together.

One day the little old lady Refugio, one of the oldest of the village, watched them at length. But what was this. That way of slowly passing his finger down her arm, from her shoulder to her fingertip, tirelessly. Then that touching of heads, and how they petted each other, just like puppies. Then she associated the scene with an old rosebush that had begun to bloom with true passion, after years and years of dormancy. Something strange is happening, she thought, because her blood circulation had accelerated and her rheumatism pains had vanished. Then from so much contemplation, she caused others to contemplate too and she saw they were emotional, enthusiastic, absorbed in that torrent of true caresses.

That night the old woman didn't sleep, the hours passed as she remembered the exact movements and searching in vain for happiness. The following morning she had made up her mind and at dusk she passed again through the plaza and the whole village was there watching and watching. She saw what she could as long as the light permitted it, and then went downriver looking for Don Miguel, who was almost as old as she was. That night she slept like a log.

The couple became the number one spectacle of the village, now no one read, even the newspaper, in the general store the television stopped glowing, in the houses the radios were turned off, no one was interested in the soccer game, not even the players wanted to wear themselves out with their running and kicking. The priest and the sexton, together with the altar boys, joined the contemplation. It was a lovely spectacle, so pure and innocent that the priest dedicated Sunday's sermon to the art of loving, loving each other without end and without rest.

Strange things began to happen in the village. The potatoes tasted like yams, the yams like papaya, the papaya like turnips, the turnips like tomatoes, the coffee bean while it was still green smelled of orange blossoms, daisies bloomed from rosebushes, gladiolus from tulips and bougainvilleas from lilies. Everyone realized that the summer was staying around too long and it wasn't raining; there wasn't even a hint of rain in the sky, only chalky white clouds. But they didn't worry, because the river brought more water than ever and it was as soothing as the sea, it caressed them to sleep with caresses that were every day more creative, more imaginative as it slowly carried out its journey.

When the old woman confessed that she was pregnant, they thought it must be her senility or maybe nostalgia for times past. She had given birth to nine children, she had almost seventy-five grandchildren, and her eighth great-grandchild was about to be born. They began to believe it when they noted that all the women, old ones and young ones, some of them almost children, were in the same state, along with the sacristan's wife, the girlfriends of the altar boys, and the priest's blessed servant.

The odor of the flowers truly intoxicated the village, they were blooming everywhere, even among the stones; the plaza was filled with them, and the paths, and the sidewalks, to the point where it was hard to walk and calmly find a place to step, without a guilty conscience for causing harm to some generous plant.

Perhaps that was why the people stopped going out, and they didn't realize that the couple wasn't there any more. They had gone their separate ways, as they had arrived, on different days.

He left first. In that village, filled with flowers, of tranquil, good people, a smiling priest who always put good before evil, he arrived at the conclusion that he had made a mistake in his calling. He wanted to be a sailor instead of a farmer. She left afterwards, perhaps a few weeks later. By then the smile had dissipated and her eyes were filling with solitude, the solitude of an island in an unruly sea where someone was shipwrecked.

Neither she nor he perceived anything different in that village, so quiet and so covered with flowers. She left as if shutting a door, he as if opening one.

When the village realized that they had gone, busy as everyone was with babies being born, almost all of them around the same date, and with the care of that enormous quantity of children, because there were many twins and triplets, another teacher was already there, and she arrived obviously pregnant, and another farm administrator, with his wife and five rather grown children.

Now in this epoch it rained day and night, the flowers had disappeared, the river ran with less music and less water, things tasted like what they were, plants produced what they were supposed to. Everyone confessed his confusion to the priest and the priest sought out his superior to do the same. He counseled him to say solemnly what he had repeated in the confessional: One swallow doesn't make summer come faster, nor does the birdsong bring the rains. Fleeting things have no transcendence and if the disorderliness were ordered, it wouldn't contain the gravity of the sin.

The couple appeared in some dreams but without doing much damage. Everyone had rediscovered that one sleeps better and more profoundly in one's own solitude and with the expectations of the era.

Translated by Linda Britt

Alicita Rodríguez

IMAGINING BISBEE

Few people live in Bisbee; the town's history makes it so. When miners decided to strike in 1917, the sheriff's deputies, with their big guns and small teeth, rounded them up like cattle, packed them into train cars, and shipped them to New Mexico—dumped the strikers, with their soot-covered faces, smack in the middle of desert. A few of the miners walked back to Bisbee, each step, each raising and dropping of the foot, taken amid the jumble of hallucinations. These are the forefathers.

And so, their progeny.

Bisbee Bob, drug dealer, father of two suspected arsonists.

Walking Bob, Francophile, tours the Côte d'Azur every summer, raves about the country's footpaths.

Bible Bob, eighty years old, thin as a pencil, eats only carrots, skin hangs in folds, scribbles in notebooks, recognizable by red rubber raincoat.

Crazy Nancy, bright lipstick, black hair, junkie. Reportedly a brutal suicide.

Library Girl, reads, looks for forest fires with *perro callejero*.

Built into the mountains, Bisbee is a town of steps. Natives decorate their steps in many ways. Some string colored electric lights along the treads. The more creative choose novelty bulbs in the shape of bumblebees or cactus trees or cowboy boots. Others paint the risers with bright colors; some imitate the designs of the surrounding Indian tribes. Still others paste tiny pieces of broken glass onto the stairs. The paths to their homes glisten and blind in the Arizona sun.

Bisbee's inhabitants want to disappear. They use P.O. boxes and first names. They hide under straw hats and melt into the horizon. They don't see movies and they only sleep with foreigners. They never get biblical with one another.

It is a town that exists only in relation to other realities: south of Tombstone; east of Nogales; north of Mexico; west of the Arizona/ New Mexico border. Bisbee often does not appear on maps. It is not there.

Helena María Viramontes

MISS CLAIROL

Arlene and Champ walk to Kmart. The store is full of bins mounted with bargain buys, from T-shirts to rubber sandals. They go to aisle 23, Cosmetics. Arlene, wearing bell-bottom jeans two sizes too small, can't bend down to the Miss Clairol boxes, asks Champ.

—Which one, *amá*? asks Champ, chewing her thumbnail.

—Shit, *mija*, I dunno. Arlene smacks her gum, contemplating the decision. Maybe I need a change, *tú sabes*. What do you think? She holds up a few blond strands with black roots. Arlene has burned the softness of her hair with peroxide; her hair is stiff, breaks at the ends, and she needs plenty of Aqua Net hair spray to tease and tame her ratted hair, then she folds it back into a high lump behind her head. For the last few months she has been a platinum "Light Ash" blond, before that a Miss Clairol "Flame" redhead, before that Champ couldn't even identify the color— somewhere between orange and brown, a "Sun Bronze." The only way Champ knows her mother's true hair color is by her roots which, like death, inevitably rise to the truth.

—I hate it, *tú sabes*, when I can't decide. Arlene is wearing a pink, strapless tube top. Her stomach spills over the hip-hugger jeans. Spits the gum onto the floor. Fuck it. And Champ follows her to the rows of nail polish, next to the Maybelline rack of make-up, across the false eyelashes that look like insects on display in clear, plastic boxes. Arlene pulls out a particular color of nail pol-ish, looks at the bottom of the bottle for the price, puts it back, gets another. She has a tattoo of purple XXXs on her left finger, like a ring. She finally settles for a purple-blackish color, Ripe Plum, that Champ thinks looks like the color of Frankenstein's nails. She looks at her own stubby nails, chewed and gnawed.

Walking over to the eye shadows, Arlene slowly slinks out another stick of gum from her back pocket, unwraps and crum-bles the wrapper into a little ball, lets it drop on the floor. Smacks the gum.

—Grandpa Ham used to make chains with these gum wrap-pers, she says, toeing the wrapper on the floor with her rubber san-dals, her toes dotted with old nail polish. He started one, *tú sabes*, that went from room to room. That was before he went nuts, she says, looking at the price of magenta eye shadow. *¿Sabes qué?* What do you think? —lifting the eye shadow to Champ.

—I dunno, responds Champ, shrugging her shoulders the way she always does when she is listening to something else, her own heartbeat, what Gregorio said on the phone yesterday, shrugs her shoulders when Miss Smith says OFELIA, answer my question. She is too busy thinking of things people otherwise dismiss like parentheses, but sticks to her like gum, like a hole on a shirt, like a tattoo, and sometimes she wishes she weren't born with such adhesiveness. The chain went from room to room, round and round like a web, she remembers. That was before he went nuts.

—Champ. You listening? Or in la-la land again? Arlene has her arms akimbo on a fold of flesh, pissed.

—I said, I dunno, Champ whines back, still looking at the wrapper on the floor.

—Well, you better learn, *tú sabes*, and fast too. Now think, will this color go good with Pancha's blue dress? Pancha is Arlene's *comadre*. Since Arlene has a special date tonight, she lent Arlene her royal blue dress that she keeps in a plastic bag at the end of her closet. The dress is made of chiffon, with satinlike material underlining, so that when Arlene first tried it on and strutted about, it crinkled sounds of elegance. The dress fits too tight. Her plump arms squeeze through, her hips breathe in and hold their breath, the seams do all they can to keep the body contained. But Arlene doesn't care as long as it sounds right.

—I think it will, Champ says, and Arlene is very pleased.

—Think so? So do I, *mija*.

They walk out the double doors and Champ never remembers her mother paying.

IT IS FOUR in the afternoon, but already Arlene is preparing for the date. She scrubs the tub, Art Laboe on the radio, drops crystals of Jean Naté into the running water, lemon scent rises with the steam. The bathroom door ajar, she removes her top and her breasts flop and sag, pushes her jeans down with some difficulty, kicks them off, and steps in the tub.

—*Mija. MIJA* —she yells. —*Mija*, give me a few bobby pins. She is worried about her hair frizzing and so wants to pin it up.

Her mother's voice is faint because Champ is in the closet.

There are piles of clothes on the floor, hangers thrown askew and tangled, shoes all piled up or thrown on the top shelf. Champ is looking for her mother's special dress. Pancha says every girl has one at the end of her closet.

—Goddamn it. Champ.

Amid the dirty laundry, the black hole of the closet, she finds nothing.

—NOW.

—Alright, ALRIGHT. Cheeze *amá*, stop yelling, says Champ, and goes in the steamy bathroom, checks the drawers. Hairbrushes jump out, rollers, strands of hair, rummages through bars of soap, combs, eye shadows, finds nothing; pulls open another drawer, powder, empty bottles of oil, manicure scissors, Kotex, dye instructions crinkled and botched, finally, a few bobby pins.

After Arlene pins up her hair, she asks Champ, *¿Sabes qué?* Should I wear my hair up? Do I look good with it up? Champ is sitting on the toilet.

—Yeah, *amá*, you look real pretty.

—Thanks, *mija*, says Arlene. *¿Sabes qué?* When you get older I'll show you how you can look just as pretty, and she puts her head back, relaxes, like the Calgon commercials.

CHAMP LIES on her stomach, TV on to some variety show with pogo stick dancers dressed in outfits of stretchy material and glitter. She is wearing one of Gregorio's white T-shirts, the ones he washes and bleaches himself so that the whiteness is impeccable. It drapes over her deflated ten year old body like a dress. She is busy cutting out Miss Breck models from the stacks of old magazines Pancha found in the back of her mother's garage. Champ collects the array of honey-colored-haired women, puts them in a shoe box with all her other special things.

Arlene is in the bathroom, wrapped in a towel. She has painted her eyebrows so that the two are arched and even, penciled thin and high. The magenta shades her eyelids. The towel slips, reveals one nipple blind from a cigarette burn, a date to forget. She rewraps the towel, likes her reflection, turns to her profile for additional inspection. She feels good, turns up the radio to . . . your love. *For your loveeeee, I will do anything, I will do anything, forrr your love. For your kiss . . .*

Champ looks on. From the open bathroom door, she can see Arlene, anticipation burning like a cigarette from her lips, sliding her shoulders to the ahhhh ahhhhh, and pouting her lips until the song ends. And Champ likes her mother that way.

Arlene carefully stretches black eyeliner, like a fallen question mark, outlines each eye. The work is delicate, her hand trembles cautiously, stops the process to review the face with each line. Arlene the mirror is not Arlene the face who has worn too many relationships, gotten too little sleep. The last touch is the chalky, beige lipstick.

By the time she is finished, her ashtray is full of cigarette butts, Champ's variety show is over, and Jackie Gleason's dancing girls come on to make kaleidoscope patterns with their long legs and arms. Gregorio is still not home, and Champ goes over to the window, checks the houses, the streets, corners, roams the sky with her eyes.

Arlene sits on the toilet, stretches up her nylons, clips them to her girdle. She feels good thinking about the way he will unsnap her nylons, and she will unroll them slowly, point her toes when she does.

Champ opens a can of Campbell soup, finds a perfect pot in the middle of a stack of dishes, pulls it out to the threatening rumbling of the tower. She washes it out, pours the contents of the red can, turns the knob. After it boils, she puts the pan on the sink for it to cool down. She searches for a spoon.

Arlene is a romantic. When Champ begins her period, she will tell her things that only women can know. She will tell her about the first time she made love with a boy, her awkwardness and shyness forcing them to go under the house, where the cool, refined soil made a soft mattress. How she closed her eyes and wondered what to expect, or how the penis was the softest skin she had ever felt against her, how it tickled her, searched for a place to connect. She was eleven and his name was Harry.

She will not tell Champ that her first fuck was a guy named Puppet who ejaculated prematurely, at the sight of her apricot vagina, so plump and fuzzy. —*Pendejo* —she said —you got it all over me. She rubbed the gooey substance off her legs, her belly, in disgust. Ran home to tell Rat and Pancha, her mouth open with laughter.

Arlene powder puffs under her arms, between her breasts, tilts a bottle of Love Cries perfume and dabs behind her ears, neck and breasts for those tight caressing songs that permit them to grind their bodies together until she can feel a bulge in his pants and she knows she's in for the night.

Jackie Gleason is a bartender in a saloon. He wears a black bow tie, a white apron, and is polishing a glass. Champ is watching him, sitting in the radius of the gray light, eating her soup from the pot.

Arlene is a romantic. She will dance until Pancha's dress turns a different color, dance until her hair becomes undone, her hips jiggering and quaking beneath a new pair of hosiery, her mascara shadowing under her eyes from the perspiration of the ritual, dance spinning herself into Miss Clairol, and stopping only when it is time to return to the sewing factory, time to wait out the next date, time to change hair color. Time to remember or to forget.

Champ sees Arlene from the window. She can almost hear Arlene's nylons rubbing against one another, hear the crinkling sound of satin when she gets in the blue and white shark-finned Dodge. Champ yells good-bye. It all sounds so right to Arlene, who is too busy cranking up the window to hear her daughter.

Edmundo Paz Soldán

COUNTERFEIT

At age seven, Weiser decided he hated school and resolutely stopped going. He still rose at dawn, nonetheless, to obey his mother (since his father's death, Weiser, an only child, had been the sole object of her hopes), and put on the required uniform and set out toward school, and returned at noon and spoke unabashedly about exams and instructors. Now and then, to keep up the sham, he had to forge praising notes from the principal, and notebooks full of excellent marks; he had to enlist ex-classmates, who appeared at his house certain afternoons to help him pretend to do homework. His mother trusted him fully; as a result she didn't bother to visit the school to see how her son was improving, nor did she suspect an absence of parents' meetings and charity gatherings, which she wouldn't have attended anyway. She kept to her schedule, paying tuition on the first of each month, which her thoughtful son would deliver to save her the bother.

All this continued without variation until graduation day, at which point Weiser invented a sudden, stabbing back pain as an excuse to stay in bed. His mother, though worried, was pleased not to have to go to the ceremony: she hadn't met a single teacher, or any of the priests who governed the school, or her son's classmates' parents—she'd have felt out of place. The following day, she couldn't help crying, seeing the diploma Weiser had forged with brazen perfection; her sacrifices hadn't been idle. Her son would go on to the university. And Weiser, telling her he'd study medicine, believed they had six tense, arduous years yet to come.

But the years weren't arduous or tense, thanks to his continuing progress in the art of imitation. Graduation day was harder, of course, to arrange. He had to bring in forty-three friends to serve as classmates, and hire sixteen actors to serve as academic body (professors, dean, rector), and rent the auditorium at the Cultural Arts Center and make the ceremony happen at the precise moment the true ceremony happened in the main lecture hall at the university.

And his mother, embracing him, cried.

Later, he opened a fake office of general medicine, where he spent afternoons from three till seven examining fake patients, hired for fear of discovery by his mother, who often made sudden, unexpected visits. Still, he didn't feel he was wasting his time; the office lent an air of respectability, a needed façade quietly veiling his true profession, which had allowed him to accrue incredible wealth: the profession of counterfeiter.

Nine years later—he had a false specialization in neurosurgery, at this point—his mother appeared at the office, complaining about unbearable headaches. He examined her, and determined that the pain would be temporary, nothing too serious. She died two months later. The coroner determined that death had come as a result of a tumor not treated in time. Weiser didn't blame himself for a moment: Looking back on his life from age seven, he could see that she, only she, was to blame for this death that might not have happened.

Translated by Kirk Nesset

Omar Castañeda

THE NEWS OF
THE AUTHOR

The news of the building of the wall
now penetrated into this world.
— FRANZ KAFKA

Finally, the news reached us about The Murder. The dark
glove of its fame spread across the country, covering the landscapes
between empires with its coarse weave. Of course, there was no
other like it. Like so many other stories of hands or reach, or exten-
sions beyond any grasp of reason, this, too, arrived late to our village. Not so late that we had already poured out our Pho and stock
pots, but we had been eating molded bread for as long as my son
had been alive. Yet, in this, we were hardly different from hundreds
of other villages scattered along the waterways, the roads. We lived
far from the imperial throne.

I remember the boatman, dark-draped, black-hatted, poling along the softer currents in the very center of the river. He waved and called excitedly. All of us ran to the bank to receive him. The officials from my union stood back. It was a premonition, I suppose, thick as fog in our heads. Our leader, the distinguished assassin of several difficult marks, stood with his hands clasped behind his back. His long, bound hair seemed a sable muffler draped over his shoulder. The blood-red ribbon at the end stood boldly out against his black pajamas. I held my son's hand. He had already killed, much to my delight. He was to be initiated into the union in the coming month. Already he had our desperate look, our hunger for recognition, our talk of higher visions, our ravenous grip.

Our mayor went down the slippery bank to receive the boatman. The mud and slickered vines made it difficult for both men. They had to embrace to keep from falling. Yet the man would only give the news to the president of our union. Our leader nodded. He wrapped his braid several times around his neck like a necklace and made his cautious way down. By this time the boatman had returned to the safety of his launch. Our leader met him on board. The waves rocked it gently, so they spoke quickly but comfortably. The men shook hands, embraced, and then the boatman left to carry the news farther on. Our leader stood facing away from us. Was he hiding his reddened eyes? He did not wave, but watched contemplatively the river swells, the current swirls, and the long poling barge disappearing toward the next village.

He would not share with the others the intimate words of the messenger until he had addressed the union first. There was no amount of coaxing to wheedle it from him. He was resolute.

Our lodge is the best along this stretch of the river. We have electricity and typewriters. The walls and aisles have towering bookshelves. These, of course, are overcrowded with mysteries, with whodunits. They are impossibly crammed vertically and horizontally so that it can be most difficult to locate a particular volume. It is a library we are very proud of, and, indeed, it must be acknowledged that we take turns dusting this interminable labyrinth of shelves. Not one of us would dare complain about our duties—what is there to complain about? Our lives are good. Furthermore, each of us has worked late through the night on some plot or another—culling the references—and each of us knows the cycle of the evening. The lamps and soft electric lights call forth the moths. The dying ones bring the toads. With their quick tongues, they devour only those flapping over the earthen floor. Early morning, half an hour before daybreak, the chickens enter and finish the dead moths. By six in the morning the long night of hunger and duty, with its litter of corpses, is nowhere to be seen. It is as if there had been no struggle at all during the wee hours, the blind hours.

"This is what the boatman said to me," our leader began. He stood at the podium, his arms outstretched, his hair loose and flowing to below his waist. He held his arms out and there were none of his traditional ribbons, ties, broaches, or jewelry. He wore a white tunic and left his hair unbound. He had kept himself as unadorned as the most devout ascetic for the news.

" 'Finally,' " our leader continued, " 'we can rest.' This is what the boatman said to me. 'Finally, The Murder has been committed. Little is known of The Author except that The Murder was done in our empire's capital—as it should be—protected by the barbarian wall, and there he has accomplished what we have all longed for. But there is no knowledge of whether The Author is one of us or someone brought from outside the wall. We do not even know if it is a man or a woman. If there are children for this genius. Finally, all we know is that The Murder has occurred.' "

And then he bowed deeply before us, religiously; his great cascade of hair fell like a black cowl about his shoulders and face.

He then thrust up and—wild! horse mane!—swept his long tresses back in an arc over his head. We were beyond gasping.

We understood this and still understand it, even though we are so far from the center of the empire that we have yet to receive details of The Murder. But the news was for us, after all, this: The Author's final coming. After all, there were many in the village who hardly bothered with the deaths we orchestrated. Others complained that we still had not quite got it right, that there was more that needed to be done, that we got near but not quite home to the authentic. Some openly disdained our butcherings as banal, unimaginative. And there were those who berated us for our apparently self-indulgent life. What did we give to our village? We killed our fellow villagers, imperfectly; we maimed and tortured to fulfill abstruse notions that only we subscribed to. We lived our lives simultaneously crying about the present and looking to some distant time beyond our meager lives when posterity would recognize our talents, our teeth. For generations beyond recollection, we, in our union, suffered attacks of apathy. And now, finally, The Author made all our travails bearable. The Murder had come to exonerate us, but not only us—everyone who lived! The Author was the arrow leading us into light.

Who knows? Perhaps The Murder, once it is finely explicated— did I say that the details haven't yet reached our village?—will bring a new purpose to our carnage. Perhaps we will be able to imitate this oeuvre nonpareil with innumerable permutations. Perhaps our small homicides will be analyzed as precursors, as earlier forms of the great evolutionary state of The Murder. Perhaps we will be asked to formulate opinions, to help decipher the less obvious conceits of the work. Perhaps a new age of cultural critique will begin, where practitioners—instead of nonpractitioners—will be seen as the experts.

Wild! Horse mane! Arc of the tresses—black optimism and freedom!

We all wear white tunics now. We all do: Hierophants of steel. Some, in our union, have perfected a knowing smile that lingers across our lips like the faint grins on maple leaves.

Norma Elia Cantú

HALLOWEEN

It's Halloween, but we haven't donned costumes—we didn't yet believe in that strange U.S. custom; only my younger siblings did, many years later. Mamagrande and her oldest daughter, Tía Lydia, have come to visit, to clean the *lápida* in Nuevo Laredo where Mamagrande's dead children are buried, to place fresh flowers in tin cans wrapped in foil, and hang beautiful wreaths; they've come to honor the dead. But it's the day before, and Mami and Papi and Bueli leave me alone with our guests and the kids; I'm fixing dinner—showing off that I can cook and feed the kids. I've made the flour tortillas, measuring ingredients with my hands, the way Mami and Bueli do, five handfuls of flour, some salt, a handful of shortening, some *espauda* from the red can marked "KC." Once it's all mixed in, the shortening broken into bits no bigger than peas, I pour hot water, almost boiling but not quite, and knead the dough, shape it into a fat ball like a bowl turned over. I let it set while I prepare the sauce I will use for the *fideo*. When it's time, I form the small *testales* the size of my small fist; I roll out the tortillas, small and round, the size of saucers, and cook them on the *comal*. As they cook, I pile them up on a dinner plate, wrap them in a cloth embroidered with a garland of tiny flowers—red, blue, yellow—and crochet-edged in pale pink. We eat *fideo*, beans, tortillas quietly because Mamagrande and Tía Lydia watch us. We drink the cinnamon tea with milk. I look outside and see a huge moon rising; it's the same color as the warm liquid in my cup. Later, Tino and Dahlia wash the dishes, and even later, the kids are watching TV quietly, without arguing. Mamagrande rocks in the *sillón* out on the porch and can't understand why some kids all ragged and costumed as hoboes and clowns come and ask for treats. I try to explain, but it's useless. My siblings want "fritos" so I cut some corn tortillas Mamagrande has brought from Monterrey into strips and heat the grease in an old skillet. I'm busily frying the strips and soaking the grease off on a clean dishrag when all of a sudden the skillet turns and I see the hot grease fall as if in slow motion. My reflexes are good, but the burning on my foot tells me I wasn't fast enough. At first it doesn't hurt, but then I feel it: the skin and to the bone, as if a million cactus thorns—the tiny nopal thorns—have penetrated my foot. I scream with pain. Mamagrande rushes and puts butter on the burn. I cry. The kids are scared. Later, Doña Lupe will have to do healings *de susto*—they're so frightened. And when Mami and Papi return they scold me for not being careful.

I miss school for two days. When I go back, my foot and ankle wrapped in gauze and cotton bandages attract attention. I'm embarrassed. When my social studies teacher, Mrs. Kazen, the wife of a future senator, concerned, asks, I tell her the truth.

"Did you go to the hospital? Did a doctor examine the burn?"

"No," I answer, knowing it's the wrong answer, but not wanting to lie.

She shakes her head, so I know not to tell her how every three hours, day and night for three days, Mami, remembering Bueli's remedies, has been putting herb poultices on the burn and cleaning it thoroughly. She's punctured the water-filled ampula with a maguey thorn and tells me there won't even be a scar. And there isn't.

Jorge Luis Borges

THE BOOK OF SAND

> ... thy rope of sands ...
> —GEORGE HERBERT (1593–1623)

The line consists of an infinite number of points; the plane, of an infinite number of lines; the volume, of an infinite number of planes; the hypervolume, of an infinite number of volumes ... No—this, *more geometrico*, is decidedly not the best way to begin my tale. To say that the story is true is by now a convention of every fantastic tale; mine, nevertheless, *is* true.

I live alone, in a fifth-floor apartment on Calle Belgrano. One evening a few months ago, I heard a knock at my door. I opened it, and a stranger stepped in. He was a tall man, with blurred, vague features, or perhaps my nearsightedness made me see him that way. Everything about him spoke of honest poverty: he was dressed in gray, and carried a gray valise. I immediately sensed that he was a foreigner. At first I thought he was old; then I noticed that I had been misled by his sparse hair, which was blond, almost white, like the Scandinavians'. In the course of our conversation, which I doubt lasted more than an hour, I learned that he hailed from the Orkneys.

I pointed the man to a chair. He took some time to begin talking. He gave off an air of melancholy, as I myself do now.

"I sell Bibles," he said at last.

"In this house," I replied, not without a somewhat stiff, pedantic note, "there are several English Bibles, including the first one, Wyclif's. I also have Cipriano de Valera's, Luther's (which is, in literary terms, the worst of the lot), and a Latin copy of the Vulgate. As you see, it isn't exactly Bibles I might be needing."

After a brief silence he replied.

"It's not only Bibles I sell. I can show you a sacred book that might interest a man such as yourself. I came by it in northern India, in Bikaner."

He opened his valise and brought out the book. He laid it on the table. It was a clothbound octavo volume that had clearly passed through many hands. I examined it; the unusual heft of it surprised me. On the spine was printed *Holy Writ*, and then *Bombay*.

"Nineteenth century, I'd say," I observed.

"I don't know," was the reply. "Never did know."

I opened it at random. The characters were unfamiliar to me. The pages, which seemed worn and badly set, were printed in double columns, like a Bible. The text was cramped, and composed into versicles. At the upper corner of each page were Arabic numerals. I was struck by an odd fact: the even-numbered page would carry the number 40,514, let us say, while the odd-numbered page that followed it would be 999. I turned the page; the next page bore an eight-digit number. It also bore a small illustration, like those one sees in dictionaries: an anchor drawn in pen and ink, as though by the unskilled hand of a child.

It was at that point that the stranger spoke again.

"Look at it well. You will never see it again."

There was a threat in the words, but not in the voice.

I took note of the page, and then closed the book. Immediately I opened it again. In vain I searched for the figure of the anchor, page after page. To hide my discomfiture, I tried another tack.

"This is a version of Scripture in some Hindu language, isn't that right?"

"No," he replied.

Then he lowered his voice, as though entrusting me with a secret.

"I came across this book in a village on the plain, and I traded a few rupees and a Bible for it. The man who owned it didn't know how to read. I suspect he saw the Book of Books as an amulet. He was of the lowest caste; people could not so much as step on his shadow without being defiled. He told me his book was called the Book of Sand because neither sand nor this book has a beginning or an end."

He suggested I try to find the first page.

I took the cover in my left hand and opened the book, my thumb and forefinger almost touching. It was impossible: several pages always lay between the cover and my hand. It was as though they grew from the very book.

"Now try to find the end."

I failed there as well.

"This can't be," I stammered, my voice hardly recognizable as my own.

"It can't be, yet it *is*," the Bible peddler said, his voice little more than a whisper. "The number of pages in this book is literally infinite. No page is the first page; no page is the last. I don't know why they're numbered in this arbitrary way, but perhaps it's to give one to understand that the terms of an infinite series can be numbered any way whatever."

Then, as though thinking out loud, he went on.

"If space is infinite, we are anywhere, at any point in space. If time is infinite, we are at any point in time."

His musings irritated me.

"You," I said, "are a religious man, are you not?"

"Yes, I'm Presbyterian. My conscience is clear. I am certain I didn't cheat that native when I gave him the Lord's Word in exchange for his diabolic book."

I assured him he had nothing to reproach himself for, and asked whether he was just passing through the country. He replied that he planned to return to his own country within a few days. It was then that I learned he was a Scot, and that his home was in the Orkneys. I told him I had great personal fondness for Scotland because of my love for Stevenson and Hume.

"And Robbie Burns," he corrected.

As we talked I continued to explore the infinite book.

"Had you intended to offer this curious specimen to the British Museum, then?" I asked with feigned indifference.

"No," he replied, "I am offering it to you," and he mentioned a great sum of money.

I told him, with perfect honesty, that such an amount of money was not within my ability to pay. But my mind was working; in a few moments I had devised my plan.

"I propose a trade," I said. "You purchased the volume with a few rupees and the Holy Scripture; I will offer you the full sum of my pension, which I have just received, and Wyclif's black-letter Bible. It was left to me by my parents."

"A black-letter Wyclif!" he murmured.

I went to my bedroom and brought back the money and the book. With a bibliophile's zeal he turned the pages and studied the binding.

"Done," he said.

I was astonished that he did not haggle. Only later was I to realize that he had entered my house already determined to sell the book. He did not count the money, but merely put the bills into his pocket.

We chatted about India, the Orkneys, and the Norwegian jarls that had once ruled those islands. Night was falling when the man left. I have never seen him since, nor do I know his name.

I thought of putting the Book of Sand in the space left by the Wyclif, but I chose at last to hide it behind some imperfect volumes of the *Thousand and One Nights*.

I went to bed but could not sleep. At three or four in the morning I turned on the light. I took out the impossible book and turned its pages. On one, I saw an engraving of a mask. There was a number in the corner of the page—I don't remember now what it was—raised to the ninth power.

I showed no one my treasure. To the joy of possession was added the fear that it would be stolen from me, and to that, the suspicion that it might not be truly infinite. Those two points of anxiety aggravated my already habitual misanthropy. I had but few friends left, and those, I stopped seeing. A prisoner of the Book, I hardly left my house. I examined the worn binding and the covers with a magnifying glass, and rejected the possibility of some artifice. I found that the small illustrations were spaced at two-thousand-page intervals. I began noting them down in an alphabetized notebook, which was very soon filled. They never repeated themselves. At night, during the rare intervals spared me by insomnia, I dreamed of the book.

Summer was drawing to a close, and I realized that the book was monstrous. It was cold consolation to think that I, who looked upon it with my eyes and fondled it with my ten flesh-and-bone fingers, was no less monstrous than the book. I felt it was a nightmare thing, an obscene thing, and that it defiled and corrupted reality.

I considered fire, but I feared that the burning of an infinite book might be similarly infinite, and suffocate the planet in smoke.

I remembered reading once that the best place to hide a leaf is in the forest. Before my retirement I had worked in the National Library, which contained nine hundred thousand books; I knew that to the right of the lobby a curving staircase descended into the shadows of the basement, where the maps and periodicals are kept. I took advantage of the librarians' distraction to hide the Book of Sand on one of the library's damp shelves; I tried not to notice how high up, or how far from the door.

I now feel a little better, but I refuse even to walk down the street the library's on.

Translated by Andrew Hurley

Juan Martinez

CUSTOMER SERVICE AT THE KARAOKE DON QUIXOTE

Customer service at the Karaoke Don Quixote is main thing we worry about. Because if customer doesn't go here, will go elsewhere, and soon no customers go here period. We treat them special. We feign bad foreign accent to make feel better. We not decide on particular region—because if customer is from said particular region, or customer's family is, is no good, no? No. Is no good. Is little Italian, little Polack, little bit here and there. Is good.

Because it gets customer singing. Customer service is number one priority for us. We say, You sing, you sing! Is person drinking? Yes! Is good, for beer and spirits make person sing, and people singing is good: They buy more beer and spirits. And intoxication is good because is no cover charge. Is good, because people like singing great works of literature, and is good because they drink more, so more profits.

First we start with *Don Quixote*. But soon we branch to post-modernist stuff, because customers want, and customers is always accurate: They say, Barth! Barthelme! Pynchon! Coover! We say, okay. We say, is good. Also postmodernists drink. Minimalists, they don't drink so much. Is poetry good? No, is no good. Poetry kara-oke, is like haiku, sonatinas—no good, no one sings. Classic is good: Melville and Tolstoy and some other peoples—big hits, big big hits.

Is reason for accent? Is annoying you? Logic? Logic is, these are shy peoples—literature peoples is shy. Is sitting around read-ing, no much dancing, maybe some drinking and then dancing, but stiff, you know? Is people reading travel, you know? The *New York Times* travel section? Also travelogues and such. Is dreaming of going elsewhere, maybe finding charming out-of-the-way spots with kindly innkeepers, lovely foreign women, also big motherly types that feed them exotic soups and ales and such. And maybe, in this fantasy of going places, they're thinking they might let go a little because no one knows them, right? So we feed that fantasy a little. Is good, is people happy. Is good business. People sing: They sing *Quixote*:

«En un lugar de la Mancha, de cuyo nombre no quiero acor-darme, no ha mucho tiempo que vivía un hidalgo de los de lanza en astillero, adarga antigua, rocín flaco y galgo corredor.»

Or sing dubbed international public domain version:

"In a village of La Mancha, the name of which I have no desire to call to mind, there lived not long since one of those gentlemen that keep a lance in the lance-rack, an old buckler, a lean hack, and a greyhound for coursing."

Is good? Business is good. We have many franchises. As for matter of customer service—customers happy, is always happy here—service-wise we are number one. Soon we open in La Mancha—is ironic, no? Waiters feign heavy American accent. Talk loud. Slow. Is good. People feel okay singing. Is happy.

Soon: IPO. T-shirts. Web site. CDs. Is good!

Carmen Boullosa

IMPOSSIBLE STORY

They were left alone. Laura suddenly felt tired. She sat on the edge of the bed to take her shoes off; made of stiff leather, they seemed to him more rigid than wooden clogs. "I'm going to put some music on," she said to him. "You'll love it. Wait a minute." She went into the bathroom and shut the door. He remained alone, wondering at everything he saw: the transparent vase on the bedside table, the table itself, the shelves full of books, when the sound of music hit him, a blow that Montezuma could never have imagined, like a coup de grâce yet full of joy, something that deafened him at first and then filled him with emotion. What music was that? When Laura came out of the bathroom, he asked her, "What am I listening to?" "There are many instruments," she explained, "interpreting the music written by a man called Vivaldi. I put it in this box where it is being played for you because Vivaldi wrote an opera with your name. He made the music, which is the sound you can hear, to honor you, many years ago, much closer to the time when the captain of La Malinche landed here than to our present day." And she thinks, How could Vivaldi have ever imagined that one day Montezuma would hear it on tape? Never! While Montezuma wonders what artifices Laura employed to make so many musicians play such strange sounds. What kind of sounds are they? What does one hear in them?

But Montezuma is not thinking. At this point he no longer thinks. He no longer wonders "what?" and "how?" Does not say, "It can't be" or "I'm a Mexica Indian. I live differently from these people who have invented other ways of being." He says nothing, remembers nothing as if what he sees might affect his being, invade his body, enter his pores, consume him. No, not consume him. Montezuma is there present, watching, conscious without speaking or forming a judgment. As if he did not have a body, only eyes or, rather, as if instead of having eyes and a head, he were just a body that explores and sees. That is the only word I can think of: see. He does not order things, or explain them, yet he misses nothing. At lightning speed he has invented within himself a way to survive, this new way of being. Not for one moment does he say to himself: "I'm Montezuma, miraculously reborn in the same geographical space where once stood the great Tenochtitlán." He never thinks of what is happening, not because he shuts his eyes but because he opens them more and more. It is as if, abolishing his original vision of life and death, of the universe and nothingness, he arises a new being made up of wonder and observation. There he is, Montezuma, watching, feeling.

Why did Laura once again take him in hand like a child? She led him to the bathroom and placed him in front of the toilet. "Have a pee in there, pass water, if you prefer to call it that, and I'll be back." And she shut the door. Standing alone by the lavatory, he undid the knot of his pants and pissed. An endless stream that could not be just the result of the chocolate drunk that morning; an ancestral flow of urine cut off (as the result of a wound?) on the day of his death and which by some stupid biological error had stayed in his body. Perhaps that was why he had been sent back to earth with his entire body, to release in this lavatory the urine he was not meant to keep in his death. With slow and ceremonial movements he once again tied up his pants, and she came back, pulled the chain, and let the water flow from two taps into the pink tile bathtub, mixing the two jets until it was full of warm water. She undressed him and helped him to get in, chatting all the time, "What a lovely bath, just for you, to calm you down and see whether you change that expression of yours and look more at ease." Montezuma got inside the bath and relaxed in the warm clear water and watched her pour a liquid in it, something that turned into bluish bubbles. Then she rubbed him with a very smooth sponge, rinsed him with clear water from the handheld hose, and helped him out of the bath, wrapping him in a soft towel.

Standing in front of him she undressed and gave herself a quick cold shower, to wake up and get rid of this hangover.

She then wrapped herself in a towel, got out of the bathroom, opened the door to the bedroom, and lay on the bed on top of the damp towel. Then she threw it aside and went naked under the covers. He watched her, let his towel slip down on the wet bathroom floor, and went naked toward the bed. Laura lifted the covers to let him lie beside her. What happened then had nothing to do with the power of desire. It would be foolish to think so; how could he desire her or she desire him? At first it was as if their bodies had stumbled, missed a step, and the sheer clumsiness had made them fall by each other's side and embrace. But after the first move, clumsy and accidental as it was, turning over at the same time from their different positions, they allowed their bodies to fall into each other's arms as if they were alien objects.

The result was of such comfort—not entirely devoid of desire—and of such relief that they could no longer let go. They were releasing each other from their suffering, their painful situation. For her, the meaningless condition of a young woman full of life, at the end of the twentieth century, living in a city once the greatest and most beautiful in the world, now the most crowded, the most populated, and perhaps the most insane of them all. For him the uncomfortable feeling of waking up centuries after his death in the very place where his city stood, recognizing nothing except the skeletons of his temples. Nestling between two clean sheets, a light eiderdown filled with goose feathers and two pillows with embroidered edges also of white cotton, Laura and Montezuma inexplicably—and this is not an author's nonsense, because if you are to consider the act you'd soon call it incredible and even idiotic, but that's what happened, and what am I to do besides just say so—Laura and Montezuma inexplicably copulated, fucked, became man and wife. You choose the term, this is your privilege, name as you like the act they performed and which I am hurrying to recount before these pages be irremediably condemned (the story is pretty well finished) to come to an end.

FOR A WHILE they seemed not to be moving, or rather to be both trotting at the same rhythm, her two hands placed on his hips pushing him away from her ever so lightly—yet such a separation between their two skins—until his body fell again hard and strong, deeper into the hollow that Laura's thighs could not hold back. For a long while they seemed not to be moving, identical as they were in their movements (one-two, one-two, their repeated comings and goings), a canvas to which the skilled artist added final touches:

drops of sweat here and there, hair tossed away, muscles relaxing in a uniform, precise rhythm.

For a while they were firm as a statue balanced by the comings and goings of the wind, still, impeccable in the exasperation of the approaching climax. Every part of their body was pleasure, their teeth and ears, their nails and their flickering eyes. But they did not, could not know this because they were standing at the edge of the place where everybody gets lost. They did not know that they were feeling pleasure, as if they were never to come out of its unconscious state.

A new element intrudes like a dagger, which tears the perfection of the canvas; the voice of Laura scoring the picture they are forming, perfect, divine in their perfection within that image which nobody could understand just by looking, a drawing of flesh and spirit (if you could distinguish one from the other), an incomprehensible work perfected by a passion without name or explanation, whose only meaning lies there in that moment torn by Laura's voice, which says in a tone too feeble to be imagined, "I am coming, come with me!"

And after this voice, so new in her mouth, Laura's body dissolves like smoke arising from a burning corpse, like steam from water before disappearing into dispersed particles, which no longer remember or know that they had been water, that they had belonged to it.

And him? The same thing happens to him. What remains of him on the bed is his atrocious dejection, the white yolks of his semen, the senseless grayish thick stain, left behind, while he returns to the air, the wisdom of rocks and water, forgetting, perhaps forever, the uncomfortable verticality of the human body. All pleasure at last without distinction, turned into complete surrender where not time or language or custom watch over one's actions, like the fattening of victims, measuring the warm fragile immensity of man, then to crash it, blunting out all flexibility, against the blind reality of the individual.

He dispersed into minute unidentifiable particles, in the fins of a fish, the bark of a tree, the bed of a river; wind and fire where the air that surrounds the earth ceases to exist. No memory, no city, immensely wise in his lack of knowledge, without wondering whether or not he would once again be called to duty or even whether he ever was. His consciousness lost in minimal deaf and blind fragments, finally exempt from pain, struggle, battles, and wars, from the vacuum and the absence of being, powerful or not, man or woman, free or slave in all the meanings of the word, like a nail in the wind, being nowhere, made of nothing, with no truths, altogether good, more good than bread, wise as a stone but without the misfortune of intelligence.

Translated by Psiche Hughes

EVA AND DANIEL

People still remember Eva and Daniel. They were both very good looking, and in all honesty it was a pleasure to see them together. But that's not the reason people remember them. They were very young when they got married or, rather, when they eloped. Her parents hardly got angry at all, and, if they did, it was for a very short time and that was because everyone who knew Daniel liked him very much and had many good reasons to like him. They eloped up north during the county fair that was held every year in Bird Island.

Both families lived on the same ranch. They worked together in the same fields, they went to town in the same truck, and they just about had their meals together; they were that close. That's why no one was surprised when they started going together. And, even though everyone knew about it, no one let on, and even Eva and Daniel, instead of talking with one another, would write letters to each other once in a while. I remember very clearly that that Saturday when they eloped they were going happily to the fair in the truck. Their hair was all messed up by the wind, but when they got to the fair they didn't even remember to comb it.

They got on every ride, then they separated from the group and no one saw them again until two days later.

"Don't be afraid. We can take a taxi to the ranch. Move over this way, come closer, let me touch you. Don't you love me?"

"Yes, yes."

"Don't be afraid. We'll get married. I don't care about anything else. Just you. If the truck leaves us behind, we'll go back in a taxi."

"But they're going to get after me."

"Don't worry. If they do, I'll protect you myself. Anyway, I want to marry you. I'll ask your father for permission to court you if you want me to. What do you say? Shall we get married?"

At midnight, when all the games were closed and the lights of the fair were turned off and the explosions of the fireworks were no longer heard, Eva and Daniel still hadn't shown up. Their parents started to worry then, but they didn't notify the police. By one-thirty in the morning the other people became impatient. They got on and off the truck every few minutes and, finally, Eva's father told the driver to drive off. Both families were worried. They had a feeling that Eva and Daniel had eloped and they were sure they would get married, but they were worried anyway. And they would keep on worrying until they saw them again. What they didn't know was that Eva and Daniel were already at the ranch. They were hiding in the barn, up in the loft where the boss stored hay for the winter. That's why, even though they looked for them in the nearby towns, they didn't find them until two days later when they came down from the loft very hungry.

There were some very heated discussions but, finally, Eva's parents consented to their marriage. The following day they took Eva and Daniel to get their blood test, then a week later they took them before the judge and the parents had to sign because they were too young.

"You see how everything turned out all right."

"Yes, but I was afraid when Father got all angry. I even thought he was going to hit you when he saw us for the first time."

"I was afraid too. We're married now. We can have children."

"Yes."

"I hope that they grow real tall and that they look like you and me. I wonder how they will be?"

"Just let them be like you and me."

"If it's a girl I hope she looks like you; if it's a boy I hope he looks like me."

"What if we don't have any?"

"Why not? My family and your family are very large."

"I'll say."

"Well, then?"

"I was just talking."

Things really began to change after they were married. First of all because, by the end of the first month of their marriage, Eva was vomiting often, and then also Daniel received a letter from the government telling him to be in such and such town so that he could take his physical for the army. He was afraid when he saw the letter, not so much for himself, but he immediately sensed the separation that would come forever.

"You see, son, if you hadn't gone to school you wouldn't have passed the examination."

"Oh, mama. They don't take you just because you passed the examination. Anyway I'm already married, so they probably won't take me. And another thing, Eva is already expecting."

"I don't know what to do, son, every night I pray that they won't take you. So does Eva. You should have lied to them. You should have played dumb so you wouldn't pass."

"Oh, come on, mama."

By November, instead of returning to Texas with his family, Daniel stayed up north, and in a few days he was in the army. The days didn't seem to have any meaning for him—why should there be night, morning, or day. Sometimes he didn't care anything about anything. Many times he thought about escaping and returning to his own town so that he could be with Eva. When he thought at all, that was what he thought about—Eva. I think he even became sick, once or maybe it was several times, thinking so much about her. The first letter from the government had meant their separation, and now the separation became longer and longer.

"I wonder why I can't think of anything else other than Eva? If I hadn't known her, I wonder what I would think about. Probably about myself, but now . . . ."

Things being what they were, everything marched on. Daniel's training continued at the same pace as Eva's pregnancy. They transferred Daniel to California, but before going he had the chance to be with Eva in Texas. The first night they went to sleep kissing. They were happy once again for a couple of weeks but then right away they were separated again. Daniel wanted to stay but then he decided to go on to California. He was being trained to go to Korea. Later Eva started getting sick. The baby was bringing complications. The closer she came to the day of delivery, the greater the complications.

"You know, *viejo*, something is wrong with that baby."

"Why do you say that?"

"Something is wrong with her. She gets very high fevers at night."

"I hope everything turns out all right, but even the doctor looks quite worried. Have you noticed?"

"No."

"Yesterday he told me that we had to be very careful with Eva. He gave us a whole bunch of instructions, but it's difficult when you can't understand him. Can you imagine? How I wish Daniel were here. I'll bet you Eva would even get well. I already wrote to him saying that she is very sick, hoping that he'll come to see her, but maybe his superiors won't believe him and won't let him come."

"Well, write to him again. Maybe he can arrange something, if he speaks out."

"Maybe, but I've already written him a number of letters saying the same thing. You know, I'm not too worried about him anymore. Now I worry about Eva."

"They're both so young."

"Yes they are, aren't they."

Eva's condition became worse and, when he received a letter from his mother in which she begged him to come see his wife, either Daniel didn't make himself understood or his superiors didn't believe him. They didn't let him go. He went AWOL just before he was to be sent to Korea. It took him three days to get to Texas on the bus. But he was too late.

I remember very well that he came home in a taxi. When he got down and heard the cries coming from inside the house he rushed in. He went into a rage and threw everyone out of the house and locked himself in for almost the rest of the day. He only went out when he had to go to the toilet, but even in there he could be heard sobbing.

He didn't go back to the army and no one ever bothered to come looking for him. Many times I saw him burst into tears. I think he was remembering. Then he lost all interest in himself. He hardly spoke to anyone.

One time he decided to buy fireworks to sell during Christmastime. The package of fireworks that he sent for through a magazine advertisement cost him plenty. When he got them, instead of selling them, he didn't stop until he set them all off himself. Since that time that's all he does with what little money he earns to support himself. He sets off fireworks just about every night. I think that's why around this part of the country people still remember Eva and Daniel. Maybe that's it.

José Emilio Pacheco

THE CAPTIVE

At six o'clock in the morning an earthquake shook the entire town from top to bottom. We ran out into the streets fearing that the houses were going to topple down on top of us. And once we were outside, we were afraid the ground would open up under our feet.

The quake was over, but the women continued to pray. A few alarmists said that there would soon be another one of greater intensity. The general anxiety was so great, we thought they would not send us off to school. Classes began an hour late. In class, we all spoke about our experiences during the cataclysm, until the professor said that at our age, fourth graders that we were, we should not be superstitious like the rest of the people in the town, nor should we ascribe natural phenomena to divine judgments or omens or the unleashing of evil forces. And in any case, the quake had caused no catastrophes: the only buildings that sustained any real damage were the colonial churches and houses.

We were convinced by his arguments and repeated them, more or less faithfully, to our parents. By the afternoon, everything had returned to normal. Sergio and Guillermo stopped by the house to get me. We went out into the lush field between the river and the cemetery. The setting sun reflected off the marble crosses and the granite monuments.

Guillermo suggested we go have a look at what had happened to the ruins of the convent that stood near town. We were usually afraid to go there after dark; but that afternoon everything seemed fascinating and explainable.

We walked past the cemetery, and, choosing the most difficult path, we climbed up the hill until it became so steep we almost had to crawl along on our bellies. We felt dizzy when we looked down, but, without uttering a word, each of us was trying to prove that the other two were the cowards.

We finally reached the ruins of the convent that rose up at the top of the hill. We walked through the portico. We stopped in front of the wall that surrounded the terrace and the first cells. We found some dead bees on the floor tiles. Guillermo went over and picked one up. Silently, he came back and joined us. We walked through a hallway where the humidity and the nitrate had corroded the ancient frescoes.

Without confessing to each other our growing fears, we found our way to the cloister, which was even more ravaged than the other parts of the building. The central patio was covered with thistles and weeds. Two rotten beams leaned against a cracked wall.

We climbed a broken staircase to the second floor. Darkness had set in, and it was beginning to rain. The first sounds of the night rose all around us. The rain resounded on the porous stones. The wind sighed in the darkness.

As he approached the window, Sergio saw, or thought he saw, in what had been the cemetery, balls of fire zigzagging through the broken crosses. We heard a thunderclap. A bat flew off the ceiling. The flapping of its wings echoed dully against the dome.

We ran down the hallway and were nearing the door to the staircase when we heard Sergio scream: his whole body was shaking, and he just barely managed to point to one of the cells. We grabbed him by his arms and, without hiding our fears any longer, went toward the cell. As we were about to enter, Sergio pried himself loose, ran through the hallway, and left us there alone.

We soon realized that a wall had fallen and, full of terror, we looked into what had been a crypt or perhaps an ossarium: pieces of coffins, disintegrated bones, skulls.

Suddenly, in the semidarkness, we saw the white tunic of a woman who was seated on an iron chair. A mummified body: intact in its infinite calm and perpetual immobility.

I felt the cold rush of fear through every vein and joint. I summoned up all my strength and approached the cadaver. With three fingers I touched the forehead's wrinkled skin: under the slightest pressure the body disintegrated, turning to dust on the metal chair. It seemed as if the entire world was falling to pieces along with the captive in the convent. Everything swam before my eyes; the night was filled with a clamor and uproar, and the walls crumbled and were laid to waste as their secret was revealed.

Guillermo then dragged me out of the cell and, heedless of danger, we dashed down the hill at full speed. At the entrance to town, we met up with the men Sergio had called to help us. They went up to the convent. When they returned, they ascertained that indeed it was a crypt from around 1800 with some pulverized remains from that period. There was no cadaver. That had been a hallucination, a product of our fear, the storm and the darkness that caught us unawares in the ruins, a delayed reaction to the shock the earthquake had produced in the whole town.

I could not sleep. My parents stayed near me. During the following days, the only person among all of those who questioned us who gave any credence to our story was the priest. He told of a legendary crime recorded in the annals of our town, a monstrous act of revenge that was carried out at the end of the eighteenth century but which nobody could prove had occurred until then. The cadaver that had dissolved under my touch was that of a woman who had been given a paralyzing potion and who, when she came to her senses, found herself walled into a tenebrous crypt accompanied only by cadavers and unable to get up from the chair in which we found her nearly two hundred years later.

TIME PASSED. I have not returned to the town, nor have I seen Sergio and Guillermo again, but each earthquake fills me with panic, for I feel as if the earth will spew up its bodies and only my hand will let them rest: the other death.

Translated by Katherine Silver

Jorge Luis Arzola

ESSENTIAL THINGS

Many things are now just a black space in my memory. But there was the sea, the fragrant journey and the galley—from Carthage?—and that boy so very like me (my friend, I believe), with his lover, that girl whose eyes spoke of desires and things of which I knew nothing then. . . . Or was I the lover, and was the boy the one who trembled to receive in his mouth the woman's small, salt breast?

But I could just as easily have been the girl. The three of us probably came from the West—from Rome, from Gaul, from some far place in the future: from the kingdom of Castile, from the Socialist Republic of Cuba? Or did we come, my two dark-skinned boys, from the past, their silken rosebuds between my lips; and the girl who, one moonlit night, behind a crate of salt, showed me, gave me the first taste of a breast perfect for my adolescent lips, the lips of a girl almost?

I was running away: the girl and her lover, and the other boy too, we were all escaping—from what, from whom, from where and to where? I was coming, going, running back home, and there was the smell of the sea and, of course, the sea itself and a port from which to weigh anchor, and a galley, a sailing ship, a vast steamship ready to weigh anchor.

No one now can clarify the precise circumstances of this story. The three of us were running away, this is all that can be known. But the point of departure was doubtless a suffocating village, and we had decided to try our luck on the vastness of the sea.

I was the friend of the lover, and while I did not desire his girl, I had never desired anyone as much as I desired that girl. And there, in that loathsome village, I used to spy on them when he rocked like a boat on the sea between her legs.

Or was I perhaps the girl? And who was spying on whom? Sometimes I felt sorry for him watching us, but it was pleasurable too, the sight of his almost frightened face watching from afar. . . . I would lay my lover down on the grass and I would sit on top of him until I had had my fill, and I would offer up to him (to the boy) the sight of my breasts erect as tremulous promises.

(Ah, gods, did they not tremble like that too, those bunches of grapes loaded onto the back of a mule being driven to market by a peasant from a vineyard near the village?)

I was the girl, I was the lover, I was the friend who dreamed of the girl sitting on top of him, not on his pubis, but on his chest, on his mouth. Then I was the lover who sensed both the veiled offers being made by my girl and my friend's covetous blushes.

And which of us planned the escape? Who convinced whom that there was a reason to escape?

I accept that it was me, the friend of the lovers. I had more than enough reasons. The girl wanted me, and I wanted her. In fact, once, as if by accident, she showed me one charming breast, while she was explaining to her lover that they had a surplus of oranges that year, enough to be able to sell some.

The important thing, though, was that the three of us decided to run away from the village together. And early one morning, we left. I remember that it was a long, hard walk until we found the sea and could feel that we were rendering null and void that now-distant, unimaginable village, which may never have been anything but my way, our way, of giving a name to our fear, although now I don't even know why I mentioned it, since I've never said anything about neighbors or judges, with which all villages everywhere are crammed.

The fact is that, one day, we found the sea and set sail joyfully, and that on another day, at last, my beloved and the boy met behind a crate of salt on the deck. At the time, I was (perhaps) in my first-class cabin drinking whiskey, or talking to the man in charge of the galley while he whipped the Scythian oarsmen, who complained ceaselessly.

But I could have been the girl. I was the girl, and sometimes I think I can remember my beloved standing there in the port—of Samos? of New York?—while our ship sailed swiftly away. I can still feel the unexpected sadness of seeing him left behind there, gesturing and shouting. . . . But before us, immense, lay the sea, and on my waist I suddenly felt the boy's hand. It was a delicate, almost girlish hand.

The sun was setting in the distance and there was a breeze and we were free. And then I no longer felt quite so sad.

Translated by Margaret Jull Costa

Sandra Cisneros

PILÓN

Like the Mexican grocer who gives you a pilón, some-thing extra tossed into your bag as a thank-you for your patronage just as you are leaving, I give you here another story in thanks for having listened to my cuento . . .

On Cinco de Mayo Street, in front of Café la Blanca, an organ grinder playing "Farolito." Out of a happy grief, people give coins for shaking awake the memory of a father, a beloved, a child whom God ran away with.

And it was as if that music stirred up things in a piece of my heart from a time I couldn't remember. From before. Not exactly a time, a feeling. The way sometimes one remembers a memory with the images blurred and rounded, but has forgotten the one thing that would draw it all into focus. In this case, I'd forgotten a mood. Not a mood—a state of being, to be more precise.

How before my body wasn't my body. I didn't have a body. I was a being as close to a spirit as a spirit. I was a ball of light floating across the planet. I mean the me I was before puberty, that red Rio Bravo you have to carry yourself over.

I don't know how it is with boys. I've never been a boy. But girls somewhere between the ages of, say, eight and puberty, girls forget they have bodies. It's the time she has trouble keeping herself clean, socks always drooping, knees pocked and bloody, hair crooked as a broom. She doesn't look in mirrors. She isn't aware of being watched. Not aware of her body causing men to look at her yet. There isn't the sense of the female body's volatility, its rude weight, the nuisance of dragging it about. There isn't the world to bully you with it, bludgeon you, condemn you to a life sentence of fear. It's the time when you look at a young girl and notice she is at her ugliest, but at the same time, at her happiest. She is a being as close to a spirit as a spirit.

Then that red Rubicon. The never going back there. To that country, I mean.

And I remember along with that feeling fluttering through the notes of "Farolito," so many things, so many, all at once, each distinct and separate, and all running together. The taste of a *caramelo* called Glorias on my tongue. At la Caleta beach, a girl with skin like *cajeta*, like goat-milk candy. The *caramelo* color of your skin after rising out of the Acapulco foam, salt water running down your hair and stinging the eyes, the raw ocean smell, and the ocean running out of your mouth and nose. My mother watering her dahlias with a hose and running a stream of water over her feet as well, Indian feet, thick and square, *como de barro*, like the red clay of Mexican pottery.

And I don't know how it is with anyone else, but for me these things, that song, that time, that place, are all bound together in a country I am homesick for, that doesn't exist anymore. That never existed. A country I invented. Like all emigrants caught between here and there.

Raúl Brasca

4 MICROSTORIES

LOVE 1

She likes love. I don't. I like her, even, clearly, her taste for love. I don't give her love. I give her passion wrapped up in words, many words. She kids herself, believes that it is love and she likes it: She loves the impostor in me. I don't love her and I'm not fooled by appearances, I don't love *her*. What we have is very common: two who persevere together thanks to one feeling that is misunderstood and another that is mistaken. We're happy.

LOVE 2

He claims that I'm in love while he is only interested in sex. I let him believe it. When his body arouses me, he attributes it to his many words. When my body arouses him, he puts it down to his own ardor. But he loves me. And I let him fool himself because I love him. I know very well that we will be happy as long as he believes that we do not love each other.

For Marcelo Caruso

THE TEST

"Only when it is cut down will you have my daughter," the sorcerer said. The lumberjack looked at the tree's slender stem with a self-satisfied smile. His first, formidable blow lightly grazed the trunk. Another, in the same place, barely deepened the gash. Night had long fallen when the lumberjack collapsed, exhausted. He rested until daybreak, then hacked away all day. And so on, day after day. The cut gradually deepened, but the trunk kept getting thicker. Time passed and the tree's foliage grew lusher, while the girl lost her youth and beauty. At times, the lumberjack would look up to the skies, not knowing that the sorcerer was warding off gales, diverting lightning bolts, and casting away wood-eating blights. The girl's hair turned gray and he kept on cutting. He barely thought about her anymore. Eventually he completely forgot about her. The day the girl died didn't seem any different to him from the previous days. Old now, he continues his fight against the enormous tree. He wouldn't know what else to do: The axe's silence would fill him with terror.

For Cristina Fernández Barragán, in memoriam

THE HOLE

He'd been digging in the sand for three minutes when the hole swallowed up his spade. Disconcerted, the boy looked to his mother. The woman saw him sink in, ran over in horror, grabbed his hands, and sank with him. Before the other bathers could react, the hole was swallowing up a parasol. They looked at each other in astonishment, saw that they too were converging on the hole and, with an instinct that had been forever buried until now, realized that they couldn't save themselves. It was as natural as dusk: the world turning inside out. Many tried to flee, slowly, with the hopeless apprehension of animals seeking shelter from the storm. But the sand slipped faster and in they all meekly fell. In turn, the hole swallowed up houses, cities, mountains. Just as an unseen hand folds back a shirt sleeve, a powerful force dragged the skin of the world within, turning it inside out. And when the last frayed remnants of seas and lands had been gulped down, the hole swallowed itself. It did not leave so much as a fleeting gap in space: Only the void remained, homogeneous and silent, incontrovertible evidence that the world had always been the other side of nothing.

Translated by Daniel Tunnard

Isabel Allende

OUR SECRET

She let herself be caressed, drops of sweat in the small of her back, her body exuding the scent of burnt sugar, silent, as if she divined that a single sound could nudge its way into memory and destroy everything, reducing to dust this instant in which he was a person like any other, a casual lover she had met that morning, another man without a past attracted to her wheat-colored hair, her freckled skin, the jangle of her gypsy bracelets, just a man who had spoken to her in the street and begun to walk with her, aimlessly, commenting on the weather and the traffic, watching the crowd, with the slightly forced confidence of her countrymen in this foreign land, a man without sorrow or anger, without guilt, pure as ice, who merely wanted to spend the day with her, wandering through bookstores and parks, drinking coffee, celebrating the chance of having met, talking of old nostalgias, of how life had been when both were growing up in the same city, in the same barrio, when they were fourteen, you remember, winters of shoes soggy from frost, and paraffin stoves, summers of peach trees, there in the now forbidden country. Perhaps she was feeling a little lonely, or this seemed an opportunity to make love without complications, but, for whatever reason, at the end of the day, when they had run out of pretexts to walk any longer, she had taken his hand and led him to her house. She shared with other exiles a sordid apartment in a yellow building at the end of an alley filled with garbage cans. Her room was tiny: a mattress on the floor covered with a striped blanket, bookshelves improvised from boards stacked on two rows of bricks, books, posters, clothing on a chair, a suitcase in the corner. She had removed her clothes without preamble, with the attitude of a little girl eager to please. He tried to make love to her. He stroked her body patiently, slipping over her hills and valleys, discovering her secret routes, kneading her, soft clay upon the sheets, until she yielded, and opened to him. Then he retreated, mute, reserved. She gathered herself, and sought him, her head on his belly, her face hidden, as if constrained by modesty, as she fondled him, licked him, spurred him. He tried to lose himself; he closed his eyes and for a while let her do as she was doing, until he was defeated by sadness, or shame, and pushed her away. They lighted another cigarette. There was no complicity now; the urgent anticipation that had united them during the day was lost, and all that was left were two vulnerable people lying on a mattress, without memory, floating in the terrible vacuum of unspoken words. When they had met that morning they had had no extraordinary expectations, they had had no particular plan, only companionship, and a little pleasure, that was all, but at the hour of their coming together they had been engulfed by melancholy. We're tired, she smiled, seeking excuses for the desolation

that had settled over them. In a last attempt to buy time, he took
her face in his hands and kissed her eyelids. They lay down side by
side, holding hands, and talked about their lives in this country
where they had met by chance, a green and generous land in
which, nevertheless, they would forever be foreigners. He thought
of putting on his clothes and saying good-bye, before the tarantula
of his nightmares poisoned the air, but she looked so young and
defenseless, and he wanted to be her friend. Her friend, he thought,
not her lover; her friend, to share quiet moments, without demands
or commitments; her friend, someone to be with, to help ward off
fear. He did not leave, or let go her hand. A warm, tender feeling,
an enormous compassion for himself and for her, made his eyes
sting. The curtain puffed out like a sail, and she got up to close the
window, thinking that darkness would help them recapture their
desire to be together, to make love. But darkness was not good; he
needed the rectangle of light from the street, because without it he
felt trapped again in the abyss of the timeless ninety centimeters of
his cell, fermenting in his own excrement, delirious. Leave the
curtain open, I want to look at you, he lied, because he did not dare
confide his night terrors to her, the wracking thirst, the bandage
pressing upon his head like a crown of nails, the visions of caverns,
the assault of so many ghosts. He could not talk to her about that,
because one thing leads to another, and he would end up saying
things that had never been spoken. She returned to the mattress,
stroked him absently, ran her fingers over the small lines, exploring
them. Don't worry, it's nothing contagious, they're just scars, he
laughed, almost with a sob. The girl perceived his anguish and
stopped, the gesture suspended, alert. At that moment he should
have told her that this was not the beginning of a new love, not
even of a passing affair; it was merely an instant of truce, a brief
moment of innocence, and soon, when she fell asleep, he would
go; he should have told her that there was no future for them, no

secret gestures, that they would not stroll hand in hand through the streets again, nor share lovers' games, but he could not speak, his voice was buried somewhere in his gut, like a claw. He knew he was sinking. He tried to cling to the reality that was slipping away from him, to anchor his mind on anything, on the jumble of clothing on the chair, on the books piled on the floor, on the poster of Chile on the wall, on the coolness of this Caribbean night, on the distant street noises; he tried to concentrate on this body that had been offered him, think only of the girl's luxuriant hair, the caramel scent of her skin. He begged her voicelessly to help him save those seconds, while she observed him from the far edge of the bed, sitting cross-legged like a fakir, her pale breasts and the eye of her navel also observing him, registering his trembling, the chattering of his teeth, his moan. He thought he could hear the silence growing within him; he knew that he was coming apart, as he had so often before, and he gave up the struggle, releasing his last hold on the present, letting himself plunge down the endless precipice. He felt the crusted straps on his ankles and wrists, the brutal charge, the torn tendons, the insulting voices demanding names, the unforgettable screams of Ana, tortured beside him, and of the others, hanging by their arms in the courtyard.

What's the matter? For God's sake, what's wrong? Ana's voice was asking from far away. No, Ana was still bogged in the quicksands to the south. He thought he could make out a naked girl, shaking him and calling his name, but he could not get free of the shadows with their snaking whips and rippling flags. Hunched over, he tried to control the nausea. He began to weep for Ana and for all the others. What is it, what's the matter? Again the girl, calling him from somewhere. Nothing! Hold me! he begged, and she moved toward him timidly, and took him in her arms, lulled him like a baby, kissed his forehead, said, Go ahead, cry, cry all you want; she laid him flat on his back on the mattress and then, crucified, stretched out upon him.

For a thousand years they lay like that, together, until slowly the hallucinations faded and he returned to the room to find himself alive in spite of everything, breathing, pulsing, the girl's weight on his body, her head resting on his chest, her arms and legs atop his: two frightened orphans. And at that moment, as if she knew everything, she said to him, Fear is stronger than desire, than love or hatred or guilt or rage, stronger than loyalty. Fear is all-consuming . . . , and he felt her tears rolling down his neck. Everything stopped: She had touched his most deeply hidden wound. He had a presentiment that she was not just a girl willing to make love for the sake of pity but that she knew the thing that crouched beyond the silence, beyond absolute solitude, beyond the sealed box where he had hidden from the Colonel and his own treachery, beyond the memory of Ana Díaz and the other betrayed *compañeros* being led in one by one with their eyes blindfolded. How could she know all that?

She sat up. As she groped for the switch, her slender arm was silhouetted against the pale haze of the window. She turned on the light and, one by one, removed her metal bracelets, dropping them noiselessly on the mattress. Her hair was half covering her face when she held out her hands to him. White scars circled her wrists, too. For a timeless instant he stared at them, unmoving, until he understood everything, love, and saw her strapped to the electric grid, and then they could embrace, and weep, hungry for pacts and confidences, for forbidden words, for promises of tomorrow, shared, finally, the most hidden secret.

Translated by Margaret Sayers Peden

Rudolfo Anaya

THE NATIVE LAWYER

After many years of not seeing each other, two friends met at a village fiesta. Manuel invited Rufo to come to his home for breakfast the following morning.

—I will come if you let me buy the eggs, said Rufo. He insisted and gave Manuel twenty-five pesos to buy a dozen eggs.

Manuel bought the eggs, and the next morning his wife boiled them for breakfast. They waited a long time for Rufo to arrive, and finally decided he wasn't coming, so they ate the eggs.

Manuel didn't feel right about eating the eggs his friend had paid for, so he went out and bought a dozen eggs.

—Put these eggs under one of our hens, he told his wife. When the chicks are born we won't sell them, and when they are chickens and lay eggs we will raise more chicks. Half of everything that is produced from this dozen eggs, I will give to my friend Rufo.

A dozen chicks were born and when they were grown they began to lay eggs. Manuel sold some of the eggs and set the money aside. The rest of the eggs he allowed to hatch. Soon he had the most thriving business in the country. And always, he put aside half of his earnings to give to Rufo.

With the money he made from the egg business he bought many ranches, cows, and sheep. He became the richest man in the entire Río Arriba region of the Río Grande valley. He told everyone that all his riches had come from the eggs Rufo had given him, and when he saw his friend again he would give him half of everything he had earned.

Finally the news reached Rufo that Manuel had grown exceedingly rich, and that everything he had earned came from the eggs he had bought for breakfast long ago. He saddled his horse and rode off to visit Manuel.

—I am glad to see you, said Manuel. Do you remember the twenty-five pesos you gave me to buy eggs? I bought them and boiled them, but since you didn't show up for breakfast my wife and I ate them.

—How did you become so rich? asked Rufo.

—I bought another dozen eggs, and from those I made a fortune. I made a promise that I would give you half of anything I earned.

Rufo shook his head.

—If all this wealth came from the money I gave you, then everything belongs to me.

Manuel was surprised.

—That's not fair, he replied. I've worked hard to accumulate this wealth. I'll give you half and that way both of us profit.

—No, said an angry Rufo, it all belongs to me! And if you don't sign it over to me I'll take you to court!

Rufo went off in search of a lawyer. He found two who said they would represent him in a suit if he gave them half of all he was awarded by a judge. Rufo agreed and the two attorneys brought a suit against Manuel.

Soon the entire region was talking about the case. Everyone thought Rufo would win. Manuel tried to find a lawyer who would represent him, but none were willing.

One day as he sat contemplating his fate, Salvador, an Indian neighbor who lived in a nearby pueblo, walked by.

—How are you, *vecino?* asked Salvador. You look very sad. Tell me, what's the matter.

—There's too much to tell, replied Manuel, and nothing you can do to help.

—I'm your neighbor, maybe I can help.

—What I need is a good lawyer, but I can't find one. Tomorrow I have to appear in court. I'm afraid I'm going to lose everything I own.

—How did this happen? asked Salvador, and Manuel told him the entire story.

—Oh, compadre, I think I can persuade the judge to rule in your favor. How much will you pay me?

Manuel was surprised. How could an uneducated Indian win his case?

—I would pay you fifty pesos.

—No, that's too much. Give me a bushel of corn.

—If you win you deserve more, said Manuel. Thank you, neighbor.

—Oh, and bring a pot of cooked *habas*, those beans I like so much.

Manuel thought that Salvador wanted the beans for lunch,

so the following morning he was ready. When Salvador arrived he wrapped the pot of fresh baked beans in a serape and off they went.

The courthouse was packed with people. Everyone wanted to know if Manuel had found a lawyer to represent him, but they saw him arrive with only Salvador at his side.

—Is he your attorney? a man asked.

—Yes, answered Manuel.

Everyone laughed, thinking the Indian could never beat Rufo's two educated lawyers.

When the judge entered he looked at Salvador and shook his head. He asked Manuel if he had a lawyer.

—Yes, replied Manuel, Salvador is my attorney.

Laughter broke out again. Salvador had lifted the lid from the pot and was eating beans. An illiterate Indian eating beans could hardly be a good attorney.

The judge banged his gavel and called for the first of Rufo's lawyers to present his case, which he did very eloquently. Then the second lawyer rose and finished by saying if all of Manuel's fortune came from the eggs purchased by Rufo's twenty-five pesos then the fortune belonged to Rufo. When he had presented the argument he sat down.

All the time Salvador was dipping into the pot and eating beans.

—It is your turn, don Salvador, said the judge sarcastically.

—Father Judge, said Salvador, I ask the court to lend me a piece of land so I can plant a crop.

—Is that all you have to say? asked the exasperated judge.

—Oh, I have to ask Manuel what he did with the eggs he bought with the twenty-five pesos?

Manuel rose and said,

—My wife boiled the eggs and we ate them.

Then Salvador asked Rufo if he had told Manuel to prepare the eggs for breakfast.

—Yes, replied Rufo. I told him to cook the eggs for breakfast.

Salvador turned to the judge. I ask your honor to lend me a piece of land to farm.

—The court is not in the business of lending farmland! exclaimed the judge. I'm tired of you asking the silly question. Is that the only defense you have?

—Yes, your honor. I can only ask the court to lend me a piece of land to farm.

By this time the judge had decided the Indian was crazy, and so it would be best to humor him.

—And what would you plant on the land? he asked.

Salvador reached into the pot and pulled out a handful of beans.

—I would plant these beans, he said.

—You are crazy! replied the judge. Those beans won't grow! They've been cooked.

—Yes, said Salvador, just as the dozen eggs Manuel bought with the money were boiled. Nothing could come from those eggs.

The surprised judge nodded. Salvador had made his point.

—What you say is true. No further product could have come from the boiled eggs, and so I must rule that Manuel keeps his property. The court is adjourned.

Manuel went home with his good neighbor Salvador, leaving everyone in awe of the native lawyer. His common sense had beaten the educated lawyers.

Raúl Leis

SEÑOR NOBOA

For Ernesto Cardenal

Señor Noboa is the owner of half a province. During the last fifty years he had extended the lands inherited from his father by squeezing small landholders so they would sell him their small properties for a pittance. This was also how the large properties he inherited had come into being.

Of the many things that Señor Noboa possesses, the most valuable is the banana tree. In association with a foreign company, his lands are covered with green-gold stalks and clusters that are watered by the sweat of thousands of laborers, who never earn more than ninety dollars a month.

Once a year Señor Noboa personally tours his lands, atop his white horse and sweating heavy streams beneath his Panama hat. None of his banana camps fails to receive a visit from the lord and

163

master. On that day, the only one all year long, something out of the ordinary happens. The peons turn their backs and refuse to look him in the face, because the legend has gone around that every time Señor Noboa visits those places a laborer dies of some illness or accident.

They all remember when three years ago a machine shredded the hands of the Chinaman Ramírez, and he died with the blood spurting from his wounds while he got paler and paler until he was white as a piece of paper. Or good old Sebastian, who was hit by a lung problem that finished him off before you could say boo. And Rafael? He got sick and died from the insecticides they used on the young banana sprouts. Not to speak of Matías; he was surprised by a coral snake in a clearing and that was it for him in spite of all the spells and invocations offered by Domingo the *curandero*, who traced the sign of the cross all over him in saliva and dark tobacco.

So that is why the people don't want to look Señor Noboa in the face, because they think it is the only way to avoid the evil spell the boss carries around with him. Señor Noboa is quite familiar with the legend that time has woven around him, and he enjoys it fully. It fascinates him to be able to instill that double fear. On the one hand, to be the omnipotent buyer/owner of all that effort of sweat-soaked labor that topples the banana stalks with lightning blows from sharpened machetes; and, on the other hand, to possess this supernatural power of causing death with the same ease as one snuffs out a candle. But he knows that his only real power is the first. The second has come about only as the result of stringing together a fortuitous series of accidents linked to the natural risks of the job like little chains of thread crocheted by a dressmaker's hands.

He spurs his horse and reaches the last of the camps, where the foreman greets him while looking only in the direction of Señor Noboa's mud-caked boots.

"So this is the troublemakers' camp," the master says to himself, and brings to mind the several attempts at strikes that have taken place around this place throughout the year. "No one is looking at me."

And he laughs inwardly, convinced that his legendary power is a potent ingredient for thoroughly crushing those who question his authority by alleging salary or health claims.

Hundreds of laborers are gathered around him with their eyes set on the clouds, the dirt, or the greenness of the forest. Without dismounting, Señor Noboa lets loose a tirade in a stentorian voice. Right to the heart of the matter. No beating around the bush. Puts them in their place. Sets the example. Threatens. Warns. A pause to wipe off the sweat.

Without looking at him, a group of peons pulls on a rope. A woven grass mat that faces the master falls, exposing a large mirror to view. Señor Noboa stares at himself in it, full length, on horseback, face to face. And Señor Noboa sees Señor Noboa as he falls from his horse. As he shudders with strange convulsions. As his face grows purple, his hands twitch. As he dies with all his might, as his mouth fills with ants. While the *curandero* Domingo vainly outlines cross after cross in saliva and dark tobacco all over the body of Señor Noboa.

Translated by Leland H. Chambers

Juan Felipe Herrera

HOW TO LIVE WITH A FEMINISTA AND (STILL) BE A MACHO: NOTES UNABRIDGED

There are seven ways.

The first involves the ability to be a *payaso*—a nimble clown with the eyes akimbo as a Chicano Charlie Chaplin's or, even better, a Hispanic legislative type—let's call him Cristóbal.

Cristóbal with a three-piece suit of propriety, hard Catholicism, and a well-defined leaning toward apologia. "Have you been there?" he asks her. "Have you eaten shoelace potatoes made out of leather and never winced?" Cristóbal utters bitter reprisals in a sweet munchkin voice.

"I've cut my long hair, shaved my mustache," he says, "just for you." Sometimes he wears tight *puto* jeans, drives upstate in the snow, and buys her fancy fuchsia-colored undergarments thinking he's on the right track—on the way to a skewed but tasty what-can-you-do-for-me *Paraíso*.

Marlon Brando for the second way.

Are you ready to graduate into true testosterone leather?

Maybe you've been in Venice, California, wearing an *Easy Rider* helmet that Raoul, a good acid buddy, gave you. Got the jacket in the outskirt boutiques of Beverly Hills for twelve dollars, caffè-latte–colored boots from Greenwich Village (got them when you purchased the fuchsia stuff on an earlier jaunt). For the Brando effect you speak slow, with a twang, and you burn internally, mutter the inadequacies of conjugal romance, kick domesticity backward, and eat very small tortes while you smolder on your lover's locked journals. This stuff can get you places fast—too fast.

For the third road you go holy.

I said *holy*, carnal.

Holier than the typical middle-class-hamster-maharishi-iconoclast. You go into 100 percent cotton, no *calzones*, no under-wear, no T-shirt. Like I said, you just go. One pair of pointed huaraches, one pair of golfer khakis pilfered from an army surplus store—if they still have them. A male anorexia mode. The idea is to put everything on a diet except your cock. Even the cock strikes a different pose. It wants to appear docile, easy to handle, silky, if pos-sible. This particular way requires mixed meditations. One part, a critique of gender politics and homoerotric art. Part two: a critique of Super Bowl as American power performance, mucho Murine for the eyeball. The woman in your life drinks a lot of Bancha tea and (still) reads de Beauvoir. This is how you communicate.

Che Guevara speaks in your ear in the fourth way. In a fancy Spanish, an Argentinean singalong where you go gravely through the city streets in search of a coin from Lesbos; a neo-grunge boy with Vietnam boots and no cologne on the pits. "This is the jungle," you tell her. "This is this." You quote your other leader, Robert De Niro in *The Deer Hunter*. You want to quote Visconti but it rubs against your seduction mobile. You want to quote Paglia but you are too Dionysian to utter a woman's language. "This is this," you repeat at the kitchen table as you devour lox, capers, and bagels. Anything goes. Cold cream on fresh-picked cranberries. No postmod cultural bull. Just pure vision — the Marxist Blendinist Epicurean kind. You are atomic and nuclear, solar and parabolic. She knows you have the semiotic scope and the androgynous look. Most of all, with a swish gesture, you can prove yourself in a minute. All your followers lean on you for change. True change. *"Cambio es cambio,"* you write in your shredded notebook.

The next boy is the Taco Boy.

Yes, I hate to admit it. El Taco Muchacho is most appropriate. He comes on light. He comes on light-colored and light-spoken. Gentle boy with the handbook of Elizabethan-Hispano manners. This is his charm and most of all his sadist-masochistic weaponry. She can't tell if she met him in the barrio over a *raspada*, cherry flavor, of course, or at a Wimin's Mural inaugural. She just can't tell where he's going to end up (of course, we know where). Genuflection, the inflection of piety and sobriety; all this is what catches the fly-girl. His sensuality and personal spice are effusive; an overkill in the form of stuttered underdog poetics and a façade of suave nurturance that filters through his melancholia and slight, hooked face.

Of course, the most post-postmodern and politically correct is the whiny, crabby, crappy, midpotbellied, and wise-beaked fellow you come to know as El Trucha.

El Trucha says he's been through the mill, he's walked up Movimiento Hill, he's seen the pumiced land, no longer idolizes Sam the Sham (you remember "Wooly Bully"). In other words, he's made ideological sacrifices. For one, he's finally let go (it required

Rolfing and a relapse into Shakti yoga) of his oldies collection. El Trucha goes shopping with her and doesn't really mind it. He drives her son to prep school on occasion and argues about the need for Trigonometry II. Her colleagues appear and he serves them amaretto with chips and salsa. You see, he's come this far. El Trucha has arrived at a quixotic, Zen fullness.

The Organic Poet sees things.

He's always saying that.

He tells her he's taking care of business, that he doesn't need anything. This is what is alluring. He doesn't need anything (we know about this one). Not even words. He works on pure gas. When he flatulates by cocking one leg over the beige sofa or in front of the half-collie that he keeps in the backyard of his suburban studio, he reminds her that poetry is "a constant flow." This fellow doesn't play games. He offers wind, that is all. No more arduous barbecues in the name of Family, Culture, and Revolution. No more addendums and grammars for a tractatus on the Meaning of Blurred Sexual Roles. "Who wants wind?" he posits as he pours garlic shards over his spinach quesadilla. Socrates and Deleuze couldn't have done better. But, the ripened Poet sees things, this is what he says.

I almost forgot: Science, the coiled shapes in the quarks and pro-stars, these are the jewels of the quantum lover—JQ.

JQ is in love with Señorita Números—bank accounts, cashier receipts, old gas bills, cuneiform integers of (her) spending power. The credit cards in her purse, for example. Her revisionist (main-streamed) feminist résumé is secondary. He measures her documents for frayed edges every other Saturday. No astrology, no literary mumbo jumbo, no Kama Sutra bath crystals, no nonsense for this carnal. Just these torso-shaped Ss with stripes running down the belly button. JQ is up-to-date. Shaved, saved, and made. Johnny Quantas is always asking her, "¿Cuánto? ¿Cuánto? ¿Cómo, *cuánto?"* After an average sexual thrust, he throws his head back twice to look at the ceiling, where he has placed the Periodical Table of Upwardly Mobile Feminist Elements. This is the cellular boy of the millennia, the push-button member that promises her pragmatism without pregnancy and nontoxic furniture.

The Magnificent Macho Seven (plus one).

For decades, I have studied their behavior. I've used agents. Sentries and mirrors. These are preliminary charters of their desires, symbolic elements in their clothing—the space and culture coordinates of their habitats. Even their penchant for late-nineteenth-century art is fascinating, especially the unexplained obsession for German woodcuts; these qualities seem to speak of potential turns in their lives. Yet, the macho ecology remains fragile. This I haven't solved. The constructions of the internal landscape have always escaped me; its tiny trees, the lack of rivers, its odd shape, tied so intimately and yet intrinsically readied for fatal rejections.

Ángeles Mastretta

AUNT CHILA

Aunt Chila was married to a man whom she abandoned, to the scandal of the entire city, after seven years of life together. Without giving explanations to anybody. One day like any other, Aunt Chila awakened her four children and took them to live in a house that, with such good judgment, her grandmother had left to her.

Chila was a hardworking woman who had enough years' experience darning socks and preparing bean and bacon soup that setting up a clothing factory and selling in large quantities cost her no more effort than she had always expended. She became the purveyor of the two most important stores in the country. She never stopped bargaining, and once a year she traveled to Rome and Paris to look for ideas and free herself from her routine.

Most people did not agree with her behavior. No one understood how she had been able to abandon a man whose innocent
eyes reflected his kindness. How could such an amiable husband,
who kissed the women's hands and bowed affectionately to any
good man, have bothered her?

"What it is—is that she's a whore," some said.

"Irresponsible," said others.

"A lizard." They shut an eye.

"Look at that—to leave a man who never gave you any reason
to complain."

But Aunt Chila lived in the present and without complaints,
as if she didn't know, as if she didn't realize, that even in the
beauty salon there were those who did not approve of her strange
behavior.

It was precisely in the beauty parlor, when she was surrounded
by women who held out their hands to have their nails painted,
their heads to have their hair curled, and their eyes to have their
lashes brushed, that the husband of Consuelito Salazar entered
with a pistol in his hand. He stood over his wife screaming, and
fished her up by her mane of hair to shake her violently like the
clapper of a bell, tossing off insults and recounting his jealousies,
reproaching the lazy girl and cursing his in-laws, all with such
ferocity that the calm women ran to hide behind the hair dryers,
leaving Consuelito, who cried gently and fearfully, prisoner of her
husband's tempest.

It was then that Aunt Chila, waving her just polished nails,
came out of a corner.

"You get out of here," she told the man, approaching him as if
she had spent her whole life disarming cowboys in saloons. "You
don't scare anyone with your screaming. You coward, son of a bitch.
We're fed up already. We're not afraid anymore. Give me the gun
if you're such a man. Brave man of courage. If there's something

you need to settle with your wife, tell it to me, because I am her representative. Are you jealous? Of whom? Of the three children Consuelo spends her time watching? Of the twenty pots among which she lives? Of her knitting needles, her housecoat? This poor Consuelito, who looks no farther than her own nose, who devotes herself to putting up with your nonsense? You came here to create a scandal in this place where we are all screeching now like frightened mice. Don't even dream of it. Throw your temper tantrum elsewhere. Get out of here—go, go, go!" said Aunt Chila, snapping her fingers and coming close to the man, who had turned purple with rage and who, without his gun, was on the verge of provoking a laughing attack in the salon.

"Until never, mister," finished Aunt Chila. "And if you need understanding, go find my husband. Good luck, and I hope you get the whole city to feel sorry for you."

She aimed him toward the door, pushing him along, and when she got him out on the sidewalk, she shut the door and locked it with three keys.

"These bastards," they heard Aunt Chila say, almost to herself. She was applauded when she came back, and she made a very big curtsy.

"I finally said it," she later sighed.

"So you, too, eh?" asked Consuelito.

"One time," answered Chila, with a look of shame. The news spread rapidly and liberally from Inesita's salon, like the smell of baking bread. And nobody spoke ill again of Aunt Chila Huerta, because there was always someone, or the friend of a friend of someone, who had been there that morning in the beauty parlor who was ready to prevent it.

Translated by Amy Schildhouse Greenberg

Louis Reyna

THE HITCHHIKER

It was on a long, hellish stretch in the city of Rialto, where on either side of the road there is only desert, with an occasional automobile carcass whizzing by, and the San Gabriel Mountains are shielded by a fiery blight.

She was hitchhiking, carefully tiptoeing along the road to avoid the rubble and the broken glass.

"What's your name?" she asked as she pulled the strands of blonde hair from her face.

"Manuel," I said. "But call me Manny."

"You're Mexican."

"I'm not from Mexico. I was born here, in L.A."

"But you're Mexican."

I sighed. "Okay, I'm Mexican."

I had the passenger side door to the step van open. She rode standing up, holding on to the inside of the door with one hand and pulling the hair from her face with the other as it blew wildly in the hot wind. The hem of her short dress kept flapping up over her thighs.

"I know a lot of Mexicans," she said. "There's a lot in my school."

"How old are you?"

"Thirteen," she said, and then added, quickly, "but I'll be fourteen next month. That's when I start the eighth grade."

"You shouldn't be hitchhiking," I said.

"Why not?"

"What do you mean 'Why not?' Because it's dangerous. Someone might do something to you."

She leaned forward and caught my eye. "Are you gonna do something to me?"

"Of course not. But someone else might. You never know."

She smiled. "Do you wanna do something to me? I know a place where we can go."

I turned to her and said in a stern tone, "I'm just giving you a ride. Don't forget that."

She leaned back against the paneled wall of the cab. "What's with you?"

"You shouldn't be talking like that."

"You're not that much older than me."

"How old do you think I am?"

She studied me. "Nineteen," she replied confidently.

I shook my head.

Her voice dropped. "Twenty?"

"I'm twenty-four."

She shrugged, not impressed.

Up ahead, on the horizon, an air force cargo plane was lumbering slowly to the desert floor on approach to Norton Air Base.

"My sister's seventeen," she said. "She's marrying a guy that's thirty-two. He's black."

"So?"

"So there's a lot of black guys in my school."

I didn't answer.

She sat on the engine cover, facing me. She had a lot of freckles and blue eyes — eyes like the sky. But not like the sky of this desert landscape, a sky that was perpetually brown with smog. She had eyes that were like the sky in a place that she and I would only see in postcards or in the movies.

She looked to the back of the truck. "What do you deliver?"

"Coffee."

"To who?"

"Factories, law offices . . . all types of places. I go to each account once a month and replenish their stock."

"Do you make a lot of money?"

"I make enough."

She reached into my uniform shirt pocket and took out a cigar. "You smoke these?"

I nodded.

She put the cigar to her nose. "My grandpa smoked cigars." She slid the cigar back into my pocket. "Where do you live?"

"In Glendale."

"Where's that?"

"It's near Hollywood."

I expected her to be impressed that I lived near Hollywood, to ask if I'd ever seen any movie stars. I expected her to admit that, one day, she wanted to be an actress. But she didn't. She just sat there looking out at the horizon, where another cargo plane was making its descent, rocking clumsily back and forth on its huge wingspan as it broke layer after layer of hot desert air.

"Look," I said, "you have to give me some idea of where I'm taking you."

She stood up, faced the windshield, and then looked intently at the road. Finally, she pointed to my left and said, "Turn here."

It was a tree-lined road that broke off from the highway. I'd driven this stretch of highway many times and had never noticed the road or even the trees. I wished I had because the trees were tall and provided good shade—an ideal spot to stop for lunch.

"Where to now?" I asked as I straightened the wheel.

"Just keep going."

The road was really bad. A dirt road. The step van rocked back and forth. She put her knee up on the engine cover for a better view. When I turned to look at the right side-view mirror I saw that her dress was hiked up to the top of her thigh. She wasn't wearing any panties. I turned away.

"Where's your house?" I asked, irritated.

She laughed. "There's no houses out here, silly."

"Then where do you live?"

"Stop here."

It was a foot trail that broke off from the road and wound its way down about fifty yards. At the bottom of the trail was a pond surrounded by more trees. I shut off the engine. A cool breeze swirled inside the cab, sending paperwork that wasn't secured on the clipboard flying.

The girl bounded out of the truck and raced down the trail. She stood at the edge of the pond, lifted her dress up over her head, tossed it to one side, and then jumped in. After a moment she came up. Her slicked-back hair and shoulders glistened in the sunlight.

I walked down the trail and stood at the edge of the pond.

"Get in," she said.

I didn't answer.

She paddled closer. "What's wrong?"

"Nothing."

"Then get in the water with me."

I shook my head.

"Why not?"

"Because it wouldn't look right, me in the water with you."

She pouted, feigning disappointment, and then paddled away.

I knelt down and tossed a pebble into the water. I watched her swim and was sure that, at some point earlier in the day, I had been in an accident on the road and was now lying in an intensive care unit dreaming this all: the girl, the pond, and the trees. At least I hoped it was all a dream because if it wasn't, then I was sure the San Bernardino County police would swoop down on us at any moment and cart me off to jail.

"Do you come here a lot?" I asked.

"Only during the summer."

"Who else knows about this place?"

"Just me," she replied, and then added, with a smile, "and now you."

"What's your name?" I asked.

"Fawn. Do you like it?"

I shrugged, "It's all right, I guess."

She grimaced. "I hate it. I think it's a stupid name. My mom named me that because it's in the title of a piece of music my father really liked, something about an afternoon with fawn, or something like that. I never met my dad, though. He was the music teacher at my mom's high school. He doesn't teach there anymore."

She paddled close again, letting the bottom of her nose skim against the surface of the water. "Do you like me?"

"Yeah, I guess so."

"Then get in the water."

I stood up. "No."

She swam away and then lowered her head in the water. I watched the air bubbles as she submerged and then there was a roar overhead. I looked up and saw the belly of another cargo plane. It was flying over the tops of the trees. I followed the plane as it made its descent, sinking into the shimmering heat that rose from the desert floor.

When the plane was out of sight, I turned back to the pond. The water was still. She hadn't come up yet. The surface of the water was like a dark green sheet of glass. Jesus, I thought . . . no one can hold their breath for this long. Still, I waited. I waited for her to spring from the water gasping for air. After another minute or so I thought, What if she does come up—dead? What if her body bobs to the surface swollen and blue in the face? I'd have a hell of a time trying to explain to the police what I was doing at this pond with a naked thirteen-year-old girl.

I took a deep breath and jumped into the water headfirst. I thrashed my arms about, feeling for the girl at the bottom. She wasn't there. All I felt was cold soil oozing between my fingers.

I came up.

After I caught my breath, I shook the water from my hair and face and looked to the trees. There she was, peeking out from behind one of the trees, giggling. I just stood there, feeling more embarrassed than angry. She waded in and started to put her arms around my waist. I took her by the wrists.

"What's wrong?" she asked.

"You're just a little girl," I said.

"But I've been with guys before."

"What guys?"

"Guys from my school, my sister's friends—some of them have been here."

"But I thought you said I'm the only other person who knows about this place."

"You are," she said. "The other guys have forgotten. And so will you."

I looked at the trunks of the trees and noticed the ground surrounding them was littered with empty beer bottles and cigarette butts.

I got out of the pond. Fawn followed me. I retrieved her dress and handed it to her. She was shivering as she put it on. We sat down. My wet uniform and work boots made gurgling sounds as I shifted uncomfortably on the hard ground.

We just sat there for a moment and then she said, "Do you still like me?"

I turned to her. "Of course I still like you. What makes you think I don't?"

She just smiled.

There was an empty beer bottle at my feet. I kicked it away. It rolled up the trail a bit and then came back down. I watched Fawn as she stared at the bottle. She seemed to know that particular bottle for who had drunk its contents and why they'd been here at the pond. I picked up the bottle and flung it into the trees. I expected her to ask me why I threw the bottle, but she didn't. She was expressionless as she studied me with those deep blue eyes and they were like the sky.

"Do you wanna get married?" she asked.

I was jolted with mild surprise and then I laughed. "No, I don't want to marry you."

She laughed. "Not me, silly! I mean do you ever think you'll want to get married to someone, ever?"

I thought about it. "Yeah, sure . . . maybe one day."

"My sister's marrying a guy that's thirty-two. She's seventeen."

I stood up. "Well, I'm happy for her."

She looked up at me, closing one eye to fight the glare of the sun. "She's been with this guy since she was fifteen. He's got a house in Duarte."

"C'mon," I said, "I'm taking you home."

She smiled.

I started up the trail. I could hear her bare feet slap against the ground as she ran to catch up. Another cargo plane passed low over the tops of the trees on approach to Norton Air Base.

The desert hadn't changed.

WHAT SHOULD RUN IN
THE MIND OF CABALLEROS

Don't start fights, just end them, quickly / stand up for yourself . . . a little / mind your own business / never touch the ball with your hands / play fair / no name-calling / no swearing, remember you pray with that *bocota* of yours / let ladies go first / open doors for everyone / don't stare at her . . . with your mouth open / don't stare at her chest / work out maybe another half hour / don't control the conversation / keep up with the mileage on your car / don't be cocky / remember people's names / eat vegetables / don't mix light and dark liquors like your *pendejo* of a *tío* / try new foods / dirty thoughts aren't dirty / don't expect a kiss on the first date / don't brag with the boys on poker night / be modest / drive defensively / manual labor clears your head—do it often / study hard / get good sleep / take risks with a clear mind / show some quiet pride

/ call her back / learn to cook *mojarras para tu Tía Juana* / write the thank-you cards the day after graduation / make new friends / don't sweat around girls / shave down not up, burns less / read / write / look smart / be dumb only at night / don't get a fake I.D. from your cousin Enrique or Sunjay or Ephthimos or Terrance / change your socks / call home / don't let checks bounce / don't buy every young lady a drink / don't stare at her legs . . . all night / don't whistle / offer assistance / bar-b-que with *carbon* instead of a gas grill, tastes better / remember every chick is a *dama* in training / pay bills . . . even late / dinner and dancing doesn't equal some "too-ty fruit-ty in your bed room-ty" / don't suggest one-night stands . . . let them happen / know how to cook / listen / be able to fix things / know your license number / wear deodorant / don't hit on her friends / learn a new language / only use your credit cards . . . never / take it slow / learn to take shots of Patrón / be there on time / be persistent with challenges / pray as much as your *madre* did and work as hard as your *padre*. You got that? NO? Read it again . . . I'll wait.

Rafael Courtoisie

THE SCRIBE

Among those who took part in the conspiracy were a laborer who helped build the Aswan Dam, the manager of a Fray Bentos cold storage plant who declared a fraudulent bankruptcy, a New Zealand wool merchant, and a Senegalese doctor.

The latter had lived for many years in London. There he met a woman, a South American doctor, and they lived together until she decided to return to her country.

The conspiracy also included others, almost anonymous, their names and occupations of little significance. The ex-worker from the Aswan Dam recruited some of them by offering payment and the promise of major benefits when the action took place. But many (the majority) were united by conviction, by faith.

A French Jesuit abandoned his position in a seminary directed by Monsignor LeFevre to join the group with enthusiasm. A member of the Albanese Communist Party did the same with equal determination.

An old woman who lived for thirty years in the suburbs of London cashed in her life insurance policy and got an advance of two thousand dollars to buy the plane tickets and join the rest of the conspirators.

From three different points of Asia Minor (not precisely from cities) came: a seven-year-old boy, blind from birth, child of illiterate parents; a woman of twenty-eight, a teacher; a fakir and circus performer who had spent ten years of his life in jail, accused of molesting minors.

The ex-worker from the Aswan Dam joined a group that made a pilgrimage from Cairo to Marruecos, by impossible roads. Each one discharged his role with dexterity and no one betrayed the cause. The only desertion was that of a fifty-year-old woman, a housewife and mother of three, who after traveling fourteen thousand kilometers decided to return to her husband. She promised that she would remain silent and kept her vow. The other that could also be considered a desertion was a suicide, the only one among the conspirators who didn't get to know the outcome.

The plan was carried out.

Then, the majority of the conspirators returned to their places, scattering throughout the world. Only one of them committed himself to write an account. It needed to be vague and anonymous and constitute a cold approximation of the truth, without mentioning a single detail besides some references to certain protagonists, without giving their names, without revealing the severity of the affair.

That, precisely, was what he did.

Translated by Patricia Dubrava

Roberto Bolaño

PHONE CALLS

B is in love with X. Unhappily, of course. There was a time in his life when B would have done anything for X, as people generally say and think when they are in love. X breaks up with him. She breaks up with him over the phone. At first, of course, B suffers, but eventually he gets over it, as people generally do. Life, as they say in soap operas, goes on. The years pass.

One night when he has nothing to do, B manages to get through to X after calling a couple of times. Neither of them is young anymore, and their voices, transmitted from one side of Spain to the other, betray their age. They renew their friendship and after a few days decide to meet up again. Both have been through divorces, suffered new illnesses and frustrations. When B gets on the train and sets off for the city where X lives, he is not yet in love. They spend the first day holed up in X's apartment, talking about their lives (in fact X does all the talking, B listens and asks a question now and then). That night X invites him to share her bed. B doesn't really want to sleep with X, but he accepts. When he wakes up in the morning, he is in love again. But is he in love with X or with the idea of being in love? The relationship is difficult and intense: X is on the brink of suicide every day; she is under psychiatric care (pills, lots of pills, but they don't seem to be helping at all), she often bursts into tears for no apparent reason. So B looks after X. His attentions are loving and diligent but clumsy too. They mimic the attentions of a man who is truly in love, as B soon comes to realize. He tries to show X a way out of her depression, but all he does is steer her into a dead end, or what she considers a dead end. Sometimes, when he is alone or watching X sleep, he thinks it is a dead end too. As a kind of antidote, he tries to remember his former loves, he tries to convince himself that he can live without X, that he can survive on his own. One night X asks him to go away, so B takes a train and leaves the city. X goes to the station to see him off. Their farewell is tender and hopeless. B has booked a couchette but he can't get to sleep until very late. When he finally falls asleep, he dreams of a snowman walking through the desert. The snowman is following a border, and probably headed for disaster. But he ignores this with a blend of cunning and determination: He walks at night, when freezing starlight sweeps the desert. When B wakes up (the train has already arrived at the Sants Station in Barcelona), he thinks he understands the meaning of the dream (if it has a meaning) and finds some degree of solace in it as he makes his way home. That night he calls X and tells her the dream. X says nothing. The next day he phones X again. And the day after. X's attitude is increasingly cold, as if B were receding further into the past with each phone call. I'm disappearing, thinks B. She's rubbing me out and she knows just what she's doing and why she's doing it. One night B threatens to catch a train and turn up at X's apartment the next day. Don't even think about it, says X. I'm coming, says B, I can't stand these phone calls anymore, I want to see your face when I'm talking to you. I won't open the door, says X, and then hangs up. B simply can't understand. For a long time he wonders how it is possible for the feelings and desires of a human being to swing from one extreme to the other like that. Then he gets drunk or tries to lose himself in a book. The days go by.

One night, six months later, B calls X. X recognizes his voice immediately. Ah, it's you, she says. Her lack of warmth is positively chilling. Yet B senses that X wants to tell him something. She's listening to me as if no time had passed, he thinks, as if we had spoken yesterday. How are you? asks B. What's new? After a few monosyllabic replies, X hangs up. Perplexed, B dials her number again. When he gets through, however, he decides to remain silent. At the other end X's voice says: Well, who is it? Silence. Then she says: I'm listening, and waits. The telephone line is transmitting time—the time that came between B and X, that B could not understand—compressing and stretching it, revealing a part of its nature. Without realizing, B starts to cry. He knows that X knows who is calling. Then, silently, he hangs up.

Up to this point the story is banal; unfortunate but banal. It is clear to B that he should never call X again. One day there is a knock at the door; it is A and Z. They are policemen and they want to ask him some questions. In connection with what, B would like to know. A is reluctant to say; but Z, after clumsily beating around the bush, comes out with it. Three days ago, on the other side of Spain, someone killed X. At first B is shattered; then he realizes that he is a suspect and his instinct for survival puts him on his guard. The policemen ask him about his movements on two days in particular. B can't remember what he did or whom he saw on those days. Naturally he knows that he didn't leave Barcelona—in fact he didn't leave his neighborhood or maybe even his apartment—but he can't prove it. The policemen take him away. B spends the night at the police station. At one point during the questioning he thinks they are going to take him to the city where X used to live and, strangely, this prospect appeals to him, but in the end it doesn't happen. They take his fingerprints and ask if he will agree to a blood test. He agrees. The next morning they let him go. Officially, B has not been under arrest; he has only been helping the police in a murder enquiry. When he gets back home, he collapses on his bed and falls asleep immediately. He dreams of a desert and of X's face. Shortly before waking, he realizes that they are one and the same. From which it is fairly simple for him to infer that he is lost in the desert.

That night he puts some clothes in a bag, goes to the station, and takes a train to the city where X used to live. The trip, from one side of Spain to the other, lasts all night. Unable to sleep, he thinks about all the things he could have done but didn't do, all the things he could have given X, but didn't. He also thinks: If I had died, X wouldn't be coming all the way across Spain in the other direction. Then he thinks: And that is precisely why I am the one who is still alive. For the first time, during that sleepless trip, he sees X's true worth; he feels love for her again, and, for the last time, halfheartedly, he despises himself. When he arrives, very early in the morning, he goes straight to X's brother's apartment. X's brother is surprised and confused, but invites him in and offers him coffee. He is half-dressed and his face is wet. B notices that he hasn't had a shower; he has only washed his face and wet his hair a bit. B accepts the offer of coffee, then says that he just found out about the murder of X, explains that he has been questioned by the police, and asks what happened. The whole thing's been awful, says X's brother, making coffee in the kitchen, but I can't see what you've got to do with it. The police think I might be the killer, says B. X's brother laughs. You've always been unlucky, haven't you, he says. Odd you should say that, thinks B, when I'm the one who's still alive. But he is also grateful not to have his innocence doubted. Then X's brother goes to work, leaving B in the apartment. Exhausted, B soon falls into a deep sleep. Unsurprisingly, X appears in his dreams.

When he wakes, B thinks he knows who the killer is. He has seen his face. That night he goes out with X's brother. They go to various bars and talk about this and that and although they do their best to get drunk, they can't. Walking back to the apartment through the empty streets, B says he once phoned X but didn't speak. What the fuck for? says X's brother. I only did it once, says B, but I realized that X got lots of calls like that. And she thought they were from me, you see? says B. You mean the murderer is the anonymous caller? Exactly, says B, and X thought it was me. X's brother frowns: I think it was one of her exes; there were quite a few of them, you know. B says nothing in reply (it's as if X's brother hadn't understood at all) and they continue in silence until they reach the apartment.

In the elevator B thinks he is going to throw up. He says: I'm going to throw up. Hold on, says X's brother. They walk quickly down the hallway, Xs brother unlocks his door and B rushes in looking for the bathroom. But when he gets there, his nausea has subsided. He is sweating and his stomach aches, but he can't throw up. The toilet with the lid up looks like a toothless mouth laughing at him. Or laughing at someone, anyway. After washing his face, he looks at himself in the mirror: His face is as white as a sheet. He spends what is left of the night dozing fitfully, trying to read and listening to X's brother snore. The next day they say good-bye and B returns to Barcelona. I'll never go back to that city again, thinks B, because X doesn't live there any more.

A week later, X's brother calls to tell him that the police have caught the killer. The guy was harassing her with anonymous phone calls, he says. B doesn't answer. An ex, says X's brother. Well, it's good to know, says B. Thanks for calling. Then X's brother hangs up and B is alone.

Translated by Chris Andrews

Ana Castillo

FOREIGN MARKET

At the market he calls out something—especially directed
at her, she senses. But she does not understand what he has said.
She turns around. He smiles. His eyes are succulent as oranges and
very black and his smile has made her forget about the cold. He
says something again, to her, momentarily he has thought that they
are compatriots, from their dark skin despite midwinter and black
hair, but when she does not reply again, he realizes his mistake.
He's not embarrassed; still, they are both foreigners, outsiders. She
is not interested in apples or potatoes which he points to, coyly
directing his succulent eyes to the scale hanging overhead. She
begins to go on her way. But he calls to her again. He puts out a
hand, wait, hold on, a universal signal facile to understand and
she does.

Later they are warming up with a café crême in a café down the boulevard. They get acquainted by writing to each other on a napkin, a pictograph-numerology revelation of vital statistics. She is thirty. She is very old, she thinks, but only writes "30." He smiles and writes "22." Now she is certain that she is old. But he puts a chafed hand, which has been out at the market since before dawn, carrying bushels and crates, spraying the sidewalk in the cold, behind her neck and draws her head to him for an abrupt kiss. He looks around and points at the cinema down the street. He turns to her questioningly and she nods. Yes, they can go to the movies. Why not?

It is four in the afternoon.

In the dark theater they act like teenagers and never watch the movie. He puts her hand on him.

She is thinking, she is thirty and left her husband and child three weeks ago. She has come to this city, this famous city, scandalously famous, because a good friend lives here now, and because it is so far away from her life that she thought she could think things through.

He walks her back to the apartment. In the entranceway, they kiss like parting lovers. He fondles her. The concierge's door is slightly ajar, then slams shut. The pretend lovers say good-bye and promise to meet at the market at two in the afternoon on Saturday. Yes, they can figure that much out using the national lingua, two on Saturday.

That evening her friend says (she is surprised at her friend's response), "Are you serious? You can't be serious! You met him at the market! I could see an Arab you met at the embassy but this one works as a vendor . . . ! He has no money to speak of. . . . You really can't be serious!"

On Saturday, punctually, she arrives at his stall. At first he appears too busy to stop. He weighs onions and mushrooms by the kilo and has hardly acknowledged her, although he has seen her. She takes a seat on a crate nearby. After a quarter of an hour and he has made no attempt to communicate, no hand gesture at all, avoids eye contact, turns to his comperes and speaks in his language, says something she does not understand but is embarrassed by anyway, she gets up to leave.

The boulevard is very wide and very long and it seems it is taking her an eternity to walk away. Then someone calls her. He is calling her by name. She does not recognize the voice but she still hopes it is him, and she turns around. It is one of the comperes. He is older. His wavy, blondish-red hair is mostly covered with a wool cap. Wait! he signals and she does. It is even colder than it was the other day. Perhaps he is bringing a message. She huddles and watches her breath stream out of her nose. When they are face to face, he says, almost supplicating, that *he* can go with her. Catching on, she shakes her head firmly and turns off. He calls her again—wait, please! She picks up her pace, the click-click of her boots sharp and fast on the asphalt, faster, faster.

Rodrigo Rey Rosa

THE PROOF

One night while his parents were still on the highway returning from someone's birthday party, Miguel went into the living room and stopped in front of the canary's cage. He lifted up the cloth that covered it, and opened the tiny door. Fearfully, he slipped his hand inside the cage, and then withdrew it doubled into a fist, with the bird's head protruding between his fingers. It allowed itself to be seized almost without resistance, showing the resignation of a person with a chronic illness, thinking perhaps that it was being taken out so the cage could be cleaned and the seeds replenished. But Miguel was staring at it with the eager eyes of one seeking an omen.

All the lights in the house were turned on. Miguel had gone through all the rooms, hesitating at each corner. God can see you no matter where you are, Miguel told himself, but there are not many places suitable for invoking Him. Finally he decided on the cellar because it was dark there. He crouched in a corner under the high vaulted ceiling, as Indians and savages do, face down, his arms wrapped around his legs, and with the canary in his fist between his knees. Raising his eyes into the darkness, which at that moment looked red, he said in a low voice: If you exist, God, bring this bird back to life. As he spoke, he tightened his fist little by little, until his fingers felt the snapping of the fragile bones, and an unaccustomed stillness in the little body.

Then, without meaning to, he remembered María Luisa the maid, who took care of the canary. A little later, when he fnally opened his hand, it was as if another, larger hand had been placed on his back—the hand of fear. He realized that the bird would not come back to life. If God did not exist, it was absurd to fear His punishment. The image, the concept of God went out of his mind, leaving a blank. Then, for an instant, Miguel thought of the shape of evil, of Satan, but he did not dare ask anything of him.

He heard the sound of the car going into the garage over his head. Now the fear had to do with this world. His parents had arrived; he heard their voices, heard the car doors slam and the sound of a woman's heels on the stone floor. He laid the inert little body on the floor in the corner, groped in the dark for a loose brick, and set it on top of the bird. Then he heard the chiming of the bell at the front door, and ran upstairs to greet his parents.

All the lights on! exclaimed his mother as he kissed her.

What were you doing down there? his father asked him.

Nothing. I was afraid. The empty house scares me.

His mother went through the house, turning lights off to right and left, secretly astonished by her son's fear.

That night Miguel had his first experience of insomnia. For him not sleeping was a kind of nightmare from which there was no hope of awakening. A static nightmare: the dead bird beneath the brick, and the empty cage.

Hours later Miguel heard the front door open, and the sound of footsteps downstairs. Paralyzed by fear, he fell asleep. María Luisa the maid had finally arrived. It was seven o'clock; the day was still dark. She turned on the kitchen light, set her basket on the table and, as was her custom, removed her sandals in order not to make any noise. She went into the living room and uncovered the canary's cage. The little door was open and the cage was empty. After a moment of panic, during which her eyes remained fixed on the cage hanging in front of her, she glanced around, covered the cage again, and returned to the kitchen. Very carefully she took up her sandals and the basket, and went out. When she was no longer in sight of the house she put the sandals on and started to run in the direction of the market, where she hoped to find another canary. It was necessary to replace the one which she thought had escaped due to her carelessness.

Miguel's father awoke at a quarter past seven. He went down to the kitchen, and, surprised to see that María Luisa had not yet come, decided to go to the cellar for the oranges and squeeze them himself. Before going back up to the kitchen, he tried to turn off the light, but his hands and arms were laden with oranges, so that he had to use his shoulder to push the switch. One of the oranges slipped from his arm and rolled across the floor into a corner. He pushed the light on once more. Placing the oranges on a chair, he made a bag out of the front of his bathrobe, dropped them into it, and went to pick up the orange in the corner. And then he noticed the bird's wing sticking out from under the brick. It was not easy for him, but he could guess what had happened. Everyone knows that children are cruel, but how should he react? His wife's footsteps sounded above him in the kitchen. He was ashamed of his son, and at the same time he felt that they were accomplices. He had to hide the shame and the guilt as if they were his own. He picked up the brick, put the bird in his bathrobe pocket, and climbed up to the kitchen. Soon he went on upstairs to his room to wash and dress.

A little later, as he left the house, he met María Luisa returning from the market with the new canary hidden in her basket. She greeted him in an odd fashion, but he did not notice it. He was upset: The hand that he kept in his pocket held the bird in it.

As María Luisa went into the house she heard the voice of Miguel's mother on the floor above. She put the basket on the floor, took out the canary, and ran to slip it into the cage, which she then uncovered with an air of relief and triumph. But then, when she drew back the window curtains and the sun's rays tinted the room pink, she saw with alarm that the bird had one black foot.

It was impossible to awaken Miguel. His mother had to carry him into the bathroom, where she turned on the tap and with her wet hand gave his face a few slaps. Miguel opened his eyes. Then his mother helped him dress and get down the stairs. She seated him at the kitchen table. After he had taken a few swallows of orange juice, he managed to rid himself of his sleepiness. The clock on the wall marked a quarter to eight; shortly María Luisa would be coming in to get him and walk with him to the corner where the school bus stopped. When his mother went out of the room, Miguel jumped down from his chair and ran down into the cellar. Without turning on the light he went to look for the brick in the corner. Then he rushed back to the door and switched on the light. With the blood pounding in his head, he returned to the corner, lifted the brick, and saw that the bird was not there.

María Luisa was waiting for him in the kitchen. He avoided her and ran to the living room. She hurried after him. When on entering the room he saw the cage by the window, with the canary hopping from one perch to the other, he stopped short. He would have gone nearer to make certain, but María Luisa seized his hand and pulled him along to the front door.

On his way to the factory Miguel's father was wondering what he would say to his son when he got home that night. The highway was empty. The weather was unusual: Flat clouds like steps barred the sky, and near the horizon there were curtains of fog and light. He lowered the window, and at the moment when the car crossed a bridge over a deep gully he took one hand off the steering wheel and tossed the bird's tiny corpse out.

In the city, while they waited on the corner for the bus, María Luisa listened to the account of the proof Miguel had been granted. The bus appeared in the distance, in miniature at the end of the street. María Luisa smiled. Perhaps that canary isn't what you think it is, she said to Miguel in a mysterious voice. You have to look at it very close. If it has a black foot, it was sent by the Devil. Miguel stared into her eyes, his face tense. She seized him by the shoulders and turned him around.

The bus had arrived; its door was open. Miguel stepped onto the platform. Dirty witch! he shouted.

The driver started up. Miguel ran to the back of the bus and sat down by the window in the last row of seats. There was the squeal of tires, a horn sounded, and Miguel conjured up the image of his father's car.

At the last stop before the school the bus took on a plump boy with narrow eyes. Miguel made a place for him at his side.

How's everything? the boy asked him as he sat down.

The bus ran between the rows of poplars, while Miguel and his friend spoke of the power of God.

Translated by Paul Bowles

Alberto Ríos

THE BACK OF MY OWN HEAD IN A CROWD

My husband Adolfo is gone. They have stolen him from me, and there is no news. He has been inside me for so many years that when they took him, they took me as well. They took what was inside me, and so there is nothing left to hold me up. Since he has been gone I might have looked to the world like I was standing, but inside I was only a pile of what was left of myself. Old wood for bones and red wires for nerves. Everyone has seen those piles of debris when walking, leaves that have been raked together, or bricks and broken cement stacked up in corners at construction sites. What was left in me was no good anymore. That's what I felt. My organs and my rib bones and my soul had simply fallen to the floor inside of me.

But I have begun to see myself other places. Not sitting here, not inside myself, but out there. First I saw myself in the mirror, of course, but I've always been there, for as long as I can remember. So, seeing my face in the mirror was not surprising, even if it looked like only half a face because I could not bear to look straight into it. But I see myself in more than that mirror now. I'm not looking for it, but there's more evidence of me. I see myself for example in the spoon as I lift it, after stirring coffee, or when I take it out of the sink having just rinsed it. When I look at it, I'm in the spoon. I see myself in there. And in the kitchen window, just a little—I'm in there, too, if the light is just right. I can see myself walking by and turning my head.

And there are other places. I'm in the long silver of the chrome handle on the front of the refrigerator. I have seen myself inside that handle many times, but this feels like something more, something different. This feels not simply like I'm seeing myself, but that I'm seeing as well all the times I've seen myself—and that makes me think that I'm adding up, and that I feel like something in my hands. And that putting my hand onto that handle is a way of touching my face again. Because I've been in so much of this kitchen, so much of it as well is in me.

I feel the heat of the toaster, and the sticky sting of the ice. I smell the rosemary leaves and startle myself with the smell, which is like the distant ringing of an inside telephone, a telephone in another room of myself. The dust around the windowsills is on my tongue, the way Adolfo is in my eyes when I close them.

There's more. I remember arranging the spices in the kitchen cupboard, and that I stood grasping for the higher shelves with my arm barely reaching. I can see myself doing it, because I've done it so many times. I keep the vanilla there, up high, even though I use it all the time, and should have learned by now. I'm caught in between this reaching and remembering having reached a thousand times. I feel as if I'm somewhere lost in the time of this kitchen, but found, too, because I can see myself, all one thousand of me. By remembering, by letting myself remember, I seem to be able to do something and at the same time see myself having done it before. It's like there's two of me at that moment, or three, or four. I see myself suddenly all the times I've reached for a bowl from the cupboard.

Since I see myself, since it's possible for me now to see myself, since I am in so many places now that I look, I can imagine myself out there as well, outside this house. I'm walking and I see what looks like the back of my own head in a crowd. And more than once. I see that so many of the backs of so many heads look like mine, so that suddenly I am so much of the crowd that I am the crowd. And we are all walking where I am walking. This makes me feel stronger, but only because I can't help it. I feel too weak to stop myself from feeling stronger.

This feeling of a strength-I-can't-help is like a disease that's growing inside me. With so much of me, so many of me, so many ears and eyes, so many nostrils and mouths in the air of the kitchen bent to the task of doing so many things, I am the kitchen itself, and the house, and outside the house, the neighborhood and the whole city, the whole world, everything. Everything is coming sharper to me, louder and more fragrant, all of it—I can taste it all. And not just what's around me. I can taste things I have tasted before, so much is the feeling. I can remember things, suddenly, but I can taste them, too, and hear them. Most of all, Adolfo.

I can hear him. I can hear his echo, his black absence. When I hear myself breathing, it's him, if only because it's been like that for so many years, our breathing together at night, falling asleep. But I can hear him out there as well, somewhere in the world. I can smell him. It's him. In this moment, I know it. If I am out there, if I can see myself out there, and he is still in me—then he is out there, too. I have thought I've seen the back of his head as well as mine, so it must be true. It's him.

If until this moment I have been without energy, have been robbed not just of my husband but of myself as well, now I am full of pepper and chili and lemon. I feel like I want to sneeze. If I have had no voice, now I have the sound of pots and of pans, and of the loud memory of all the glasses and plates that through the years have broken on this floor and startled the house. And if I think about going outside, when I think of that crowd, I am an army of myself, so that if moving has been difficult, now I am full of butter and oil, and all of the pilot lights on the stove combined. I am sliding forward in spite of myself. I am melting forward.

If I have felt no pulse, now I hear clearly the loud ticks of the cheap tin kitchen clock, right there above the stove. That clock. It is a beast itself with an electrical tail that kept us up in the beginning when we first brought it home, but which then became part of us, me and Adolfo. We shared that pulse and this kitchen, and our story in this world. We shared one life. All of us and all of this.

Sitting here at the table, my elbows stick a little bit on the blue plastic of the tablecloth as I lean a little harder against it. My fists push up at the base of my ears. My face suddenly fills the empty space between my hands. And I can hear the clock, loud as anything. That animal in the clock is alive. I know what this means, what it has to mean. I know what I have to do.

But I get ahead of myself.

Marisella Veiga

FRESH FRUIT

I was up the first time about five, made coffee, and heated up some milk for it. When I turned on the kitchen light, the dog came and stood near the stove. He seemed cold. Right before lunch I usually boil some meat and bones for him, but it was not time for that feeding, so I gave him a little warm milk instead. I snapped the light off and went to sit on the porch, where I usually have my coffee and listen to the roosters and the occasional car traveling along the highway.

The young woman across the street, Susana, went to work earlier than usual today. The driveway gate clanked loudly when she closed it, as if it was meant as a shout to someone inside the house, "There, you have it!" I'd like to see someone actually walk away from his home that easily.

She started that old car with tremendous faith. It's as loud as a motorcycle. Sometimes, as the car warms up, she looks over to see if I am on the porch and waves. In the morning she is relaxed, friendlier. By late afternoon, she is tired and a bit arrogant, thinking that what she does all day is more important than what I do. I can tell by the excuses she makes when I call her to come over for a short visit.

"I just got home from work and have to shower," she yells from across the street, one hand busy with a set of keys, the other holding a briefcase. Other times, when she's tired, there's a longer litany: "I'm hungry. There's no food in the house. I have to go to the market, then make dinner." There's a plea in her voice on those days, yet I do not do anything to alleviate her exhaustion. What she means is that there's no time for an old lady on the schedule unless a hot meal is included.

She'll push her plate away at the end of the meal, thank me, smoke a cigarette, and five minutes later cross the street to her house without being any sort of company afterward. My husband, Wilfredo, is just like that.

Susana, of course, has the option to not make anyone anything. Every morning at the corner cafeteria she reads a newspaper while having breakfast. Someone cooks it and somebody else takes the dishes away when the meal is done. She does not even see the faces of the people performing these services. Throwing away money, that's all. I told her she could pay me less and have more delicious food, but I don't think she's interested in saving money either, or forming a home with a husband.

Why? For one, though I have advised her, she has not bothered to invest in a red dress. It's an attractive color that suits her, and would appeal to a man, and one never knows. A husband could help her along, and she, in turn, could help him. When I told her my idea, she said, "Red? I don't like that color at all."

When Wilfredo and I were first married, we rented a small apartment in this neighborhood, near the sea, and spent Sundays on the beach. Years later, he bought this house and a few years after that a farm in the mountains, so our home would not lack fresh fruit or vegetables. I haven't seen the farm in years; I don't leave the house, but he drives up there often and returns with the back of his jeep loaded with bunches of plantains. He hangs them on hooks to ripen in the garage.

I give them out to neighbors as a way of showing appreciation for their attentions to me. Whenever I tell Susana to take a couple, she hesitates. Oh, the diet she is currently on does not allow for much of anything fried, and that's how she likes them. A little prompting and she takes three thick ones home, hiding them in the briefcase. I know she eats them up fast, fried as *tostones*, not waiting for them to ripen for a sweeter-tasting dish. No, she is an impatient sort who likes to take hard bites of hot salty starches.

She refuses things like custards, although I have seen her eyes widen when I've brought one out to the table and set it next to her coffee. No sweets. Give her salt, the sea, the beginning of the meal and she's happy. I know. Now, I want the sweet, the fruit that comes after the meal is done.

He's home. I heard the car horn sound, a warning so I am not frightened when someone begins jiggling the padlock on the porch door. When Wilfredo returns in the evening, he greets me with a kiss on the cheek, though he is coming from his mistress's house. We have lived in this house for twenty years now, and she has lived in another one, which he also owns, all along.

I tolerate his nightly visits with her. I have no choice. In a way, they are a relief because he does not look at me anymore to satisfy his longing. He thinks I think I'm too old for sex. He doesn't leave her, won't abandon me, and the neighbors know that in the end he sleeps in this house every night. One might say I am no longer acting completely as a wife.

He does not allow his mistress to cook for him. That is why I believe that, after all these years, he loves me most because he comes home twice a day to my table.

The young woman across the street, despite all her American ways, which she learned at school, does not know how to do this. Yes, she is free to wander beyond her gate, walk into a restaurant any time of day, like any mall, and buy meals made by someone cooking anonymously in the kitchen. She has money, a way to ride around town. She speaks English and French and travels to the other islands. She drinks beer and sometimes stays out late, while I sit on my porch waiting for Wilfredo to arrive. I don't get bored.

Her house is empty all day until she walks into it. She can stroll along the shore of the sea anytime, but there, nobody gives a damn. There she goes, out to dinner alone again, taking a book along for company. I'll start frying up plaintains. Wilfredo will be home in an hour.

After the meal and some conversation, he will turn off the lights in the dining room. I'll wash the dishes and close up the kitchen, and finally bring the dog inside the house for the night. We will go through the rest of the rooms, turning off the lights in the entire house, before going our separate ways.

Eduardo Galeano

CHRONICLE OF
THE CITY OF HAVANA

His parents had fled to the north. In those days, he and
the revolution were both in their infancy. A quarter of a century
later, Nelson Valdés traveled from Los Angeles to Havana to visit
his homeland.

Every day at noon, Nelson would take the *guagua*, bus number
68, from the hotel entrance, to the José Martí Library. There he
would read books on Cuba until nightfall.

One day at noon, *guagua* 68 screeched to a halt at an intersec-
tion. There were cries of protest at the tremendous jolt until the
passengers saw why the bus driver had jammed on the brakes: A
magnificent woman had just crossed the street.

"You'll have to forgive me, gentlemen," said the driver of *gua-*

gua 68, and he got out. All the passengers applauded and wished him luck.

The bus driver swaggered along, in no hurry, and the passengers watched him approach the saucy female, who stood on the corner, leaning against the wall, licking an ice cream cone. From *guagua* 68, the passengers followed the darting motion of her tongue as it kissed the ice cream while the driver talked on and on with no apparent result, until all at once she laughed and glanced up at him. The driver gave the thumbs-up sign and the passengers burst into a hearty ovation.

But when the driver went into the ice cream parlor, the passengers began to get restless. And when he came out a bit later with an ice cream cone in each hand, panic spread among the masses.

They beeped the horn. Someone leaned on it with all his might and honked like a burglar alarm, but the bus driver, deaf, nonchalant, was glued to the delectable woman.

Then, from the back of *guagua* 68, a woman with the appearance of a huge cannon ball, and an air of authority, stepped forward. Without a word, she sat in the driver's seat and put the engine in gear. *Guagua* 68 continued on its route, stopping at its customary stops, until the woman arrived at her own and got off. Another passenger took her place for a stretch, stopping at every bus stop, and then another, and another, and so *guagua* 68 continued on to the end of the line.

Nelson Valdés was the last one to get off. He had forgotten all about the library.

Translated by Cedric Belfrage with Mark Schafer

Cristina Peri Rossi

THE UPROOTED

You see them frequently, walking down the streets in big cities, men and women floating on air, suspended in time and space. Their feet lack roots, and sometimes they even lack feet. Their hair doesn't have roots, nor do they have soft vines to tie their trunks to any type of ground. They are like algae propelled by the ocean currents and, when they finally attach themselves to any surface, it is by chance and only momentarily. They immediately begin to float again, and there is a certain nostalgia in it.

Their rootlessness confers upon them a unique, imprecise air, which is why they seem awkward everywhere and are not invited to parties or houses, because they appear to be suspect. It is true that, on the surface, they do the same things other humans do—they eat, sleep, walk and even die, but perhaps the careful observer might discover a slight and almost imperceptible difference in the way they eat, sleep, walk, and die. They eat hamburgers at McDonald's or sandwiches at Pollo Pokins, be it in Berlin, Barcelona, or Montevideo. And what's even worse, they order outlandish dishes from ridiculous menus, made up of gazpacho, cioppino, and English cream. They sleep at night, just like the rest of the world, but when they wake up in the darkness of a miserable hotel room, they experience a moment of uncertainty—they don't recall where they are, or what day it is, or the name of the city they live in.

The absence of roots gives their glances a characteristic feature—a blue and watery tonality, evasive, like that of someone who, instead of acquiring strong nourishment from roots attached to the past and to the land, floats in space, vague and undefined.

Although at birth some of them had some knotty threads, which would have undoubtedly become solid roots with time, for some reason or other, they lost them, they were taken away from them or amputated, and this unfortunate circumstance turns them into a sort of victim of the plague. But instead of arousing compassion in others, they usually inspire hostility—they are suspected of being guilty of some obscure fault, the dispossession (if there was one, because it could be a matter of a deficiency from birth) implies their guilt.

Once they are lost, the roots are irretrievable. The exile stands in vain at a street corner, next to a tree, glancing sideways at those long appendages that unite the plant to the earth—the roots are not contagious, nor do they adhere to foreign bodies. Others think that if they stay long enough in the same city or country, someday they will be granted fake roots, some plastic roots, for example, but no city is that generous.

Nevertheless, there are optimistic exiles. They are the ones who attempt to see the good side of things and declare that lacking roots allows them great freedom of movement, it avoids uncomfortable dependencies and facilitates travel. In the midst of their speech, a strong wind blows, and they disappear, swallowed up by the air.

Translated by Sean Higgins

Daniel Alarcón

THE VISITOR

It had been three months and I thought things would have
gotten easier. The children still cried at night. They still asked
about their mother. On clear mornings, I took them to the cemetery, which was all that was left of the old town. From that hill we
could see the remains of the valley, and the sharp scar where the
mountain had slipped. The planes flew only on clear, cloudless
days, and we watched for them in the skies above us: whirling,
seesawing, their shaky wings trembling in the mountain wind. The
children waved. We counted the parachutes drifting down and
down. It was a game we played. I taught Mariela and Ximena to
differentiate between German and French as we sifted through the
aid packages. I helped Efraín pull the parachutes from the mud
and clean them off.

The first day we huddled together to stay warm. The sky was heavy with dust after the landslide. We'd been at the cemetery burying the little one, who was only a few days old when he died, who Erlinda, my wife, hadn't had the heart to name. The children didn't understand. Erlinda had stayed in town, still recovering. We lowered him into the earth. Then there was a shaking. The mountain broke free. I held our three children close to me. A stew of ice and rock and mud rumbled down the valley.

We stayed at the cemetery that first night. Some of the coffins had been shaken from the earth. I made a lean-to with the planks of wood. The earth shook every hour or so, and I was afraid. Only the summit of the cemetery hill was still poking out from beneath the slippery mud. There was just room enough for me and my children.

On the second day, the sun came out, and the mud began to dry. I took two of the longest planks and told the children to wait for me. Efraín wanted to come, but I told him to stay and take care of his sisters. Help is coming, I said. I laid the planks out one in front of the other, and made my way across the mud toward where our house had been. I oriented myself by the plaza, which I could still make out. The tops of the four palm trees rose out of the mud, but the cathedral and the other buildings had been buried. I saw no one. The planks sunk a little into the mud as I walked.

I stepped over the buried town. We'd moved here from the south end of the valley when it was time to start a family. We'd made a life here. I tended herds I did not own. Erlinda sold what she could in the market. We worked and we saved. We'd tried to buy a small plot of land on the eastern folds of the mountains, but had been spurned. Those lands are reserved for important families, they'd told us, not for you. Just before the youngest was buried, we'd talked of leaving. To the city, to the sea. I remember Erlinda and her confusion. We worried about our children, about the future. We would never leave. This was home. It had been home.

I made it, finally, to where my house had stood, to where my wife must have been buried. I'd taken a cross from the cemetery, scavenged from one of the wrecked graves, and I planted it in the mud above my home. Erlinda, I prayed, had felt no pain and hadn't had time to be afraid. She had died in her sleep, I prayed.

Across the valley, the mountainsides were green and blooming. My children were hungry. I sat and prayed, and then took my planks and continued on toward the hills.

I found herbs and fruits there, and grazing sheep and goats that now had no owner other than me. The sun warmed my cheeks. Across the valley, across the muddy strip of earth, I saw the cemetery hill. The children sat together; I waved to them. We would be better off here, I decided. These were the best lands. I went back for the children. While the girls waited, Efraín and I made two more trips, crossing the thick mud with careful steps, carrying more planks. With the remains of the shattered coffins, we made a new home on the eastern slopes.

In the weeks after, Efraín seemed to be growing every day, and I was proud. He took care of the girls. He made my life easier. The girls asked him about their mother, because they knew not to ask me anymore. Efraín gave them the same simple answer I had given them: that things were different now. This would usually set them crying, Mariela folding herself into her sister's embrace. I would hold them, but I had nothing to give them. I tried to be strong. I dreamed of Erlinda every night. Each day, I went to see her, to tell her about the children, about our new home. I told her I missed her. Every week or so, I pulled the cross out and replanted it so it wouldn't tilt or lean as the mud settled. From our new home we could see everything, and everything, I told Erlinda, was ours: the cemetery hill, the four palm trees, the green eastern slopes, and the grazing herds. Erlinda, my wife, was resting.

Some days I stole away from the children. Efraín disappeared with his sisters to play and I to gather parachutes from the hillsides. I would find myself crying. I cried for the town and for my wife, for myself and the children. I cried for my fourth child, the buried child. The children seemed to have forgotten him: his smallness, his labored breathing, and even the events of that day. And I tried to forget him too: in the way of our grandparents, who withheld their love from a child until he had survived two winters. When I was Efraín's age, I lost a sister. For a time, our home was quiet and heavy, but then she was buried and never spoken of again.

The children survived my moods. Sometimes I asked, "Do you remember where we used to live?" and their blank stares told me they hadn't understood my question. I envied them and their youthful amnesia. Under the sweep of mountain sky, I felt alone.

"Where did we live?" I asked them.

"With Mother," was all they ever said. We gave our emptiness a name. That name was Erlinda.

So we stayed there, on the other side of the valley from the cemetery, on the foothills above the martyred town. Parachutes slipped through the heavy clouds, swinging gently in the passing wind. No one came to see the town or its graves. We waited. We were there when the visitor came.

His name was Alejo. He carried a bundle of clothes wrapped in a blanket. He'd come from over the mountains, from the city. "I've been walking," he told me, "for two weeks." Alejo yawned as he sat, and I heard his bones creaking. "I have news."

"Tell it then," I said.

"There are twenty thousand dead in the city."

"Twenty thousand?" I asked.

The visitor nodded. He took off his shoes.

"And in the north?"

"Seven thousand when I left."

"The south?"

"At last count, sixteen thousand."

My head felt light. "On the coast?" I asked, though I knew no one on the coast.

"There are no towns left standing."

"My God," I said.

His face was cracked by the wind. He rubbed his feet. Ximena brought us tea in earthen bowls. We sat quietly.

"What are people saying?" I asked.

He cupped his bowl in his calloused hands. He let the steam kiss his face. "They're hardly speaking at all."

It was getting cold.

From the pile of clothes, Mariela brought our visitor a jacket. "Guess where this jacket came from!" she asked cheerfully. "Guess!"

The visitor smiled gently and shrugged his shoulders. We were all bundled and wearing the bright clothing of survivors.

"France!" my daughter said, beaming,

I smiled. "We counted thirteen parachute drops in one day," I said.

"Thirteen?"

My son and I had collected nearly fifty parachutes. We would build tents with them, for when the rains come.

We sat in silence for a moment.

"What do we have for our visitor?" I called to the children. We'd been inundated with aid, some of it useful, some of it less so. A box of oversize bathing suits from Holland. Postcards from New York that wished us well. A package of neckties from Denmark. I'd picked a red one, which I used to tie back my hair. Efraín offered Alejo a selection of ties. Erlinda would have been proud. "Please take one," he said, bowing ceremoniously.

The visitor picked an orange tie and smiled at me. He wore it as a headband, then picked a shorter green one, which he tied on Efraín. "We're a tribe now," the visitor said, laughing. Efraín smiled too.

It was overcast, the sky a color of bone. The fog sank from the silver mountains. "How many did you lose here, friend?" the visitor asked.

We could still see the cross. I pointed across the muddy plain at my resting wife. "Only one," I said.

Efraín had picked out headbands for his sisters. My children were a row of Danish neckties. "Only one," they said in a chorus.

VOLAR

Judith Ortíz Cofer

VOLAR

At twelve I was an avid consumer of comic books—
Supergirl being my favorite. I spent my allowance of a quarter a day
on two twelve-cent comic books or a double issue for twenty-five. I
had a stack of *Legion of Super Heroes* and *Supergirl* comic books
in my bedroom closet that was as tall as I am. I had a recurring
dream in those days: that I had long blond hair and could fly. In
my dream I climbed the stairs to the top of our apartment building
as myself, but as I went up each flight, changes would be taking
place. Step by step I would fill out: My legs would grow long, my
arms harden into steel, and my hair would magically go straight
and turn a golden color. Of course I would add the bonus of breasts,
but not too large; Supergirl had to be aerodynamic. Sleek and hard
as a supersonic missile. Once on the roof, my parents safely asleep

in their beds, I would get on tiptoe, arms outstretched in the position for flight, and jump out my fifty-story-high window into the black lake of the sky. From up there, over the rooftops, I could see everything, even beyond the few blocks of our barrio; with my X-ray vision I could look inside the homes of people who interested me. Once I saw our landlord, whom I knew my parents feared, sitting in a treasure-room dressed in an ermine coat and a large gold crown. He sat on the floor counting his dollar bills. I played a trick on him. Going up to his building's chimney, I blew a little puff of my superbreath into his fireplace, scattering his stacks of money so that he had to start counting all over again. I could more or less program my Supergirl dreams in those days by focusing on the object of my current obsession. This way I "saw" into the private lives of my neighbors, my teachers, and in the last days of my childish fantasy and the beginning of adolescence, into the secret room of the boys I liked. In the mornings I'd wake up in my tiny bedroom with the incongruous—at least in our tiny apartment—white "princess" furniture my mother had chosen for me, and find myself back in my body: my tight curls still clinging to my head, skinny arms and legs and flat chest unchanged.

In the kitchen my mother and father would be talking softly over a café con leche. She would come "wake me" exactly forty-five minutes after they had gotten up. It was their time together at the beginning of each day and even at an early age I could feel their disappointment if I interrupted them by getting up too early. So I would stay in my bed recalling my dreams of flight, perhaps planning my next flight. In the kitchen they would be discussing events in the barrio. Actually, he would be carrying that part of the conversation; when it was her turn to speak she would, more often than not, try shifting the topic toward her desire to see her *familia* on the Island: *How about a vacation in Puerto Rico together this year, Querido? We could rent a car, go to the beach. We could . . .* And he would answer patiently, gently, Mi amor, *do you know how much it would cost for all of us to fly there? It is not possible for me to take the time off . . .* Mi vida, *please understand. . . .* And I knew that soon she would rise from the table. Not abruptly. She would light a cigarette and look out the kitchen window. The view was of a dismal alley that was littered with refuse thrown from windows. The space was too narrow for anyone larger than a skinny child to enter safely, so it was never cleaned. My mother would check the time on the clock over her sink, the one with a prayer for patience and grace written in Spanish. A birthday gift. She would see that it was time to wake me. She'd sigh deeply and say the same thing the view from her kitchen window always inspired her to say: *Ay, si yo pudiera volar.*

Robert Lopez

ASUNDER

This is to be without ceremony.

This is to be the marriage of two disparate ideas.

Concerning someone in particular and the kind of woman who signs the guest book at her own son's wake. On the surface it's complicated. Deeper down it has to do with something else altogether.

Someone in particular wanted to compose a story without characters and details. Without a setting, either. No themes, no ambiguities. Being that someone in particular doesn't consider himself a writer he feels he can dispense with many of the rules and regulations.

And then the kind of woman who takes twenty-five pills a day.

No flashbacks, no dialogue, no obscure academic references.

What's more is someone in particular is shamefully ignorant when it comes to the rules and regulations. For instance, he has no idea what a split infinitive is.

And then the kind of woman who sends her twelve-year-old grandson a birthday card with a five-dollar bill taped to it and writes *I am broke* under her signature.

Any use of simile or metaphor or foreshadowing or alliteration or onomatopoeia would be unnecessary in such a story. Nothing at all synecdochical.

Even if someone in particular knew what any of that meant.

To heavily second chance the lonely alone.

And then the kind of woman who applies lipstick at inappropriate times and identifies people by their ethnicity, all of them savages.

Who'd come running when her husband would whistle for her to come running.

Which is not to say someone in particular doesn't respect those who are cognizant of the rules and regulations and adhere to said rules and regulations. That someone in particular doesn't consider himself a writer should in no way reflect upon any of those people.

A story without exposition or a conflict or an arc and with nothing at all at stake.

And then the kind of woman you cannot believe actually raised two children and held down several jobs and who derives a queer satisfaction from having her picture taken and is the kind of woman you can say is the kind of woman for years and never run out of she is the kind of womans.

Joan of Arc.

Any assumption that someone in particular is the author of the lines *This is to be without ceremony* and *This is to be the marriage of two disparate ideas* would be premature at this time.

Joan of Arc being the one who led four thousand French soldiers into Orléans to expel the English in 1429, all at the tender age of sixteen. Then she was taken prisoner by the Burgundians. Then she was burned at the stake in Rouen. Then they made her a saint. Someone in particular has a hard time swallowing any of this.

Some of this can be considered adulterous.

Then the kind of woman who is afraid to answer the door lest she be attacked by the Savages probably knows next to nothing about Joan of Arc. The arc of that particular story clearly being Joan herself. Joan was also what was at stake, too.

Derivative. Superfluous.

Someone in particular has given little thought to how long such a story should be. If he ever decides to write it, that is.

A story not subjected to editors or critics or awards or anthologies.

It goes without saying someone in particular has his own problems.

Right around this time the marriage seems headed for trouble.

No plot, no backstory. Research is something someone in particular wouldn't have to do for such a story.

Someone in particular does not feel he is in any way obsessed with the kind of woman who dyes her hair at the age of eighty-four. He does, however, feel he sometimes devotes too much time to thinking of her. Point being he can stop whenever he wants to.

The actual relationship between someone in particular and the kind of woman who discusses regularity in mixed company isn't worth mentioning. She in no way dominates his consciousness. Someone in particular often goes weeks without giving the kind of woman who spreads *lite* butter on *lite* bread a single thought.

Nothing linear. Nothing avant-garde. No discernible style whatsoever.

And he has never had a single dream in which she has made

even a guest appearance. So she is not a part of his subconscious at all.

Essentially a story with no language to get in the way of the telling.

Or is it unconscious? Do dreams belong to the subconscious or the unconscious? Regardless.

Point being someone in particular has a life of his own.

A life that has nothing to do with the kind of woman who harps ceaselessly on the fact she is all alone.

Retaliation. Misogyny. Blatant disregard.

Connubiality.

Marriage without consummation is subject to annulment.

Someone in particular originally conceived of his story in his native language and then translated it into its present form. It is fair to say it has lost something in the translation.

And then the kind of woman who identifies people by their ethnicity is actually bilingual.

Nothing that may pay homage to something done long ago. Or echoes this or calls to mind that. Nothing ahead of its time.

The sanctity of the institution.

None of this should be taken literally. Nor should it be taken figuratively, orally, rectally, intravenously, three times a day, on an empty stomach, with milk, or lying down.

Not realism, impressionism, minimalism, dadaism.

The someone in particular knows his proverbial goose has been long ago cooked.

The someone in particular intended to compose a story disregarding all of the inherent trappings common to such endeavors while still addressing the life and impact of the kind of woman they write stories about. If someone in particular could somehow allude to the great women of history like Joan of Arc doing some kind of juxtaposition then that would be an unexpected bonus.

Someone in particular realizes he possesses certain gifts. He plans on getting up early tomorrow to exchange them for something more practical. Like a toaster oven. Or a cutting board.

A story that cannot be dissected or explicated by any would-be dissectors or explicators.

Here comes the bride. All dressed in white.

What certain explicators might call an off rhyme. Or is it slant rhyme?

Someone in particular would like to hit it big posthumously.

Does anyone know what comes after all dressed in white?

This way he will have nothing to live up to.

No movements, not neo-this or post-that.

Da-Dum-Ta-Da-Dum-Ta-Da-Dum-Ta . . . Daaa.

And then the kind of woman who lives well past a hundred, burying husbands, sons, daughters, grandchildren, and as yet unborn and distant progeny.

Involve. Revolve. Dissolve. Absolve.

Given such an ill-conceived union between someone in particular and the kind of woman who sits in the back seat of cars because the front passenger side is the *death seat*, two things happen, both unfortunate. One is it makes the kind of woman who believes everything she is told more important than she actually is. And secondly, there is never an appropriate ending to end with, such a story as this and such a woman as she.

Alejandra Pizarnik

DEVOTION

Below the tree in front of the house, death and a girl sat at a table drinking tea. A doll was sitting between them, unspeakably beautiful, and death and the girl watched her more closely than the sunset while they spoke above her.

"Have a little wine," said death.

The girl looked around her without seeing anything on the table but tea.

"I don't see any wine," she said.

"That's because there is none," replied death.

"Then why did you say there was?" she asked.

"I never said there was wine; I only asked that you have some," said death.

"Then you made a mistake by offering it," said the girl, becoming angry.

"I am an orphan," said death, apologizing. "No one took the time to give me a proper education."

The doll opened her eyes.

Translated by José Chaves

Hernán Lavín Cerda

THE ETERNAL DOG

A famous photographer named Martín Brugnoli remembers that there would always be a dog in the photos of his family album, though his family never really liked animals that only caused hives, sinus trouble, migraines, and other allergic reactions. Brugnoli knew his family had borrowed the dog just for the portraits, in the same way they would pose in front of a limousine that wasn't theirs. This phenomenon allows him to recognize that the portraits revolve around a borrowed dog, a social cosmetic that organizes the image in such a way as to be more adorable and respectable to others. No one knows to this day that dog's name or what kind of dog it was that wagged its tail as if it were someplace other than in the photo that contained it. We can't deny the dog appears to be happy, apart from the momentary lapse of boredom.

His tail is an allegorical symbol, a dual object, a cinematic representation.

One could say that a manufactured expression composes the portrait, so as to defend our family from the embarrassment of being in the public eye. It is the makeup that conceals the face. One could also say that every portrait has a hidden face; maybe that is why it originated as an art destined for the dead.

Translated by José Chaves

Mario Benedetti

THE EXPRESSION

Milton Estomba had been a prodigious child. At six years old he could play Brahms's Sonata No. 3, Op. 5, and, at eleven, he received unanimous public and critical acclaim for a series of concerts in the principal capitals of Europe and America.

Nevertheless, when he turned twenty, one could note a distinct transformation in the young pianist. He had begun to worry too much about his pompous gestures and affectations of the face: the furrowed brow, the passionate gaze, and other refined affects. He called all of this his "expression."

Little by little, Estomba became a specialist in "expressions." He had one to play *Patética*, another for *Niñas en el Jardín*, and another for *Polonesa*. He practiced them in front of the mirror before each concert, but an enthusiastic public took the expressions to be spontaneous and welcomed them with wild applause, bravos, and foot stamping.

The first disturbing symptom came during a Saturday recital. The crowd noticed something strange was happening, and during their applause, they were overcome with a sense of bewilderment. The truth was: Estomba had played *Catedral Sumergida* with the expression of *Marcha Turca*.

The catastrophe repeated itself again only three months later and was diagnosed by the doctors to be an amnesic gap. The gap in question corresponded to the musical scores. In a period of twenty-four hours, he had forgotten every nocturne, prelude, and sonata he held within his wide repertoire.

The astonishing thing, the really astonishing thing was that he didn't forget a single pompous gesture or affectation that had accompanied his playing. Although he could never play the piano again, he had this consolation. To this day, on Saturday nights his most faithful friends come to his house to attend a mute recital of his "expressions." Among them, it is of unanimous opinion, *Appassionata* is his best.

Translated by José Chaves

Socorro Venegas

JOHNNY DEPP

I haven't seen this young man since—sad, listless in an absence that even he didn't notice. His own absence. The first time he told me about his life, he explained to me why he had no shadow. He gave me a chaste peck on the lips, as if he were a child, and kept staring at the sea, his hand covering his left eye.

I had just graduated from nursing school when I came to this clinic for addicts. I was sent to take care of him. My job was to keep him company, to talk to him. But he didn't talk to me, he only said yes, no, and asked for small things—a glass of water, a book. So I enjoyed the beach, beside the silent companion.

I read his medical file. He had gone through the darkest valleys of heroin. I don't know how he was still alive. It was clear that he didn't want to live—overdose, trouble with the law, several suicide

233

attempts. I began to wonder who cared so much to save him, who paid the bill for the most exclusive, expensive clinic. He had no visitors.

Dr. Van der Graff was in charge of psychotherapy. One morning, when Johnny—he only responded to this name—was swimming in the pool, the doctor approached me and asked if Johnny ever talked to me. I told him no. I couldn't help but ask him if he thought Johnny had suffered any brain damage. "Look at him," the doctor pointed his chin toward Johnny, who was taking slow strokes under water. "He's not the person we think he is. He's an actor named Johnny . . . Johnny Depp. He really believes that." While the doctor gave an account of his theories on multiple personality, Johnny reached the edge of the pool, wiped his face, shook his long hair, and looked at me. His glance was a flock of blackbirds flying over me.

"You think you're an actor," I asked, wanting to provoke him. It didn't work. He flashed me a condescending smile, his lips shut tight. He returned his gaze to the sea. Then I told him a lie. "If you like, we could get on one of those sailing boats you sometimes see in the distance." Johnny's smile turned into a serious expression, as if he contemplated what he was going to say. In the end, he remained silent, but his eyes showed a restlessness that I took as the beginning of something, some progress. I kept him company while he was having his afternoon snack, and left him in his room.

Days later he had an anxiety attack, but it was not as severe as the previous ones, they said. One afternoon he wanted to take a walk on the beach again. He walked slowly and let me walk beside him. Before he always walked ahead of me. From time to time he turned to find his footprints. He seemed to enjoy this. I stopped suddenly. I was frightened—Johnny had no shadow. Mine stretched out, lingered on the foam that waves left under our feet, but he had no shadow. I told him so as calmly as possible when he shot me a quizzical look. Then he came close and gave me a chaste peck. I didn't know what to say. Johnny covered his left eye, as if to see something on the horizon, then kept walking. I preferred to walk behind him.

Those long walks ended beside a few crags that received the calming embrace of the sea. He sat there. He gestured for me to sit next to him. "You think I'm crazy, don't you?" he asked me. I told him no. "I'm alone," he added. I told him again about his shadow. "Stars have no shadow," he answered. And he told me how he lost it. "While we were shooting *Arizona Dream* . . . have you seen it? With Faye Dunaway and Lili Taylor. You must see it. One day when we didn't film, I went to see a wise Indian, an old man. He told me I was living in fear of my shadow. And he took it from me to take my fear away. But there's nothing to worry about. It's not lost somewhere. I have it inside. Do you understand? Inside." He pointed with his finger to the veins in his arms, his scars from needles and anxiety.

His straight black hair almost touched his shoulders. A lock of his hair fell over his face. He was thin, he ate little. Also a bit haggard, pale, pale brown. He had a sharply outlined chin, manly and firm. His smile was shy. There was a sadness in his eyes, a sadness of a blackbird. Johnny let me observe him. I realized that I enjoyed what I was looking at, so I turned my gaze toward the sea.

"What happens in the movie, what was it, *Arizona's Dream?*" I asked him.

"It's a weird movie, you know? I like those movies, they are my favorites. Faye plays a woman who dreams of flying. Lili, Faye's daughter in the movie, dreams of reincarnating as a turtle," he said.

"And you?" I asked. "What was your dream?"

Johnny didn't answer. The wind blew through his hair. He brought his hands to his temples and said, "I'm tired." We went back.

Van der Graff was closing Johnny's file. He was going to discharge him. While he jotted down his conclusions, he asked me again if Johnny told me something. I told him that the other day we had talked about one of his movies. The doctor frowned. "His movies?" he asked, his icy blue eyes piercing me.

That afternoon, the head nurse told me that Johnny would leave the next morning, that he was already "clean." The rest of the day, I felt very irritable. I found Dr. Van der Graff and told him about the shadow. He shrugged and told me that sometimes people have illusions, superstitions . . . anyway, Johnny's case was closed. I went for a walk with Johnny at the usual time. It was a cold afternoon, so he had a white blanket over his shoulders. His pensive walk irritated me even more. He said nothing, he was not going to say good-bye. He would be gone, and that was it. I stopped. He noticed that he was walking alone and turned to look at me. He took off his blanket and gave it to me. "The boat," he whispered. "Take this sail for your boat . . . "

Through the window of his empty room, I saw Johnny leave in a black limousine, like the ones that carry Hollywood stars. Stars without shadows.

Translated by Toshiya Kamei

Antonio José Ponte

IN THE COLD OF
THE MALECÓN

"**H**e chopped the meat into small pieces. Too small."

"Like his apartment," the mother commented.

"Yes. . . . And you want to know what I thought, seeing him cut the meat in the kitchen of the tiny apartment?"

She could imagine.

"I thought how strange that we've had a son."

Because they behaved like those old married couples, very attached to one another, who could never have children and in old age each becomes the child of the other.

"It would've been stranger not to have one."

"He was slicing the green bananas into rounds and then removing the skin from each round. You never did it that way."

"No."

She made a pretense of high spirits.

"But the apartment, describe it. What's it like?"

The father began to place all the rooms of the apartment within the room where they were sitting.

"It could all fit in here," he said finally.

So then he hasn't managed to get away from us, the mother thought.

"And tell me if he ate the meat."

The meat was a present they'd sent him.

"He cooked some of the small pieces and we ate them, and during the meal he talked about his work."

"He told you he'll have to move farther away, right?"

"How'd you guess?"

"It's a pretext of his."

"Could be, yes."

"He needs pretexts to defend himself from us," the mother said aloud. "Did you see things that weren't his? I mean: Does he live alone?"

"There was nobody else with us, no. There was one thing that seemed odd to me."

"What?"

"He didn't want the meat to lose the blood in cooking. He ate it very rare."

"And you?"

"Me? The same as always."

The mother nodded.

"While you were eating you asked him to take you to see the whores."

"After we had just finished eating. The pieces of meat were hard to stick a fork into. He asked me what I felt like doing. We had three hours before my train left and could take advantage of the time."

"Go on. Go on."

"Near his apartment are some movie theaters. Or we could walk around a little. . . . Then I told him I'd like to see the whores again."

"See them again?" The mother burst out laughing. "They can't be the same ones, they'd be wrecks by now."

The father laughed too.

"Of course."

"He knows where to find them," the mother mused aloud.

"He said we could go but that it was a bad night to walk along the Malecón. We might not find any."

"Why a bad night?"

"The surf. The waves crash over the top of the wall of the Malecón. You can't stay there without getting splashed."

"But finally you did find some."

"After a lot of walking. They were on the edge of the sidewalk, being careful of the waves and looking at the cars passing by."

"And they didn't look at you?"

The father suddenly felt ridiculous.

"At me? I'm old."

"At him."

"One woman looked at him for a moment. Just a moment, that's all. Like when you mistake someone in the street and realize the mistake immediately."

"And then?"

"She went back to looking at the street so she wouldn't miss any cars."

"Keep going."

"And that was all. We went back to his apartment to have coffee. I really liked the coffee, it gave me a lift. I asked him if he'd seen how that woman had looked at him."

"Yes."

"And in spite of how strange it was being his father, it felt right, the two of us in the nice warmth of his apartment, the two of us there and those women outside in the cold of the Malecón."

There the story ended. The two old people were silent for a while.

"Tell me again," the mother asked.

"What do you want me to tell you?"

"The way she looked at him, the woman you found."

Translated by Cola Franzen

Carmen Tafolla

TÍA

When she was eighty-two, she lost her eyesight. Cataracts. Same year, she lost her husband. Two years later, the cholesterol and blood sugar were responsible for a severe loss of hearing. The niece who took care of her was the one whom everyone turned to when someone got sick. Nice lady. Let her move in and cooked for her, *con mucho cariño*. Husband said, "Oh, well. It's just like when we had our babies. I don't mind."

By eighty-nine, she was having some serious problems with the diabetes. In two years, she lost two legs. "It's okay," said the niece, "I'll take care of her. She doesn't need to walk." But then the different parts of her started falling off. By ninety-six, the whole day was bathing, giving medicine, changing diapers, and listening to groans. The night was worse. The husband left. The niece was now taking care of her aunt, an older sister, and her father. The aunt began to cough and some internist said she should be in the hospital. So they put her in. The niece came by every evening. Covered her with a bathrobe that only had to cover a shape two and a half feet long. The doctor said it wouldn't be long.

But after two months, the doctor had been transferred to a different hospital, and one of his eager and eminent replacements had dropped dead of a heart attack.

In the third month, the hospital social worker recommended that she be moved to the "extended care" unit. The niece still came every evening, sitting by her side, holding the space that used to be her hand, and finally checking her watch and going home with a sigh to prepare for her father's doctor visits the next day. "I feel like running away from home," she said, "but there's no one to take care of everyone. Nobody who'll do it. They'd all come hunt me down to do the family chores. Sometimes this sitting by Tía's side is the only quiet time I have."

The hospital social worker was reassigned to a different unit; faces came and faces went. When they had to weigh her, they used the baby scales. She was under forty pounds. "She can't last much longer," said the young doctor, new to the beat and soon to be gone.

She didn't speak anymore, but she coughed and she groaned, and the night nurse said to the niece, "Prepare yourself, honey; she doesn't have long. But she's going to a better place." After a while, the night nurse went on to a better position with a private foundation. Finally, Medicare said they couldn't cover any more hospital days that year. So her niece came with a lap blanket, wrapped her gently, and carried her home.

The niece was having chest pains regularly these days and her own children had all moved out of state. Her grandchildren were asking what she was going to leave them, what the market value of her house was, and if she had a DNR order. A living will?

The niece changed the diapers more easily now that the aunt's weight had dropped even more. And the other sick family members had passed on and released her of her other extra duties. The ex-husband never came by. And the brothers and sisters that had been too busy to take care of the aunt were still too busy to take care of the niece.

The niece lit a *vela* once a week right after her trip to the grocery store, but soon she had made arrangements with a teenage neighbor to run the errands for her for a small fee. Life got quieter, and the niece quit counting the years going by. Sometimes she felt that the only thing that got her up each morning was the knowledge that she had to change the diaper and prepare the corn *atole*. *Atole* that she spoon-fed her *tía*, and occasionally tasted a spoonful of as well.

But finally the morning came when the clock had wound down, the spirit had run out, and the niece did not rise from her bed.

The house was quiet for a long time.

"WELL, IT'S OLD but I'm really happy with it. A good place for graduate work. You wouldn't believe this place! It's really, well . . . I dunno . . . like home. *Una casita chiquita, calladita*, but it's got something . . .

"And there's a *vela* to the Virgin of Guadalupe at a little altar and hand-crocheted doilies on the couch. Yeah, I got it with the furniture and everything. There's gobs of stuff here! The family didn't think a garage sale would be worth the trip down here, so they sold the whole thing at a flat rate and great terms, even let me move in right away and prorate the rent . . . I can hardly wait to open up some of these trunks!"

She was right. The place was cozy. She noticed it changed her lifestyle right from the beginning. She started buying candles to the Virgin of Guadalupe and lighting them at the altar, and for some reason, she began cooking *atole*. There were so many pillows piled on the bed in the second bedroom, and several of them seemed to be antiques. She promised herself to get to that room as soon as she cleared away some of the stuff in the kitchen.

By the end of the first week, she was feeling the rhythm of the house, and at night she was dreaming—of a flow like the ocean's tide—an in and out, a soothing repetitive pattern that sounded like life itself, like breathing. She quit working on the dissertation and began writing in her journal—writing between pots of *atole* or *sartenes* of *frijol con queso*, and sometimes a homemade *caldo* steeped all day till the nutrients filled the air, and she felt she could almost inhale their sustenance. And the dreams of tides, of ins and outs, of the breath of life, began to fill her waking hours as well.

One night, in the middle of the night she dreamed she was walking to the second bedroom and opening the trunk, peering inside, and seeing things she recognized from long, long ago. She even picked it up, this thing she had never touched, but had somehow never forgotten. It was rounded and pulsing and smelled of corn being toasted, warmed, prepared. Then she had approached the bed and looked beyond the pillows until her own breathing had tied her to the universe. In the morning, she couldn't remember if she had really gone to that room or merely dreamed of it.

The months passed. Her sense of peace deepened. There were three constants in life: the *atole*, the *vela* to the Virgin of Guadalupe, and the in-and-out of breathing that she heard more and more clearly each day, heard with something more than her ears, more than her heart, heard maybe with the life spirit that kept her going. She or the house or the air—or maybe someone else—was breathing.

By the time she met the niece's aunt, there was no surprise inside her. There was only the desire to cook *atole* and the dedication to continue the breath of the ocean's life. If she could keep her alive, she could keep the universe alive. Tía was tiny by now, no more than an armful. And there was nothing left to lose except her heartbeat and that obstinate, soothing breath.

She fed her *atole,* or maybe the old woman inhaled it. All she knew was that the rhythms of her life had changed, and they followed the inhale and the exhale of the large cloudy brown eyes. When she was not cooking or buying *velas,* she wrote. And when she had ceased to light *velas,* the person who followed her read the writings.

These writings.

AND THEY knew that if you listened very closely, you could hear her inhale, the universe, still alive. Do you hear it? Do you hear it now? Between the flickers of the *vela* in your living room. Between your footsteps as you walk to the kitchen, thinking of smooth life-giving *atole*—thinking of sustenance so soft, so strong you can inhale it, in the particles of the air, thinking of . . . life . . .

Hilma Contreras

HAIR

At twelve o'clock, just as they were about to close, a new and youthful voice asked:

"Can you sell me a bottle of Alka-Seltzer?"

The two of them looked at the newcomer, surprised by such an anachronism.

"What beautiful hair," Doña Irene complimented her.

The girl smiled, shaking her chestnut mane with a haughty grace that seemed like a provocation.

The druggist wiped his face with his handkerchief.

"How can she stand it!" he exclaimed a few minutes later. "I die of heat just from looking at it. How dreadful!"

But she lived right across from them. Her name was Natividad. She would come home from school dressed in showy tight-fitting pants, flaunting her torrent of hair, which reached down to her hips.

It brought him to despair.

"If they'd let me," he would repeat peevishly, "I'd cut it all the way to her nape."

To underscore his threat he brandished a pair of scissors, clicking them in the air.

One afternoon his gentle wife had a fit of laughter that dissolved into a feigned cough, because to make matters worse, the girl showed up with bangs down to her eyes.

Luciano began to live a terrible obsession. If he lifted his eyes from his work, there was the hair, on the street, on the balcony, at the window, on the terrace. There came a moment when, his understanding perturbed by the suffocating impact of all that hair, the prescriptions he handled lost all sense.

It wasn't summer yet. But summer's breath, like that of a puffing beast, filled the air.

"It's so hot!" Luciano said, sticking his head out the pharmacy door. "The air feels like fire."

"It's not that bad," commented Doña Irene, serenely seated in the undulating space in front of the electric fan. "But you're making yourself needlessly hot with all these comings and goings."

The pharmacist felt his wife's placid gaze on his back and could not repress an unpleasant prickly sensation.

"Well," he declared impatiently. "I'm leaving. Have the delivery boy help you close up when he gets back."

Doña Irene opened her mouth and placed her plump hands on the glass showcase, rendered speechless by surprise.

Men, she told herself thoughtfully, *are as complicated as entangled spools of thread. So it's hot . . . what else is new! Just like yesterday, like tomorrow, like always. The secret lies in not getting excited.*

Luciano turned the corner around the pharmacy in a great hurry, entered the first driveway, and practically ran up the stairs to the second floor, where they had lived since they had decided to open the business on the ground floor.

FLESHY, neither tall nor short, small-waisted, with Greek-vase curves, Natividad would come out on the terrace when the eaves sheltered it like a large visor of luminous shadow. She would pause for a moment on the only step on the threshold, glance olympically over her shoulder, arching her body, bending a knee to enhance the enticing line of her profile, and after shaking the dense beauty of her mane with a self-satisfied gesture, she would sit chastely in a native-wood rocking chair in the midst of her pots of geraniums. Between rocking her chair and glimpses at the book she was read- ing, her eyes would assess the effect that her self-display produced on passersby.

That day one of her glances captured the admiration on the face of the pharmacist watching her from his apartment balcony.

Behind him Doña Irene called out.

"María! It smells like something's burning on the stove . . . María!"

LYING NEXT to the body of his profoundly asleep wife, Luciano experienced the torments of yearning for a dream that eluded him. He tossed and turned in bed, sweating, irritated by Doña Irene's wheezing breaths. Around midnight, having reached the point of exasperation, he got up and went out on the balcony, anxious for a breath of air.

The moon was shining brightly on Natividad's terrace. Its fixed and translucent light stained with black shadows the old oak tree in the garden. The girl rocked in her chair, apparently also unable to sleep. She noticed the pharmacist and smiled at him. The greenish nocturnal silence started buzzing in Luciano's ears. She was look-ing at him and smiling. She would rock for a few seconds and turn to stare fixedly at him. Luciano decided to go down.

When she saw him open the garden gate, she stood up, startled. The movement unveiled her naked body.

"What beautiful breasts you have!" he said admiringly, his eyes moist with emotion.

Instead of covering herself, Natividad tossed her head back with an arrogant gesture.

Luciano extended his arm. His hand filled with life.

She moaned in protest.

"No . . . let me go."

Ignoring her, he grabbed her brusquely by the shoulders to kiss her. His fingers got tangled in her hair. He tried to gather it in a bundle on her nape but the locks escaped his fingers, winding themselves around his arms, brushing against his face. He felt suf-focated with heat.

"I only want to kiss you," he panted. "Don't be upset . . . Be good, I'm not going to hurt you . . . "

Frantic, he exclaimed:

"Damned hair!"

It was like a hot noose around his throat. He was choking as he kissed her, with no time to free himself from the never-ending hair, quivering with desire and fear.

The ardor of the struggle awakened Doña Irene.

"That nightmare again," she grumbled as her arm reached clumsily for her husband in the semidarkness. "Don't drown, Luciano. . . . Wake up!"

Luciano sat up abruptly, half-crazed by anguish.

"The hair," he mumbled. "The hair . . . "

"What are you saying? . . . Come, lie on your side and it will be all right. . . . Where are you going?"

"To . . . I don't know. I'm soaked in sweat."

Once completely awakened, he said:

"Don't get up. I'll go get another pair of pajamas myself."

"Suit yourself. . . . But don't you start reading at this late hour . . . "

It was cool on the balcony. He breathed anxiously. All was still on the terrace, which was bathed in a moonlit brightness that made the chirping of the crickets reverberate. Leaning against the rail, Luciano stared for a long time at the exuberance of the geraniums. He was overcome by a furious desire to bite them so they would burst once and for all, driving away that unbearable feeling of lust.

DOÑA IRENE changed position in her eagerness to resume her interrupted sleep. *This husband of mine*, she sighed, *is suffering from nerves. I hope to God it's nothing serious . . . I hope he's not going to go on like some men who go through crises at a certain age . . .* She made another effort to fall asleep, sprawling on her back on the bed while she chased away her worries and concentrated on the soporific task of mentally writing numbers on the dark night of her eyelids. A frenetic weight suddenly fell on top of her. She barely had time to utter:

"Ooh . . . Luciano . . . "

Translated by Lizabeth Paravisini-Gebert

Daniel A. Olivas

LA GUACA

There was a man who owned the finest restaurant in the village. Though no name adorned the establishment, the villagers dubbed it La Guaca, the tomb. The man, as well, had no name, at least that the villagers knew. He was a complete mystery, a man apparently with no family, no origin, no history. They called him El Huérfano, the orphan.

One evening, as the villagers gorged themselves on enchiladas, tamales, and other delectable dishes, El Huérfano rose from his usual seat at the corrner table and cleared his throat. The room fell into silence.

"I plan to take a bride," said El Huérfano to the startled villagers. "But," he cautioned with a raised, elegant finger, "she must be perfect in every way."

251

Most of the families had at least one unmarried daughter because the revolution had taken from this earth most of the village's eligible young men. So this announcement raised great hope in the hearts of the parents and their daughters.

"I invite all of the village's señoritas to feast here tomorrow night," said El Huérfano. "No one else may come. And I will choose my wife from among the guests."

"How will you choose?" an older woman asked. But El Huérfano turned and disappeared through a back door. A great cheer filled the void because this mysterious but wealthy man would make someone's perfect daughter a bride.

The next evening, all of the village's single women swarmed La Guaca dressed in all their finery. Though El Huérfano was not the handsomest of men, times were hard and there was little chance of living a comfortable life without a marriage of convenience. Remarkably, all of the women found seats in La Guaca and they waited. The tables sighed with great platters of food and bottles of fine brandy. Finally, after what seemed an eternity, El Huérfano appeared.

"As you know," he began, "I search for the perfect wife."

The room murmured in anticipation.

"Before you sits a great feast," he continued, noticing one particular beauty who sat motionless amid the others. "But it is poisoned."

A horrified gasp rose from the young women.

"The poison is so potent, it will kill in a matter of minutes." El Huérfano now whispered, "But it will not harm a perfect woman. If you wish to leave, please do. Otherwise, enjoy your dinner."

Only one woman stood and left. The others slowly served themselves and commenced eating, each believing that she would survive. After a few minutes, the first victim fell. And then there was another and yet another. Finally, only the most beautiful woman was left. She stood and walked to him.

"You shall be my wife," he said as he moved his lips to hers.

She leaned forward and they kissed. El Huérfano could taste the wonderful feast from the beauty's lips. But then his eyes bulged and he fell back.

"No!" he sputtered as he dropped to the floor.

"Yes, my love," said the beautiful woman. "Yes."

Sergio Ramírez

THE CENTERFIELDER

The flashlight passed back and forth over the prisoners' faces and stopped on a man, stripped to the waist and glistening with sweat, sleeping face up on a cot.

"That's him. Open up," said the guard through the bars.

The rusty lock made a noise as it resisted the key, which was tied to the end of an electrical cable the jailer wore around his waist to hold up his pants. Inside, the guard slapped the rifle butt against the wooden cot; the man sat up, using a hand to shield his eyes from the light.

"Get up, they're waiting for you."

The man groped for his shirt; he shivered, though it had been unbearably hot that night and the other prisoners were either sleeping naked or in their underwear. The one hole in the room was high up so that air circulated only near the ceiling. He found his shirt, and slipped his bare feet into his laceless shoes.

"Speed it up," the guard ordered.

"I'm coming, can't you see?"

"No lip, huh, or you'll get it."

"Yes, I know."

"You sure do." The guard let him go first. "Get going," he said, jabbing the rifle into the prisoner's back. The cold steel made him shrink back.

They entered the courtyard; in back, near the wall, the leaves of the almond trees shone in the moonlight. The meat market beyond the wall began killing steers around midnight and the breeze carried back the odor of blood and manure.

What a great yard to play ball in. The prisoners must choose sides among themselves or challenge the guards to a game. The centerfield fence will be the wall, some three hundred and fifty feet from home base. If the ball was hit that deep, I'd have to make a running catch by the almond trees and, after snagging the ball by the wall, the infield would seem far off and I'd barely be able to hear the yells for the relay and I'd see the runner rounding second while I'd jump up for a branch, straddle it in one motion, and I'd reach the branch level with the wall bristling with pieces of broken bottles and I'd bring my body across carefully, first my hands, then my feet, and jump down on the other side even if I cut myself as I dropped and I'd land on the pile where they dump garbage, bones and horns, tin cans, broken chairs, rags, newspapers, dead animals, and as I ran along, I'd be caught by thistles, fall into a rushing creek, but I'd get up, with the barrage of rifle fire sounding hard and dry, but kind of dull behind me.

"Stand still. Where you think you're going?"

"To piss."

"You're so scared you're pissing in your pants, shithead."

The town square resembled it, with the guarumo trees by the church atrium, and me patrolling centerfield with my glove. I was the only fielder with a cloth glove—the others fielded barehand—and at six p.m. I'd still be out there and though I could barely see, no hit would get by me; I knew the ball was coming by its hum and it would drop in my hands like a dove.

"Here he is, Captain," the guard said, sticking his head through the half-opened door. The air conditioner hummed inside.

"Let him in and get out."

He heard the door lock behind him and he felt caged in the bare room with a gold-framed picture and a calendar with huge red and blue numbers hung on a whitewashed wall, a chair in the center of the room, and the captain's desk in back. The air conditioner had recently been set in the wall because the plaster was still wet.

"What time did they pick you up?" asked the captain without raising his head.

He remained silent, confused, hoping with all his might that the question was for someone else, perhaps someone hiding under the table.

"Are you deaf? I'm talking to you. When did they catch you?"

"A little after six, I think," he said so softly that he wondered if the man had heard him.

"Why do you say a little after six? Can't you remember the right time?"

"I don't have a watch, sir, but I had eaten dinner, and I eat at six."

Dinner's ready, my mother shouted from the sidewalk. One more inning, mum, I'd answer, I'm coming. But son, can't you see? It's dark already, how can you go on playing? Yes, I'm coming, one more inning, and the organs and violins started playing for the church rosary just when the last out reached my hands and we'd won the game again.

"What work do you do?"

"I'm a shoemaker."

"In a shop?"

"No, I fix them at home."

"You were a ballplayer?"

"Yes, I was."

"They called you 'Flash' Parrales, right?"

"That's because I had a quick snap when I threw home."

"You were on the team that played in Cuba?"

"Yes. Twenty years ago. I played centerfield."

"But they dropped you."

"When we got back."

"Your throw home made you quite a star."

He was about to smile, but the man eyed him angrily.

The best play I ever made was when I caught a fly by the church, glove stretched, my back to the infield, and fell flat on my face on the steps with the ball. My tongue bled, but we had won the game and they carried me home on their shoulders and my mother, who was making tortillas, left the corn meal to cure me, feeling sorry for and proud of me just the same, you'll always be dumb as a mule, son, but an athlete.

"Why did they drop you from the team?"

"I fumbled a fly and we lost."

"In Cuba?"

"Yes, against the team from Aruba. It was a little dove that slipped through my hands and two runs scored. We lost."

"Several players were dropped."

"Well, we drank too much. You can't drink and play at the same time."

"Hmm."

"Can I sit?" he wanted to ask, for his legs were wobbly, but he stood pat as if they had glued down the soles of his shoes.

The captain wrote for what seemed ages. Then he lifted his head; a red insignia glowed on his army cap.

"Why did they bring you in?"

He shrugged, looking helpless.

"Aha. Why?"

"I don't—"

"Don't what?"

"Don't know."

"So you don't know why?"

"No."

"I've got your record right here." He showed him a folder. "I'll read you a few lines so you'll know all about your life," he said standing up.

In the outfield, I can hardly, if ever, hear the ball hitting the catcher's mitt.

But if the batter connects, a dry whack explodes in my ears and all my senses perk up. And if it's a fly heading toward me, I wait for it with love, patience, spinning under it till it reaches me and I catch it at chest level as if my hands had made a nest for it.

"Friday, twenty-eight July, at five p.m., a green Willys jeep with a canvas top stopped in front of your house and two men got out; the dark-skinned man wore khaki pants and sunglasses and the blond wore blue jeans and a straw hat. The one with glasses carried a Pan Am bag, the other a guard's duffel. They stepped into your house and didn't leave till ten, without either bag."

"The one with glasses," he began, then stopped to swallow a huge wad of saliva, "happened to be my son."

"I know that."

There was silence again, and he felt his feet growing wet in his shoes, as if he had just crossed a stream.

"The bag they left had machine-gun ammunition and the duf-

fel was full of explosives. How long had it been since you had seen
your son?"

"Months," he whispered.

"Speak louder. I can't hear you."

"Months. I don't know how many. He left the rope factory after
work one day and we didn't see him again."

"You weren't worried?"

"Sure, a son's a son. We asked about, we searched, but got
nowhere." He pressed his false teeth together; they seemed to be
slipping.

"But you knew he was holed up in the mountains?"

"We heard rumors about it."

"What did you think when he showed up in a jeep?"

"That he was coming back. He greeted us, but left after a few
hours."

"And he asked you to keep an eye on his things?"

"Yes, he'd send for them."

"Ah."

He took out more papers, typed on a purple ribbon, from the
folder. He shuffled through them and put a sheet on the table.

"It says here that for three months you dealt ammunition, small
arms, explosives, propaganda, and that enemies of the state slept
in your house."

He said nothing. He only pulled a handkerchief and blew his
nose. He looked thin and worn out under the lamp, as if he had
turned into a skeleton.

"And nothing smelled fishy, huh?"

"You know how it is, sons—"

"Sons of bitches, like you."

He lowered his head and glanced at his shoes, tongue out and
soles caked with mud.

"How long?"

"What?"

"Since you've seen your son?"

He looked him in the face and took his handkerchief out again.

"You know that they killed him. Why ask me?"

Last inning against Aruba, 0 to 0, two outs, and the white ball floated toward my hands. I went to meet it, I waited, stretched my arms and we were about to be joined forever when it struck the back of my hand, I tried trapping it as it fell, but it bounced off and I saw a man, far away, dusting himself off at home plate, and all was lost. I had to soak my injuries in warm water, mum, because you always knew that I could field even if I'd die doing it.

"Sometimes you want to be good, but can't," the captain said walking around the table. He slid the folder in a drawer and turned around to shut off the air conditioner. Unexpected silence flooded the room. He unhooked a towel from a nail and wrapped it around his neck.

"Sergeant—" he called.

The sergeant snapped to attention at the door and once the prisoner had been removed, he turned to the captain.

"He was a ballplayer, so invent any crap you want: say he was playing ball with some prisoners, in centerfield, when the ball hit the wall and he climbed up an almond tree, jumped the wall, and we shot him as he ran across the meat-market yard."

Translated by David Unger

Ignacio Padilla

CHRONICLE OF
THE SECOND PLAGUE

The records of the second plague come down to no more than speculations—loose dates and contradicting theories that still circulate in the medical faculty of the University of Kent. Some of its more distinguished members seriously question the spread of the epidemic, but the majority concur in their view that Sir Richard de Veelt based his medical findings not on his observation of the epidemic itself but on another document of unknown origin, barely detectable in the notes the distinguished crown counselor forwarded to Europe some months before he disappeared.

Judging by the oblique nature of his notes, Sir Richard must have found that other notebook in some obscure corner of the St. Martin Mission, perhaps blurred and damaged by the humidity of the Amazon, perhaps at the mercy of termites in the ruins of a chapel. There was no important heading that might have given the celebrated explorer some idea of what was in those incomplete pages, nor had anyone taken the trouble to hide them in a strongbox. To whom would they have mattered, these pages? What would anyone who did not have de Veelt's knowledge have made of the hundreds of normal cardiograms, the records of glucose in perfect equilibrium, blood pressures enviably level? To establish its very existence, what that anonymous report revealed came precisely from what was not said, or, as de Veelt himself suggests, in the utter disregard shown by the victims of the second plague toward their invisible infection. Truly, no man in his right mind could have perceived an illness in so asymptomatic an appearance, an illness the first sign of which was perfect health. If you add that this particular epidemic struck St. Martin in the wake of a fierce outbreak of bubonic plague, it is no wonder that the contrast alone led sufferers and doctors alike to consider the second plague as a blessing rather than as the onset of a new epidemic even more destructive than death.

It is difficult to imagine just how much time de Veelt was able to spend with these pages, or what he managed to glean from them. Perhaps he had them for a few hours, enough to discover with some dread that he had contracted the disease and that his habitual infirmities had completely disappeared. He ought then to have consigned these notes to the cemetery of neutral texts, as out of sight as the sickness they identify. Perhaps later the counselor wondered if the substance of that record, so neat and perfect, had raised the same alarms in the inquiring spirit of some missionary, or in the mind of whoever, ages before, had written them down just as he had now read them—terrified, dwelling in this jungle retreat on the ironies of so macabre a god, who had relieved St. Martin of the bubonic plague only to visit on his creatures a second epidemic more in keeping with his sinister personal clock.

How could anyone have made this clear to the inhabitants of St. Martin, while they were rejoicing in their new health as a well-deserved miracle? The fact that these people had survived the ravages of bubonic plague left them with the firm conviction that they had paid up the quota of pain that divine providence exacts from each person, each place. When the second plague began to make its presence felt, there was a death in every dwelling, a hanging smell of burning flesh, and a solid carpet of rats as big as dogs waiting for their own cremation in the atrium of the church. In Sir Richard's considered opinion, scenes of that nature must have at least stimulated the native population with a will to live beyond their natural limits, and in that way the cruel memory of past pain seemed reason enough for them to believe that the sores, the tears, and the yellow vomit had immunized them against death, as happens when viruses carry vaccines for other infections. In that way, unable to understand their own helplessness and given to disobeying the laws of nature, the people of St. Martin had chosen to ignore death, or, as the counselor suggests, quoting his hypothetical notebook, to assimilate it with a superhuman vitality.

Even so, it would be wrong to charge the public health authority with negligence for having suspected nothing when the hospital, formerly packed with the sick and the dying, suddenly emptied dramatically and reassuringly. Now we know from other sources that the colonial government at one point saw the hospital desertion as a logical reaction on the part of the people to the increased charges levied by the medical services during the bubonic plague. But Sir Richard's notes do not go in for such speculation—his attention is more taken up with the astonishing results obtained by the notebook's author when he examined certain victims of the disease. There is a note on how cirrhotic livers continued to function perfectly, how bodies had ceased to register infection, and how minds had come to reject utterly notions of pain and death.

De Veelt acknowledges having read in the notes a record of hundreds of similar instances, in which the writer has tested patients' extremities with a scalpel, or has struck them to the point of drawing blood, without seeing any alteration in their fundamental good humor. Either from timidity or from extreme skepticism, the investigator had finally to admit his complete impotence when confronting these desperate and mutilated bodies, or in seeing flame applied to the flesh of those who showed the same indifference to their wounds as someone listening to an incomprehensible foreign language.

Sir Richard's comments in the latter part of the notebook are extremely laconic. It is difficult besides to separate from them his vision of a St. Martin turned into a kind of leper colony whose abandoned and deformed inhabitants began one day to conceive of an infirmity that would restore them to life. About that time, the patients would take to mutilating themselves, and wandering among the disintegrating buildings of the mission. In the end, their bodies, already embarked on a process of slow but inevitable disintegration, would have accepted a kind of life that was fragmented and infected, but nevertheless would retain sufficient vitality to devour Sir Richard de Veelt while he was reading the last pages of the notebook, in the certainty that one day the particles of his physical body, still squirming with life, would be dispersed by the wind that blew from the Amazon.

Translated by Alastair Reid

Lisa Alvarez

"CIELITO LINDO"

When the twelve-piece mariachi band her uncle had booked to serenade his wife on their fiftieth wedding anniversary started playing and filled up the church's basement room with the blast of five trumpets, Linda decided to sit next to her father after all because she knew they wouldn't be able to speak over the music and so she would get credit, good daughter credit she imagined, but at the same time she wouldn't have to say a thing or listen to what he had to say about her mother (*after all these years still "that crazy woman" if he was sober or "that bitch" if he was drunk*) or her own sorry life (*manless, childless, pointless in his view*). Linda also imagined that if she, his nearly fifty-year-old daughter, sat next to him, her presence might dissuade him from hitting on the younger female guests. She'd already seen his eyes wander as the generation of family grandchildren, now in their late twenties and early thirties, arrived, accompanied by their friends. The women wore dancing dresses cut just low enough to raise his hopes. He was drinking tonight, she noted, something dark and on the rocks.

Her father was handsome in a kind of craggy roosterlike way. He'd aged well and knew it. Still had all his hair, more than most men forty years younger. Tonight he dressed up in dark jeans and cowboy boots, a fine white shirt unbuttoned to show a puff of chest hair that belied his seventy-plus years. He always did that with his shirts and it embarrassed her, the sight of that patch of burnished skin and curling white hair. Linda wondered if, had she been a boy, the son her mother claimed he always wanted, she would feel different, feel pride, a kind of male camaraderie rooted in perhaps her own hopes as a middle-aged male swimming in the same hairy gene pool.

Linda sat and watched her father move in rather gentlemanly appreciation of the music, his head nodding, his eyes beaming. It was as if he and not his brother-in-law had paid for the band and made the arrangements, a kind of easy but dishonest sense of proprietorship that she often saw him deploy at family dinners and parties. As if he, along with the other *tíos* and *tías*, had helped out or pitched in when, as she well knew, all he'd done again was show up.

When the mariachis launched into the inevitable "Cielito Lindo," her aunt and uncle stood in front of the musicians. They swayed together, which was as close as they would ever get to dancing, and the crowd began to stand too and sing along to the music they had heard their whole lives, in restaurants and on street corners, in movie houses and on car radios. It meant something to them all, if perhaps not the same thing, this song with its *ay ay ay ay*, with its command to sing and not cry. Some people, she noticed, knew all the words, and some knew only the chorus. Linda was one of the chorus singers.

Her father drained his glass, got to his feet, and began to sway, to sing. He knew all the words. He even turned to Linda and smiled as if she too, his daughter, was a lovely woman, worthy of such a song. Her father knew how to look at a woman and make her feel like that, she thought. Pretty. It didn't take much. Something about the full attention of his eyes. He bent down and reached out his hand, the gentleman again, a gallant gesture, to raise her to her feet. And when he did, when her old father leaned toward her, she noticed his white dress shirt was undone one button more than his usual two. And when Linda stood beside him and glanced again, she saw that instead of his usual wife-beater undershirt (*How she hated that name however true it might be for him*), with its white ribbing and scoop neck, it appeared to her that her father was wearing a white camisole with a bouquet of embroidered flowers at its center. She looked away. Linda herself had worn such things as a girl, to dances in this very basement and yes, like her father, had left her blouses unbuttoned to the flowers, hoping perhaps something else would show as well and someone else would notice.

Linda watched as the bows of the violins cut the air with a kind of violence but, unable to help herself, her eyes shifted back to the garland of tightly stitched pink rosebuds with their satin petals and green leaves that adorned her father, his puff of chest hair rising now like a cloud above a garden.

Linda wondered what this girl's undershirt meant, with its tiny flowers: *Where did it come from? Whose was it? Had her father picked it up off the floor of some woman's bedroom and mistaken it for his own? Had he donned it like a strange trophy? Had the shirt made its way into his laundry cycle at his apartment building and gone unnoticed? Did he know? Should she tell him?*

Her father sang now, full-throated, and when she looked at him in profile, Linda saw his strength and handsomeness, perhaps what her mother had seen, yes, over fifty years ago now. But she also saw all those years gone and she knew there were not that many left for him now. Linda could see what her father could not: those flowers, that white hair, the mistakes a person makes.

Daniel Chacón

DAY OF THE DEAD

When I was two months old, my dead mother held me in her arms. My brother Vern showed me the black and white photo. In front of golden drapes that reached the ground, she held me with one arm, and, with the other hand free, she touched my nose. The lamp in the room made me bright, a little bundle wrapped in white, glowing on her hand and face. "Wow. That's Mom?" I said.

I was fourteen and had never seen her before because she died two months after the photo was taken. She looked nothing like I had pictured. She was sexy and tall, wearing tight nylon pants and a snug blouse.

"She's pretty beautiful, isn't she?" Vern said, sitting shirtless on his bed. He was nineteen, but even with the room lights dim, he looked to be in his thirties—splotchy beard, bony arms and chest. In less than a year he would die of AIDS.

"I want you to have it," he said.

"Thanks," I said. I took it back to the house, and when I went to bed I held it on my chest. After I was sure Mr. and Mrs. Martin were asleep, I flicked on the light and looked at it again. Under the brightness, I could see her much clearer. She had light brown hair and a face shaped like a heart. Then I noticed she wasn't wearing a bra, her breasts shaped like . . . simply like the sloping breasts of a beautiful woman. I ran my finger up and down her image. "Hi, Mom," I said. "I'm your son."

AT SCHOOL, I showed the photo to my best friend, Raul Galivan. "I'd do her any day," he said.

"That's my mother, you idiot," I said.

"No shit?" He grabbed the photo and looked closer. "I think I see her nipples," he said.

Jimmy Strunk, an eleventh grader who didn't have a mother or father, walked by and looked over my shoulder. He had a scar that ran from his chin to his neck and red hair and freckles. He said, looking at the photo, "Damn. That lady's so fine I'd eat the corn out of her shit."

"That's sick," I said. "That's my mother."

"So what are you going to do about it?" he said. Shortly after he would turn eighteen, he would go to prison for murder.

"I'm just saying it's my mother," I said.

ONE DAY Mrs. Reinholt, the Spanish teacher, told us about the Day of the Dead. We would erect altars, she said, called *ofrendas*, and we would display them in the cafeteria as a class project. "Bring a photo of someone who died, that you were close to," she said. On tables, around the photos, we would place things that the deceased liked while they were still among us. Things they liked to eat or drink.

I would use her picture for the altar, I decided. I called Vern at the hospital to ask what things Mom liked. He was five when she died so he didn't remember much. "Wait a minute," he said. He coughed away from the phone. Then he said, out of breath, "I think she liked grapefruit."

"What about Dad—would he know?" I asked.

"Do you really want to call Dad?" he asked.

Even if he were sober enough to recognize my name and voice, he would think I wanted money. He would live a long time—an old, unhappy man.

"No, I guess not," I said.

I TRIED to picture Mom opening presents under a Christmas tree but couldn't picture what she would want to pull from the boxes. I decided maybe she did like grapefruit, so that's what I put around her photo. I also placed bowls of candy, loaves of bread, and *calaveras*, sugar skulls. The Spanish class had about twenty tables in the cafeteria.

For two days I spent the entire lunch period before the *ofrendas*. The one time Raul Galivan talked me into going outside to watch some girls play volleyball, I felt my mother calling me to come back, so I left him in the sun and returned to the cafeteria. Before her altar, I felt peace, like resting in shadow. Except when Jimmy Strunk walked by. He would bend over her table, look at the photo, and then make a masturbation gesture with his fist.

One day I went in the cafeteria and her picture was missing.

"Well, shit, what do you expect?" said Raul. "With that nipple and all."

I stood in the crowded cafeteria and yelled, "Whoever took that photo, I'm going to kick your ass!"

Raul tried to talk sense into me. "Did you forget you don't know how to fight?"

Some of the varsity football players who sat together laughed. Then some of the *cholos* hanging out on the other side of the cafeteria laughed at me too. One yelled, "Oh, we're so scared."

But I was beside myself. "I'm not kidding. I'll make this my fucking crusade. I want that picture back."

Then I saw him sitting alone, like he always did, in the corner of the cafeteria, laughing and watching as he ate a sandwich. Jimmy Strunk, his curly red hair disheveled and high on his head like an afro. I pointed at him, "I'll kick your ass, Jimmy."

He stood and walked over to me, slowly. I could hear from around the cafeteria: "Boy's going to get his ass kicked." "He's dead." Even the jocks and *cholos* didn't mess with Jimmy Strunk, yet here I was, the smallest kid in school.

Jimmy stood right in front of me. "What're you going to do, huh?"

"Did you take my mother's picture?" I said—cried really—my voice cracking.

He looked around, and everyone was watching. The scar running down his chin was purple. "What if I did?" he said, looking in my eyes.

"I'll kill you," I said, looking in his.

"Ooooh!" said the students.

"Do it," he said, coming in closer. "Do it." He was so close I could smell the bitter tuna on his breath. "Do it," he breathed.

Suddenly I pictured the photo. My mother cooed at me and smiled, her eyes wide with awe, as if she held a miracle. Then she looked up at the camera, right at the lens. "Do it," she said. "Do it."

So warm. Like shadow.

"Here," said Jimmy, pulling the photo from his back pocket

and handing it to me. "It was just a fucking joke." He walked back to his seat and sat alone. Everyone watched me; some came up to me and patted my back and talked to me. But I kept watching him, alone in the corner, where he finished chewing his bitter sandwich.

2 MICROSTORIES

THE WOODEN BOAT

My older brother, who's almost twenty and has a goatee that Apá does not like, has stopped wearing bandannas. He's sold his watch chain and doesn't iron his khakis the way he used to, the pleats as sharp as knives.

He's good to us now, good to Apá, better to Mamá, and he's been starting on me lately.

Sitting on a railroad tie tugged away from the tracks across the road, he takes a piece of wood already fashioned by the sun and the earth and the air and the water from Apá's hose, and it's enough for my brother's hands. He sits me next to him and lets me watch. The knife he says he always had to carry inside his right sock is for different things now, and he carves the fibers and splinters the wood, until a sudden, odd little boat emerges on his fingertips. "You like it, little bro?" he asks me and smiles, his lips pressing and blowing away the sawdust like the magician I believe he is.

But I couldn't nod at him or say anything or even reach out to touch it. Because as the boat appeared, in the harbor of his hands, I spied the dried flecks on the knife tip, and my mouth said nothing, but my heart thought of that bad guy slit last night, up the street, the sirens in the alley, the fading feet.

ASTILLA

My friend Diego, because he was older, was tough. Not tough enough to live forever. When it was still rumor—that a shotgun blast hit his left side, that he had flown from the back of a car, that he was riding a bicycle and not looking—it did not matter. I was sad when I heard, only sure that Diego had taken the trip to the hospital, mumbling, gurgling blood, but not making it.

When we were young, we played baseball in a clearing completely surrounded by peach trees. All the kids in the neighborhood, everything we owned crude, the bases smashed chicken buckets, the ball ragged from a chewing dog. We owned the wooden bat not used anymore by the older kids, heavy tape around the tip to keep it together. In that clearing, where everyone ran circles, ate free peaches, it was Diego who did not mind picking me from the last of the bunch, and it was Diego who corrected my throw, got my stance right. He showed the rest of us and could shield the taunts.

The day I heard about the accident, I thought of that baseball field and the day the bat gave me a splinter. Diego took me aside, letting the game go on, seeing the long splinter dug deep into my palm. He saw me crying, and he pulled in over me like a wing to block all the joking. My hand tight in his, tighter when he pulled a pocketknife. With great care, my wrist in his hand not letting me pull away from the blade, he pierced my skin, slowly, and brought the splinter out, no blood. He made me kiss the splinter for luck, and then he blew it away into the grass of the clearing and our stomping feet. He made it better, Diego, who brought out both bad and good in us, made it surface without the expected pain, when he held our hands and made us dig deep.

MANUELITO

Nicomedes Suárez Araúz

MANUELITO

Manuelito was born in Loén, and every night since his
birth a blue rider on a black horse would come up next to his bed
and with his black machete would cut Manuelito's throat. Each
night it inevitably happened.

In the morning, his mother, Doña Elcira, would find blood
clots, shaped like hearts, beating on her son's pillow. Worried, she
would stay up all night watching over his sleep, hoping to find out
the reason. Nevertheless, she never discovered any clues.

Each night the rider would arrive with his machete and each
morning Doña Elcira would cast away little hearts of blood. Yet
despite this odd nightly event, when Manuelito turned sixteen he
looked like a full-grown man. The night of his sixteenth birthday,
anticipating the arrival of his nightly visitor, he stayed on watch,

waiting for him with a machete. When the blue rider arrived, he approached Manuelito's bed and arched his body. He was about to give him the blow when Manuelito hit him first with his weapon, severing the rider's neck. A laughter of ringing glass bells invaded the room and echoed in his body.

Through the night the dried-up blood clots came back to life and began beating fast like the hearts of little birds.

Since then, Manuelito beheads the blue rider each night, and with every year that Manuelito adds to his age, the blue rider's age diminishes by one year. And the blood clots scattered among the grass, trees, ponds, gravel, and sand beaches beat weaker and weaker with every year that passes.

Translated by Sandra Reyes

Pablo Medina

ZAPATA

Mostly we drove through the swamp on our way to the Bay of Pigs, where the fishing was the best to be found anywhere on the island. The one road through went straight, with hardly a curve, into Playa Girón, which was to be the site of the ill-fated exile invasion in 1961. The sun was already setting when the first line was cast and it was only after the first light of dawn had tinted the eastern edge of the sky that we returned, laden with fish and ready to sleep through the morning.

From the car window, Zapata Swamp appeared as an endless expanse of brackish water and mangrove with an occasional *carbonero*'s shack. At times, columns of smoke in the distance rose toward the sky from, one imagined, for they were never seen outright, slow-burning coal ovens.

It happened that on a summer's day when I was eight years old and things were slow at the farm (the cane wasn't harvested until January), my mother's cousin Berto took a group of us crabbing in the swamp. We reached Zapata before dusk and stopped the jeep by a dirt road. To the right was a cow pasture; to the left, water as far as the eye could see—an inland shallow sea. Each of us, except my uncle Jaime, who carried a lantern, was handed a burlap sack and a hook fashioned out of a clothes hanger. The boys (two cousins and I) were told to stay close to Jaime. As the sun went down, the crabs started creeping onto the road, at first only a few, then, as it got darker, more and more came until the road was covered with them. They were ocher-colored, about a foot long each, with claws as big as my hand, and they made eerie clacking and rasping noises as they crawled over each other. It was my first time crabbing and I was terrified, frozen in place by the morbid sensation that I could, at any time these creatures so wished, be devoured alive.

Everyone else was busy hooking the monsters by the large claw and dropping them into the sacks. This had to be done quickly, so as not to allow the crab to latch on to the hand holding the sack. "Those claws can really mangle a thumb," Berto had warned me with a cackle. Soon all the sacks but mine were filled and more were brought out. Jaime suggested we go into the cow pasture, where we would find the females with their egg sacks bursting. To do this we had to crawl under a barbed-wire fence, the last strand of which lay dangerously close to the ground. Berto, his brother Raelo, Jaime, and my two cousins made it through easily, but as I slid under, I felt something hard under me. Thinking it was a crab (it was, most probably, a rock), I jerked up, slashing my back on one of the barbs. Within a minute or two my shirt was soaked with blood, and surrounding me was a cloud of mosquitoes as thick as coal smoke. I could barely see, I could barely breathe; I could not talk or even cry because I didn't want to swallow a mouthful of insects. My uncle took me back to the jeep, rolled up the windows, and told me to wait.

It was a hot night, as hot as it can get in the interior of Cuba. The inside of the jeep felt like a slow-burning oven. I was wet with my own blood; I was tired, alone, afraid, constantly watching the darkness outside, horrified that one of the *carboneros*, people who were said to practice the lowest of aberrations, from pederasty to infanticide, would show up. I waited in that metal coffin in such darkness I could not even see my hand in front of my face. I tried rolling the window down a crack to get some fresh air as the ferrous smell of my blood was making me nauseous, but within minutes a few mosquitoes had snuck in. Unable to see anything, I sat helplessly and listened to them buzzing around my ears until I could not bear it any longer. I leaned forward on the seat and waited for one of the little suckers to bite my bloody back. When I felt the prick, I threw myself backward hoping it would be too drunk with pleasure to escape. I don't know how many of the mosquitoes I crushed into oblivion; my strategy, however, kept me from going insane. It took me twenty years to recognize the value of that exercise. No matter how helpless the situation might really be, one's sense of helplessness will only be increased by inactivity. Few house fires will be put out with a garden hose, but the mere attempt will save one from the vise of despair.

The rest of the group showed up an eternity later with more crabs. The sacks were tied to the sides and top of the jeep, and we were ready for home. I felt the tension in every organ seep away in a long sigh of relief: bath, sleep, bath, sleep. But when Berto turned the key, nothing happened; the motor gave not even a whimper. The battery was dead. Now there were six of us inside the car swearing, cursing, and the crabs all around clacking and rasping.

Sometime after midnight we saw lights coming toward us in the distance. A truck full of soldiers with their Thompson machine guns and M-1s dangling limply over the sides pulled up next to us. A flashlight looked us over and fixed on Berto's face. He covered his eyes with his hand as if making a halfhearted salute. For a moment, there was absolute silence inside the cab — even the crabs stopped moving.

During the last years of the Batista dictatorship, groups of soldiers and police acting on their own (but with tacit official approval) roamed the interior in search of suspected sympathizers of the revolution. Of these groups, the most notorious was one led by a man named Masferrer. They called themselves Los Tigres de Masferrer. I had heard stories of how they ripped open the wombs of pregnant women and tied naked men on the ground, close to a mound of red ants, after spreading molasses on their groins. I had seen Los Tigres photographed in *Bohemia*, a Cuban magazine, holding skulls of men and women they had supposedly tortured and killed. I was repulsed and, at the same time, fascinated by their sometimes ingenious methods. Their irrepressible brutality appealed to that part of me that sprinkled salt on toads and dropped live chameleons in jars of alcohol. This night, however, there was no fascination, only unadulterated trepidation.

Eventually, Berto got out and walked over to the truck's passenger seat. A low, barely audible murmur increased to loud talk and then open, if somewhat forced, laughter on Berto's part. A few minutes later he returned. "It's Captain Medeiros. He'll tow us to Jagüey." In the town the good captain woke up a mechanic, who jump-started the jeep.

Berto gave the mechanic a sack of crabs. He did not give the captain anything, not then.

We arrived at La Luisa in the early morning hours and we found Mina waiting up. When she saw me, miserably dirty and pale, her face opened like the dawn that was just beginning to spread over the *ceibas* in the back of the house, and she smiled. She took off my shirt, washed and disinfected my back, and prepared some café con leche and a couple of slices of warm bread with homemade butter. That was the most delicious bread I have ever tasted.

Luisa Valenzuela

CAT'S EYE

I.

They are walking down the hallway in the dark. She turns
around suddenly and he cries out. "What is it?" she asks. And he
says: "Your eyes. Your eyes are shining like a wild animal's."

"Oh, come on," she says, "look again." And nothing, of course.
She turns to him and there's nothing but pure, calming darkness.
He puts his hand on the switch and turns on the light. She has her
eyes closed. She closed them against the light, he thinks, but that
really doesn't put his mind at rest.

The dialogue between the two of them changes after that vision
of phosphorescence in her eyes. Green eyes casting their own light,
now so brown, hazel as her I.D. says; brown or hazel, that is, con-
ventional there in the everyday light of the office. He had planned
to propose a job to her, and a green phosphorescence had imposed

itself between the two of them (*ignis fatuus*). Outside is the Calle Corrientes, so edificed and unedifying. Inside the office, jungle noises conjured up by a pair of shining eyes. Okay, okay, starting like this, we'll never know how our objective narrative of events comes out. The window is open. We want to note the fact that the window is open to somehow explain the jungle noises, although if noise can be explained by noise, the light in her eyes in the hallway has no rational explanation on account of the closed door between the open window and the reigning darkness.

That she turned toward him in the hall—that's undeniable. And afterward, those glowing eyes—to what end were they looking at him? With what threat or demand? If he hadn't cried out . . . ? On the fourteenth floor, in the office, he asks himself these questions while he talks to her—talks to a pair of eyes—and he doesn't know very well what he'll be saying in the next instant, what's expected of him and where the trap into which he has slowly slid is—was. Tiger's eyes. He asks himself as he talks with her with the open window behind them: If he had been able to stifle the cry or intuit something more . . .

II.

At three in the morning a suspicious noise awakens you and you remain very quiet in bed and hear—sense—that someone is moving there in your room. Some man. A man who has forced the door; who surely now wants to force himself on you. You hear his velvet footsteps over the carpet and feel a light vibration in the air. The man is getting closer. You don't dare move. Suddenly, within you, there is something beyond terror—or is it terror itself?—and you turn in the darkness and confront him. On seeing what you suppose is the glow of your eyes, the guy lets out a shriek and jumps through the window, which, since it's a hot night, is wide open. Among other things, two questions now arise:

> a) Are you the same woman as the one in the previous story?
>
> b) How will you explain the presence of the man in your house when the police begin their investigation?

Answer to a)

Yes, you are the same woman as in the previous story. For this reason, and bearing in mind the foregoing events, you wait until 9:00 a.m. and go running to consult an ophthalmologist. The doctor, a conscientious professional, puts you through all manner of examinations and finds nothing abnormal about your vision. It's not really your vision that's the problem, you suggest without going into detail. The doctor then scans your retinas, and discovers a black panther in the depths of your eyes. He doesn't know how to explain this phenomenon to you. He can only inform you of the fact and leave the explanation to wiser or more imaginative colleagues. You return to your house stunned, and to calm down you begin to tweeze some hairs from your upper lip. Inside you, the panther roars, but you don't hear her.

The answer to b) is unknown

Green eyes of a black panther, phosphorescent in the darkness, unreflected in mirrors as might have been expected from the very beginning, had there been a beginning. The man from the first story is now her boss and, of course, has no desire to give her orders for fear that she'll suddenly turn out the lights and make him face those eyes again. Luckily for him, the panther doesn't lurk elsewhere in her, and the days go by with that peculiar placidity associated with the habit of fear. The man takes certain precautions every morning. Before leaving for the office, he makes sure the electric company has no plans to cut the power in the neighborhood. He keeps a flashlight within easy reach in the top drawer of his desk, leaves the window wide open so even the last shimmer of day can enter, and does not permit himself even a hint of darker sentiments toward her as he has permitted himself toward previous secretaries. Not that he wouldn't like that. He would like to take her dancing some night and then to bed. But the terror of facing those eyes again doesn't even allow him to entertain the notion. All he permits himself is to wonder whether he really saw what he thinks he saw or if it was merely the product of his imagination (an optical illusion of someone else's eye). He decides on the first alternative, because he can't believe his imagination is that fecund. To keep her docile, he speaks to her in musical tones, though she doesn't appear to be stalking him as she takes dictation.

Buenos Aires cannot permit itself—cannot permit him—the luxury of a conscious hallucination. We who have known him for some time can be sure that his fear has nothing to do with the imaginative. We are not that fond of him, but we'll see if, with time, we'll give him the opportunity to redeem himself. Nor is she any big deal either. It's the panther that saves her, but a panther like this one, *che non parla ma se fica*, doesn't have much of a chance inside someone so given to apathy. She begins to suffer from darkaphobia or whatever they call it, and she only frequents well-lighted places so no one will find out her useless secrets. The panther sleeps with open eyes while she's awake; perhaps it is awake while she's asleep, but she's never able to ascertain that. The panther needs no food, nor any kind of affection. The panther is now called Pepita, but that's about all. The boss begins to look upon her favorably, but never looks her in the eyes. She and the boss wind up together in broad daylight on the office carpet. Their relationship lasts quite a while.

The denouement is optional:

— Once a year, Pepita goes into heat. The boss does what he can, but the woman remains cockeyed.

— She ends up pushing the boss out the window because the eyes are the window of the soul and vice versa.

— Pepita moves from the eyes to the liver and the woman dies of cirrhosis.

— She and the boss decide to get married and their light bills are incredible because they don't ever want to be in the dark.

— Pepita begins to misbehave, and the woman finds herself forced to leave her beloved and go to live with an animal trainer who mistreats her.

— Ditto, but with an ophthalmologist who promises her an operation.

— Ditto, but with a veterinarian because Pepita is sick and the woman is afraid of going blind if the panther dies.

— Every day the woman washes her eyes with Lotus Flower Eye Bath and is very serene because Pepita has converted to Buddhism and practices nonviolence.

— She reads that in the United States they have discovered a new method of combatting black panthers, and she travels, full of hope, only to find, once there, that the reference was to something completely different.

— She leaves the boss due to his insalubrious habit of screwing in bright light and she plugs herself into a job as an usherette in a ritzy movie theater where everyone appreciates the fact that she has no need for a flashlight.

Translated by Christopher Leland

Julio Ortega

EPILOGUE: MIGRATIONS

1

Monday morning walking down the hill toward the bus stop, I was expecting to see Charlie but he was not there.

He had been there on Saturday morning when I took Kara to the children's reading hour at the bookstore. I had explained to my daughter that Charlie wakes up early for his morning drive. At the bus stop he greets each bus, inspects it, talks to the driver, and, most often, decides to wait for the next bus.

His baggy clothes and loose hat, his large ears and broken speech make the driver smile, as if dealing with a child. The passengers avoid Charlie politely, but he recognizes me, and even if he does not address me directly, he raises his voice in my direction, and I acknowledge his stuttering news. At times Charlie is already sitting on the bus quietly and as close as possible to the driver. It is clear that he is not going anywhere, just taking the whole round-trip along his favorite route.

I have never seen him with a relative, but likely he lives in the vicinity with some family member. I stopped short of asking the driver. Charlie was part of the human accidents of language, not part of us.

2

On my bus ride I was reading *The Frog*, John Hawkes's recent novel, where a frog talks inside a child. I felt that there were other voices; even from the stories I used to read as a child, woven in the same sweet fiber, evolving as memory itself. I know there is another tale behind any reading; but I felt like I was walking into a lost one.

The next page soon carried me into Saint Paul's Cathedral, among the poor children at its doors, skinny and dirty, begging and playing; and I felt how hard these boys had to work, in those stories for middle-class readers. Then, my question was, how much did these lengthy nineteenth-century narratives of survival recover real suffering? Borges has written that a fact of life is only converted into language afterwards, as memory. If so, the present pain is not only elusive but lacks a language of its own. Perhaps Heraclitus's river flows in the reverberance of speech.

Marx and Fourier start their visions of a new world by speaking of children and their suffering and both convert such rough force into the power of eloquence. Thanks to deduction and hyperbole, Marx and Fourier reshape time-present with the names of the future.

But I was not concerned with the nature of truth in the one writer and the quality of vision in the other. My questions were moving in another direction. Why, in order to talk of suffering children, do I need to go back to Saint Paul's and Notre Dame? Wouldn't any story on today's children of migration be enough?

I wrote a poem.

3

I wrote as I rode along in the bus, and my lines seemed to follow the straight road as well as the regular stops and sharp turns into downtown, while more passengers climbed in, among them vociferous high school kids, with their colorful dresses and bulky pants, and their black hair still wet. These students belonged not to Marx's first chapter but to Fourier's triumphant morning; they were full of their own force, laughing, mumbling, and kidding around. I wrote my first stanza, in large letters, amused by the flow of words, moving ahead by the compulsion to answer a question, perhaps a rhetorical question.

These boys and girls are my story, I thought, but in what role or function? Most of them spoke high-pitched Spanish, and sometimes, on the bus, I have amused myself by deciphering their national accents. There are at least twenty different Spanish accents in Latin America, and I could identify some of them—the most obvious Mexican, Argentinean, Cuban; the more recondite, perhaps Dominican or Guatemalan. But for these kids Spanish was already crossed with English. Maybe this was another language, not simply a mixture of Spanish and English but the jargon of Fourier's coming Hordes, the language of the first inhabitants of our new century. It was a physical affirmation of talking here, of being now.

I tried to go back to my poem but I was stopped by another question: How could I be sure of these teenagers' national origins? Was I using names of origin to give them a place instead, when it was clear that they were moving toward a new language? These boys and girls were the last product of migration, and perhaps both their speech and their ethnic origins were a force of meaning that was still evolving beyond our language.

I was digressing in a domestic ride. I erased a couple of lines and started over.

4

This was my first poem in English. From time to time I feel the impulse to write a poem, most of the time half a poem, but always in Spanish. My English is merely Spanish making its way across the dubious sea of translation — that other migratory condition of naming.

English, in this regard, is impeccable — it assumes that for each thing there is exactly one word, as if language were a true map of the world. Spanish is more tentative, and sometimes decorative. It allows us not one name but two, and even the possibility of over-naming, or renaming. Anyhow, this need to say something (to say more is already a Spanish dilemma!) about my reading of *The Frog* between Charlie's stuttering and the voices of migrant children, had moved me into the muddy depths of language, with only my pen to find a way.

In any case, I was ready to risk writing this story in English precisely because I am not an accomplished bilingual — I love English iambic and some terse English prose, but I could never contribute to its poetic diction or its hard clarity. In Spanish, the vocalic sound of poetry can be both elemental and architectural; you believe you touch the sound.

My poem, after all, fell between two languages too, but it didn't explore the English/Spanish borderlands.

It started as a matter-of-fact sort of poem, despite the reflective mood. I have always admired the capacity of some major poets to write with other languages crossing back into their own. It was the case with César Vallejo, in Paris, when he was composing his major poem on the Spanish Civil War. He wrote about the dead body of a militiaman: "Su cadáver estaba lleno de mundo" ("His cadaver was full of world"), using a French idiom: *plein de monde*, full of people, crowded.

I sent the first version of my poem to Guy Davenport, who welcomed me into the English language, and had a suggestion: I should translate my poem into my own Spanish and he would try to translate it into English!

I was not capable of rewriting in Spanish a poem that I had already overwritten in English, much less when the poet and translator Alita Kelley, to my surprise, pointed to another subtext: she discovered a bibliography of more or less recent French theoretical discourse as a reference. Alita explained that she could read the Spanish behind my English, but that she couldn't follow the abstruse French! I suddenly had two translators of a poem that I still had not quite written.

Like any good translator, Alita is always ready to turn her suggestions into a paper on the linguistic protocol of bilingual writing, and invited me to prove her point at the next conference of American translators. My poem in progress had already grown into a good example of the limits of writing in another language and the unlimited readings of such a futile enterprise.

I think I know now how the mind of a translator works. My discovery does not involve the talents of a man or woman but the exchange processes of language itself. Some years ago, in Austin, I helped my dear friend the Brazilian poet Haroldo de Campos translate a group of poems from Vallejo's most obscure book, *Trilce* (1922). Haroldo used to repeat José Lezama Lima's motto: "Only that which is difficult can be stimulating." He wanted to try the most impossible poems of that book, a book so obscure that it is untranslatable even into its own Spanish language.

Then, I thought I saw on the page a column of exchanging names: one word of the poem was rotating along the whole language; and I believe I saw the secret of a permanent substitution. The revelation—or the fatigue—proved that the locus of any name is a void, that any word is as good as another; but that only one word can have the value of the whole.

Yet even now I am not being faithful to the experience of working with Haroldo. I lose it at the very moment I attempt to fix it.

No less telling is the case of Gregory Rabassa. Greg becomes another person when he translates a book. To translate Luis Rafael Sánchez he moved to Puerto Rico and became a local. He has also been, many times, a Brazilian; but also Argentinean, and even Colombian. I am not only saying that he becomes fully involved with the vernacular, but that he actually transforms himself into an eloquent native.

Was there, for the inmigrated writer, a space of exchange, uncharted perhaps, formed by the crossing of languages? Was this notation another genre, simple marginalia, a sort of pretext as good as any other to keep talking about poetry?

Too many questions for a handful of words.

5

Migrations

Children, I thought, had never worked so hard
as they do in the first chapter of Marx's Capital.
And I did not think of poverty
and indignation, nor of wasted children
at the doors of London (recovered
by Fourier as hordes migrating to a new world),
but of language, a garden of horror
larger than mine and yours

—as if children,
lacking a discourse of their own,
should hold on to English (having only their Spanish),
to the hard edges of a master narrative.
And so the children of a lost City
unfold a form of moral life,
its denial

—an epilogue to our reading.
The rest is reality,
the larger dark sea of literal language.
And then I went down to a new shore,
to the Spanish river of children
crossing your page.

6

It was a long trip. It started with Charlie.

I know now that what he lacks is a connecting language—the language of associations that Rosmarie Waldrop encountered between the early Spanish chronicles of the discovery and the discoveries of Alexander von Humboldt, the German traveler who wrote in French of his visit to the new Spanish-American shores. "There are no inferior races; all are destined equally to attain freedom," wrote Humboldt, who made of the power of connecting the road to "humanization."

Charlie is unable to read, he would not have made a good traveling companion for Baron von Humboldt. But he is my fellow-traveler, and I could tell him the story of a frog speaking inside a boy as the magic voice of a memory to which both of us belong.

Now I understand why he announces the names of the buses that arrive at our shore. He is waiting for his own story among the departing ships.

7

Once in a conference at the Crystal Room, John Hawkes felt short of words and turned to me demanding the name he just lost. "Plotting," I guessed and, happily, was right.

"I know so little Spanish that I am losing my English!" he said.

ABOUT THE AUTHORS

DANIEL ALARCÓN was born in Lima, Peru, and grew up in Birmingham, Alabama. He is the author of a book of stories, *War by Candlelight* (2006 PEN/Hemingway Award Finalist), and *Lost City Radio*, a novel published in more than a dozen countries. He has won numerous prizes, including a Whiting Award (2004), Guggenheim and Lannan Fellowships (2007), and a National Magazine Award (2008). He is associate editor of *Etiqueta Negra*, an award-winning magazine published in Lima, and Visiting Scholar at the Center for Latin American Studies at the University of California, Berkeley.

ISABEL ALLENDE was born a Chilean citizen in Lima, Peru, in 1942. She is a fiction writer, translator, dramatist, children's author, and journalist known worldwide for works such as her novel *The House of the Spirits* and her story collection *The Stories of Eva Luna*. Her most recent book is a memoir, *The Sum of Our Days* (2008). Her novels and stories have been adapted for movies, plays, opera, and ballet, and she and her books have won major awards in a dozen countries. In 2003, she became an American citizen.

LISA ALVAREZ grew up in Los Angeles. Her essays and short stories have appeared in the *Los Angeles Times*, *OC Weekly*, *Santa*

Monica Review, and the anthologies *Latinos in Lotusland: An Anthology of Contemporary Southern California Literature* and *Geography of Rage: Remembering the Los Angeles Riots of 1992.* With Alan Cheuse she edited *Writers Workshop in a Book: The Squaw Valley Community of Writers on the Art of Fiction*; with Louis B. Jones she directs the Squaw Valley workshops. She is a professor of English at Irvine Valley College.

RUDOLFO ANAYA, groundbreaking writer, teacher, editor, translator, and leader in the Latino literary community, was born in 1937 in Pastura, New Mexico. He is the author of short stories, epic poems, nonfiction, plays, children's books, and novels, including the award-winning *Bless Me, Ultima*; *Tortuga*; and *Alburquerque*. He retired from the faculty of the University of New Mexico at Albuquerque in 1993.

JORGE LUIS ARZOLA was born in Cuba in 1966. Arzola became nationally known with his book *Prisionero en el círculo del horizonte*. His other works include *El pájaro sin cabeza*, *La bandada infinita*, winner of the Premio Alejo Carpentier, Cuba's most prestigious award, and *Todos los buitres y el tigre*. His work has appeared in various English-language magazines and anthologies, including *Grand Street* and *The Voice of the Turtle*. He lives in Germany.

FERNANDO BENAVIDEZ, JR., born into a family of musicians and storytellers, grew up in Brownsville, a South Texas town in the U.S.-Mexico border region where most of his stories come from. He is a graduate fellow at the University of Maryland, College Park, pursuing a Ph.D. in Chicano literature in order to explore the complexities of Chicana/o identity, his interest in what Ramón Saldívar calls "the difficult dialectic between a Mexican past and an American future for Mexican Americans living on the border," and the developing canon of "American" literature itself. His short stories have appeared in several journals, including *Pindeldyboz*, *Meat: A Journal of Writing & Materiality*, and *Fourth River*.

MARIO BENEDETTI, born in Uruguay in 1920, was a prolific writer of poems, short stories, novels, essays, and plays and the 2005 recipient of the Menéndez Pelayo International Prize. Exiled by the military dictatorship that ruled Uruguay from 1973 to 1985, he lived in Buenos Aires, Lima, Havana, and Spain. He died in May 2009 in Montevideo.

ROBERTO BOLAÑO, prolific novelist, poet, and short-story writer, was born in Santiago, Chile, in 1953. In 1968, he moved with his family to Mexico City, where he was a founder of the Infrarealist Poetry Movement. He returned to Chile in 1973, just a month before Pinochet seized power, and was arrested. After his release he lived in El Salvador, Mexico, France, and Spain, where he died in 2003. His first full-length novel, *The Savage Detectives*, received the Herralde Prize and the Rómulo Gallegos Prize. The posthumously published translation of his novel *2666* won the 2009 National Book Critics Circle Award.

JORGE LUIS BORGES, one of the most widely acclaimed writers of the twentieth century, was born in Buenos Aires in 1899 and died in Geneva in 1986. He began writing in the 1920s and, in spite of losing his sight to hereditary blindness in the 1950s, produced a vast body of work, including poems, essays, short stories, translations, criticism, and screenplays. He was also a public lecturer, university professor, editor, and librarian, appointed head of the National Library in 1955. Among his works are *History of Infamy* (short nonfiction stories and literary forgeries), *Labyrinths: Selected Stories and Other Writings*, *The Garden of Forking Paths* (short stories), *Dr. Brodie's Report* (short stories), *Dreamtigers* (poetry and short prose pieces), and *The Book of Sand* (short stories).

AÍDA BORTNIK was born in Buenos Aires in 1938. She is known internationally for her original screenplays *The Official Story*, which won an Academy Award for Best Foreign Film in 1985, and *The Old Gringo*. Bortnik's more recent films include *Wild Horses* and *Ashes from Paradise*.

CARMEN BOULLOSA, born in Mexico City in 1954, is a fiction writer, poet, dramatist, and essayist. "Impossible Story" is excerpted from her novel *Llanto, novelas imposibles*. Her fifteen novels also include *Antes*, which won the Xavier Villaurrutia Prize in Mexico; *La milagrosa*, which won the Liberatur Literature Prize at Frankfurt in 1996; *La otra mano de Lepanto*, which in 2007 was named one of the Top 100 Novels Published in Spanish over the last quarter-century; and *La novela perfecta*. She was awarded the 2008 Café Gijón Prize, one of Spain's most distinguished literary awards, for the novel *El complot de los románticos*. She received the Anna Seghers Prize from the Arts Academy of Berlin for the body of her work. Her play *Los Totoles* won two prizes awarded by critics in Mexico. She has taught or lectured at universities in the United States, Europe, and Latin America, and since 2001, she has lived in New York, where she has been Distinguished Lecturer at City College since 2004.

RAÚL BRASCA, born in Buenos Aires in 1948, was educated in chemical engineering and was a professor in that field at the University of Buenos Aires until 1988. In that year he won the first-place short-short story award in *El Cuento* magazine in Mexico City. Since then his writing has won other awards and has been published in numerous languages. He has also published the work of many others, as editor or coeditor of a dozen anthologies. Recent books of his own stories are *Últimos juegos* (Spain, 2005), *L'edonista e altri racconti* (Italy, 2006), and *Todo tiempo futuro fue peor* (Argentina, 2007).

LUNA CALDERÓN is a hybrid Latina—she was born in Brazil and raised in Mexico and the United States. By day she is a mental health administrator. By night she is a reader, writer, knitter, and dreamer. She received her M.F.A. from Mills College. She is awaiting publication of her first young adult novel. She lives in northern California.

NORMA ELIA CANTÚ was born in Nuevo Laredo, Tamaulipas, Mexico, and grew up in Laredo, Texas. Her work has won numerous awards, and she is known internationally as a poet, fiction writer, folklorist, and scholar of Chicana cultural production. Author of the award-winning *Canícula: Snapshots of a Girlhood en la Frontera* and co-editor of *Chicana Traditions: Continuity and Change, Telling to Live: Latina Feminist Testimonios*, and *Dancing Across Borders: Danzas y Bailes Mexicanos*, she has just finished a novel, *Cabañuelas*, and is working on another novel, tentatively titled *Champú, or Hair Matters*, and an ethnography of the Matachines de la Santa Cruz, a religious dance drama from Laredo, Texas. She is a professor of English and U.S. Latina/o Literatures at the University of Texas at San Antonio.

OMAR CASTAÑEDA was born in 1954, in Guatemala City, Guatemala, but grew up in Michigan and Indiana and became an American citizen in 1986. He returned frequently to Guatemala to research his novels, short stories, and children's books. Among his commendations are an Ernest Hemingway fellowship and a Pulitzer nomination. He was a professor at Western Washington University when he died of a heroin overdose in 1997.

ANA CASTILLO, born in Chicago in 1953, is a poet, novelist, short-story writer, essayist, editor, teacher, and activist. Her fiction includes the novels *The Mixquiahuala Letters*, *Sapogonia*, *So Far From God*, and *The Guardians*. Her awards include the Before Columbus Foundation's American Book Award, the Carl Sandburg Literary Award in Fiction, and the Mountains and Plains Bookseller Award. Since 2006, she has lived in New Mexico.

DANIEL CHACÓN is author of the story collections *Chicano Chicanery* and *Unending Rooms* and the novel *and the shadows took him*. He is coeditor of *The Last Supper of Chicano Heroes: The Selected Works of José Antonio Burciaga*. Visit his Web site at www .soychacon.com.

SANDRA CISNEROS was born in Chicago in 1954. Her poetry, short stories, novels, and children's books have been translated into more than a dozen languages and have won many regional, national, and international awards. By 2009, the twenty-fifth anniversary of its U.S. publication, her novel *The House on Mango Street* had sold over two million copies. *Caramelo* (2002) was selected as a notable book of the year by several major newspapers and won the Premio Napoli. Cisneros is the president and founder of the Macondo Foundation, an association of socially engaged writers working within their communities, and the Alfredo Cisneros Del Moral Foundation, which provides grants to Texas writers. She is writer in residence at Our Lady of the Lake University in San Antonio.

JUDITH ORTÍZ COFER is the author of ten books, including a collection of short stories, *An Island Like You: Stories of the Barrio*, the novel *The Meaning of Consuelo*, the young adult novel *Call Me Maria*, the poetry collection *A Love Story Beginning in Spanish: Poems*, and the collection of essays *Woman in Front of the Sun: On Becoming a Writer*. Her work has appeared in magazines such as the *Kenyon Review*, *Southern Review*, and *Glamour*, and numerous textbooks and anthologies such as *The Norton Introduction to Literature*, *The Pushcart Prize*, and *O. Henry Prize Stories*. She received an honorary doctorate from Lehman College of CUNY in 2007 and is a professor of English and creative writing at the University of Georgia. Forthcoming is a multigenre collection based on her experiences living, writing, and teaching in the Deep South, tentatively titled *Peach Pit Corazón*.

HILMA CONTRERAS was born in San Francisco de Macorís, Dominican Republic, and educated in Paris, where she started writing in the 1930s. Contreras, who received the Dominican Republic National Literary Award in 2002, is said to be the first Dominican woman to write short stories, published in her books *Cuatro cuentos*, *El ojo de Dios*, *Entre dos silencios*, and *Facetas de la vida: cuentos y minicuentos*. Her work covers a wide spectrum of themes and styles, ranging from her political novel, *La tierra está bramando*, to fantastic tales. She died in 2006 at the age of ninety-five.

RAFAEL COURTOISIE was born in Montevideo in 1958. He is a poet, fiction writer, and essayist who has published nineteen collections of poetry, ten collections of short fiction, and five novels. He has won numerous prizes, including the International Jaime Sabines Poetry Prize, 2002, and the Uruguayan National Prize for

Fiction. He was a participant in the International Writers Workshop at Iowa in 2006, and that same year took part in a Roman seminar on his novel *Caras extrañas*, which was published in Italian in 2005. Courtoisie has traveled and taught extensively in the United States and throughout Latin America. In 2008 he published the novel *Goma de mascar* and a collection of poems, *La biblia húmeda*.

MARCO DENEVI (1922–1998) was an Argentine writer, lawyer, and journalist whose first novel, *Rosaura a las diez*, was a best-seller in several languages and was adapted for film. His story "Secret Ceremony," which won a prize judged by Octavio Paz, was made into a film starring Elizabeth Taylor. Among his other writings are *Los expedientes*, *El cuarto de la noche*, and *Falsificaciones*.

JUNOT DÍAZ, born in Santo Domingo, Dominican Republic, in 1968, emigrated to New Jersey in 1974, and now lives in Boston. He is the author of the story collection *Drown* and the novel *The Brief Wondrous Life of Oscar Wao*, which won the John Sargent Sr. First Novel Prize, the National Book Critics Circle Award, the Anisfield-Wolf Book Award, the Dayton Literary Peace Prize, and the 2008 Pulitzer Prize. His fiction has appeared in the *New Yorker*, *African Voices*, *Best American Short Stories*, *Pushcart Prize XXII*, and *The O'Henry Prize Stories 2009*. He has received the Eugene McDermott Award, a Lila Wallace-Reader's Digest Award, the 2002 Pen/ Malamud Award, and the Rome Prize from the American Academy of Arts and Letters. He is the fiction editor at the *Boston Review* and a professor at the Massachusetts Institute of Technology.

JOSEFINA ESTRADA was born in Mexico City in 1957. She is a short-story writer, novelist, and journalist. For six years, she ran a creative writing workshop in a women's prison and, in 2002, published an anthology of work written by her students there. Her own work includes the short-story collection *Malagato*, the novels *Desde que Dios amanece* and *Virgen de medianoche*, and the collection of articles about Mexico City, *Señas particulares: La muerte violenta en la Ciudad de México*, which won the Concurso de Crónica Urbana Salvador Novo. Her work has previously appeared in English in *Storm: New Writing from Mexico*.

ANTONIO FARIAS has published short fiction in *Chicken Soup for the Latino Soul, Latino Boom, Urban Latino Magazine*, and *Bilingual Review*. He holds a master's in comparative literature/ creative writing from the University of California, Berkeley, and has taught Comparative Ethnic Studies at U.C. Berkeley, Colgate University, and Hunter College. He has lectured widely on the history of collaboration among underrepresented populations in the United States, the unsteady rise of the Latino middle class, and the emergence of postethnic identities and coalitions. He is chief diversity officer at the U.S. Coast Guard Academy. Outside of work, he spends the bulk of his time helping his eight-year-old daughter imagine a better world (and that vegetables are the new candy). He is finishing a novel and a collection of short stories. Visit his Web site at www.incanfisherman.com.

EDUARDO GALEANO was born in 1940 in Montevideo, Uruguay. Military coups in the 1970s forced him to flee twice: from Uruguay to Argentina and then from Argentina to Spain. In 1985, he returned to Montevideo, where he lives today. Among his many books are *Las venas abiertas de América Latina* (*The Open Veins of Latin America*), the trilogy *Memoria del fuego* (*Memory of Fire*), and the short-story collection *El libro de los abrazos* (*The Book of Embraces*). Galeano is a regular contributor to the *Progressive* and the *New Internationalist*, and has also been published in the

Monthly Review and the *Nation*. Among his awards are the Premio Casa de las Américas, the American Book Award, and the first Cultural Freedom Award from the Lannan Foundation.

GABRIEL GARCÍA MÁRQUEZ, Colombian novelist, short-story writer, screenwriter, and journalist, was born in 1927. Considered one of the most significant authors of the twentieth century, he is known worldwide for works such as One *Hundred Years of Solitude, Autumn of the Patriarch, Chronicle of a Death Foretold,* and *Love in the Time of Cholera.* In 1982, he was awarded the Nobel Prize in Literature for his novels and short stories.

DAGOBERTO GILB was born in Los Angeles to a Mexican mother illegally in the United States and a Spanish-speaking Anglo father from East Los Angeles. After earning bachelor's and master's degrees from the University of California, Santa Barbara, he worked in construction in Los Angeles and El Paso. In 1993, he received a Whiting Writers' Award, and his story collection *The Magic of Blood* won the 1994 PEN/Hemingway Award and the Texas Institute of Letters Award for Fiction. His novel *The Last Known Residence of Mickey Acuña* was a *New York Times* Notable Book of the Year. Other publications include the story collection *Woodcuts of Women; Gritos,* a collection of essays, which was a finalist for the 2004 National Book Critics Circle Award; and *The Flowers: A Novel.* He is editor of *Hecho en Tejas: An Anthology of Texas Mexican Literature.* He lives in Austin, Texas, and is a professor in the creative writing program at Texas State University, in San Marcos.

STEPHEN D. GUTIERREZ is the author of *Elements,* winner of the Nilon Excellence in Minority Fiction Award, and of *Live from Fresno Y Los: Stories* (Bear Star Press, 2009). In addition, he has published individual short stories and creative nonfiction pieces in top magazines, and has had four short plays produced in the San Francisco Bay Area. Originally from Los Angeles, he now lives in Castro Valley, California, and directs the creative writing program at California State University, East Bay. He is married, with one son.

JUAN FELIPE HERRERA was born in Fowler, California, son of Lucha Quintana and Felipe Herrera, storytellers and brave border-crossers. He is the founder and cofounder of various poetry and experimental word troupes: Teatro Tolteca, Teatro Zapata, TROKA, Manikrudo, and recently, in Riverside, The Verbal Coliseum. His next book is *Put a Poem Wherever You Go!* (Harper Collins).

ENRIQUE JARAMILLO LEVI was born in Colón, Panamá, in 1944. A poet, short-story writer, essayist, university professor, and promoter of culture, he founded the Association of Writers of Panama, was Coordinator of Cultural Dissemination of the Technological University of Panama, and also founded the 9 Signos Grupo Editorial. In 2005, as a short-story writer, he won the Ricardo Miró National Literature Competition; he is the author of ten books of poetry, eighteen of stories, seven of essays, and two of dramatic works, as well as numerous anthologies of Mexican, Central American, and Panamanian literature. Three of his books were published in 2008, two of them collections of stories, *Justicia poética* and *Secreto a voces*, and another of essays, *Por obra y gracia*.

HERNÁN LAVÍN CERDA has published more than fifty books of poetry, essays, and fiction, and his work has been anthologized in Latin America, Spain, and the United States. Among his recent books are *La sublime comedia* (2006) and *Visita de Woody Allen a Venecia* (2008). He was born in Santiago in 1939, studied at the University of Chile, and was a poet, journalist, editor, and literary critic there, winning the Premio Vicente Huidobro in 1970 for his novel *La crujidera de la vida*. Soon after, he fled the dictatorship of Pinochet, and since 1974 has been a professor in Hispanic letters at the National Autonomous University of Mexico. In 1992 he became a member of the Chilean Academy of Language.

RAÚL LEIS is a Panamanian citizen born in Isla Providencia, San Andres, Colombia, in 1947. His story collections include *Viaje alrededor del patio: cuentos de vecindario, Remedio para la congoja,* and *¿Quieres que te lo cuente otra vez?* He is also a noted writer of plays, poems, and children's books, for which he has won awards that include the Premio Plural de México and Panama's Ricardo Miró. He is a founder of the Panamanian Center for Studies and Social Action (CEASPA) and associate professor of sociology at the University of Panama; his articles and books in the field of sociology have been published nationally and internationally.

ROBERT LOPEZ is the author of two novels, *Part of the World* and *Kamby Bolongo Mean River*. His fiction has appeared in dozens of journals, including the *Threepenny Review, Bomb, Alaska Quarterly Review, New England Review, New Orleans Quarterly, Willow Springs,* and *Denver Quarterly*. He teaches at The New School, Pratt Institute, and Columbia University. "Asunder" will also appear in a collection of stories due from Dzane Books in December 2010.

JUAN MARTINEZ is a doctoral student in literature at the University of Nevada, Las Vegas. His work has appeared in *Glimmer Train, McSweeney's, River Teeth, West Branch, Conjunctions, Redi-*

vider, the *Santa Monica Review*, and elsewhere. He is working on a novel. Visit his Web site at fulmerford.com.

ÁNGELES MASTRETTA was born in Puebla, Mexico, in 1949. In 1985 she published her first novel, *Arráncame la vida (Tear This Heart Out)*, which won the Premio Mazatlán in Mexico and became a critical and popular success in the Spanish-speaking world, and then in translation into fifteen languages. Among her other books is *Women with Big Eyes*, from which the story "Aunt Chila" comes, and *Mal de amores*, which was awarded the prestigious Premio Rómulo Gallegos—the first time the prize was granted to a woman.

PABLO MEDINA, born in Cuba, is the award-winning author of eleven books of poetry, fiction, nonfiction, and translation, among them *Points of Balance/Puntos de apoyo* and *The Cigar Roller*. His story "Zapata" is a chapter from his memoir, *Exiled Memories: A Cuban Childhood*. In 2008, Medina and fellow poet Mark Statman published a new English version of García Lorca's *Poet in New York*. Medina's work has appeared in various languages, among them Spanish, French, German, and Arabic. He was on the board of the Associated Writing Programs from 2002 to 2007, serving as board president in 2005–2006.

LUPE MÉNDEZ is a writer, educator, and performer. Originally from Galveston Island, Texas, for the last decade he has lived in Houston, where he works with both Nuestra Palabra: Latino Writers Having Their Say and the Brazilian Arts Foundation to establish free poetry and creative writing workshops open to the public. When he is not playing capoeira or teaching, he serves the Houston area arts community as a poet, organizer, and host for such events as the former Latino Book and Family Festival and the Word Around Town Tour, a weeklong summer festival that showcases talented poets and spotlights local venues. "What Should Run in the Mind of Caballeros" was originally a spoken word piece (now lengthened) that serves as a performance opener. Visit his Web site at www.thepoetmendez.org.

AUGUSTO MONTERROSO was born in Tegucigalpa, Honduras, in 1921. His mother was Honduran and his father was Guatemalan. In 1936, his family settled in Guatemala, where he published his first short stories. Exiled to Mexico City in 1944, he also lived in Bolivia and Chile before returning to Mexico City, where he worked as a writer, editor, and academic until his death in 2003. Although he wrote one novel (albeit composed of a collection of short pieces), the rest of his publications were short stories (many of them mini or micro length), including the collection *La oveja negra y demás fábulas* (*The Black Sheep and Other Fables*). In 1988, he received the Águila Azteca, the highest award to foreigners in Mexico; in 1997, the Guatemala National Prize in Literature for his body of work; and, in 2000, Spain's Prince of Asturias Award.

MANUEL MUÑOZ was born and grew up in Dinuba, California, graduated from Harvard, and received an M.F.A. in creative writing from Cornell. His work has appeared in many publications, including the *New York Times*, *Boston Review*, *Edinburgh Review*, and *Swink*, and has aired on National Public Radio's *Selected Shorts*. His story collections are *Zigzagger* (2003) and *The Faith Healer of Olive Avenue* (2007). In 2008 he won a Whiting Writers' Award and in 2009 the O. Henry Award. He lives in Tucson and is a professor in the creative writing program at the University of Arizona.

CARMEN NARANJO, born in Costa Rica in 1930, is a poet and essayist as well as a fiction writer. She has won awards for her fiction, which includes seven novels and four collections of short stories. She has only recently become known in the United States as her short stories have been translated into English.

DANIEL A. OLIVAS is the author of *Devil Talk: Stories; Assumption and Other Stories; The Courtship of María Rivera Peña;* and a children's book, *Benjamin and the Word*. He has been widely anthologized and has written for numerous publications, including the *Los Angeles Times, MacGuffin, THEMA, Exquisite Corpse, La Bloga, El Paso Times,* and the *Jewish Journal*. He is the editor of *Latinos in Lotusland: An Anthology of Contemporary Southern California Literature,* which brings together sixty years of Los Angeles fiction by Latino/a writers. For the last twenty years, he has practiced law with the California Department of Justice in the Public Rights Division. He makes his home in the San Fernando Valley with his wife and son.

JULIO ORTEGA, born in Peru in 1942, has taught Latin American literature for the last twenty years at Brown University. His novel *Ayacucho Good-Bye* was adapted for the theater by Yuyachkani and became part of the movement for human rights in Peru. *Emotions,* poems (2000), *The Art of Reading,* stories (2007), *Poetics of Change* (1984), and *Transatlantic Translations,* essays (2006), are his other books in English. His work has appeared in the *Boston Globe Magazine, Antaeus, Agni, Sulfur, Bomb, Michigan Review,* and other journals; with Carlos Fuentes he edited *The Picador Book of Latin American Stories* (1998). Among his awards are the March Prize in Mallorca for short novels and the Rulfo Prize in Paris for short stories.

JOSÉ EMILIO PACHECO, renowned writer, translator, and teacher, was born in 1939 in Mexico City. After studying at the National Autonomous University of Mexico, he published his first short-story collection, *The Blood of Medusa*, in 1958. Since then, he has written over a dozen novels, short stories, and volumes of poetry in both Spanish and English. His poetry has received numerous national and international awards, including the Federico García Lorca International Poetry Prize (2005) and the Premio José Asuncion Silva for the best Spanish-language book published between 1990 and 1995. For his meritorious service to literature, Pacheco was honored with an induction into the Mexican Academy in 2006. He is also noted for his translations of the writings of such luminaries as Albert Einstein and Samuel Beckett.

IGNACIO PADILLA was born in 1968 in Mexico City. He received a bachelor's degree from the Universidad Iberoamericana, a master's in English literature from the University of Edinburgh, and a Ph.D. in Hispanic-American literature from the University of Salamanca. In 1996, he was one of six writers who proposed what became known as the Crack Manifesto, urging Mexican writers to move beyond magical realism, developing their own style based on principles embodied in the works of writers like Julio Cortázar and Jorge Luis Borges. Padilla's fiction and criticism have won many awards, including the 1999 Mexican literary awards José Revueltas, for his literary essay "Los funerales del alcaraván: historia apócrifa del realismo mágico," and Gilberto Owen, for his short-story collection *Las antípodas y el siglo* (*Antipodes*); and the 2000 Premio Primavera de Novela for his novel *Amphitryon*.

EDMUNDO PAZ SOLDÁN was born and grew up in Bolivia. He is the author of seven novels, including *Turing's Delirium* (2007) and *Los vivos y los muertos* (2009), and three short-story collections, including *Norte* (2006). He won the National Book Award in Bolivia and the prestigious Juan Rulfo Prize, and was a finalist for the Rómulo Gallegos Prize. His work has been translated into eight languages. He is a professor at Cornell University. One of the few McOndo writers who live in the United States, he is frequently called upon as the movement's spokesperson by the American media.

CRISTINA PERI ROSSI was born in Montevideo, Uruguay, in 1941, and was exiled to Spain in 1972. Her fiction, poetry, and essays have been translated into ten languages. Among her works are the collection of short stories *Por fin solos* and the novel *La nave de los locos* (*The Ship of Fools*).

VIRGILIO PIÑERA was born in 1912 in Cárdenas, Cuba, and died in Havana in 1979. In the 1950s, he lived in Argentina, returning to Cuba permanently in 1958. His work includes several collections of short stories, notably *Cuentos fríos* (*Cold Tales*) and *Pequeñas maniobras*, essays on literature and literary criticism, numerous dramatic works, and three novels.

ALEJANDRA PIZARNIK was born in Avellaneda, Argentina, in 1936. She published her first book of poetry a year after entering the Universidad de Buenos Aires, then two more before moving to Paris, where she lived from 1960 to 1964. She studied the history of religion and contemporary French literature at the Sorbonne, worked for the literary journal *Cuadernos*, and published translations, criticism, and more poetry. On her return to Argentina more books followed, including the prose work *The Bloody Countess* in 1971. She died in 1972 of an overdose of Seconal.

PEDRO PONCE is the author of two fiction chapbooks, *Alien Autopsy* and *Superstitions of Apartment Life*. His stories have appeared in numerous journals, including *Ploughshares, Many Mountains Moving, Opium, Sleepingfish,* and *Hotel St. George,* and have been anthologized in *The Beacon Best of 2001,* edited by Junot Díaz, and *You Have Time for This: Contemporary American Short-Short Stories.*

ANTONIO JOSÉ PONTE was born in Matanzas, Cuba, in 1964. He studied hydraulics at Havana's Technical University and worked for five years as an engineer in eastern Cuba before turning to screenwriting. He twice won the National Critics' Award for his essays and poems. He is also a novelist and short-story writer whose story collections include *In the Cold of the Malecón and Other Stories* and *Tales from the Cuban Empire.* His work appears regularly in a variety of journals and magazines, including *La Habana Elegante* and *Encuentro de la Cultura Cubana.* Since 2006 he has lived in exile in Madrid.

SERGIO RAMÍREZ was vice president of Nicaragua from 1985 to 1990 and made an unsuccessful bid for president in 1996, after which he retired from active politics, but not the intellectual and literary life. As a young law student he founded the magazine *Ventana* and became a leading figure in the literary movement of that name; since then he has published more than thirty books, including nine of fiction, beginning with *Cuentos* in 1963 and, more recently, *Margarita, está linda la mar,* which won Spain's renowned Alfaguara Prize and was published in English translation as *How Beautiful the Sea* in 2007. Among his other awards are France's Laure Bataillon Prize for best foreign novel and the José María Arguedas Premio Latinoamericano de Novela; he has been named

Chevalier de l'Ordre des Arts et des Lettres and has received the Bruno Kreisky Human Rights Prize. He now lives with his family in Nicaragua, continues to write for Spanish-language newspapers worldwide, and in recent years has been a visiting professor at the University of Maryland and at Berlin's Free University.

RODRIGO REY ROSA was born in Guatemala in 1958. He later lived in New York and Morocco, where he met Paul Bowles, who translated many of his works into English. His ten short-story collections and novels, which include *The Beggar's Knife, Dust on Her Tongue, The Pelcari Project*, and *The Good Cripple*, have been widely translated. His film *What Sebastian Dreamt* premiered at the Sundance Film Festival in 2004. That same year he was awarded Guatemala's Miguel Ángel Asturias National Prize in Literature.

LOUIS REYNA was born and grew up in Los Angeles and now lives in Kansas City, Missouri. He works retail. His story "The Hitchhiker" is part of a collection in progress titled "'Cancer' and Other Stories."

ALBERTO RÍOS was born in 1952 in Nogales, Arizona. His father was born in Mexico; his mother, in England. His memoir, *Capirotada*, about growing up on the Mexico-Arizona border, won the Latino Literary Hall of Fame Award and was the One Book Arizona choice for 2009. Ríos is also the author of ten collections of poetry and three collections of short stories. His work has been widely anthologized, taught, and translated, and his many awards include the 2007 PEN/Beyond Margins Award, the Western States Book Award, for *The Iguana Killer: Twelve Stories of the Heart*, and six Pushcart Prizes. He is a professor in the English department at Arizona State University.

TOMÁS RIVERA was born to Spanish-speaking migrant workers in 1935. A field laborer with his family, he was often forced to miss school. But he was determined at a young age to be a writer and in 1956 enrolled in junior college. He graduated from Southwest Texas State College in 1958 and taught both English and Spanish in high schools for most of a decade, earning an M.A. in Spanish Literature and, in 1969, a Ph.D. in Romance Languages and Literature from the University of Oklahoma. A year later, he was the recipient of the first award for Chicano literature, the Premio Quinto Sol, for his classic novel about the migrant farmworker experience, . . . *y no se lo tragó la tierra*, published in three translations: . . . *And the Earth Did Not Part*, . . . *And the Earth Did Not Devour Him*, and *This Migrant Earth*. He became a university professor and administrator in Texas, and for five years, before his death at the age of forty-eight, he was chancellor of the University of California, Riverside, the first Mexican American to hold the position at the University of California. Many plazas and school are named after him, as is a professorship at the University of Texas, a library at the University of California, and an institute at Pomona College. Yet Rivera remains best known for his short stories, poetry, and literary essays. In 2008 Arte Publico Press published a paperback second edition of *Tomás Rivera: The Complete Works*.

ALICITA RODRÍGUEZ holds a Ph.D. from the University of Denver and an M.F.A. from New York University. Recently, her work has appeared in the literary magazines *Denver Quarterly*, *TriQuarterly*, *Ecotone*, and *Fiction International* and in various anthologies, including *Wreckage of Reason* and *New Stories from the Southwest*. She is the founding editor of *Marginalia*. Originally from Miami, she now lives in Colorado with her husband, Joseph Starr, and their three dogs.

ANDREA SAENZ is an immigration attorney and a former editor-in-chief of the *Harvard Law Record*. Her fiction has appeared in the *Paterson Literary Review*, *Crazyhorse*, *CALYX Journal*, *Rosebud*, and *BorderSenses*. She lives with her husband and daughter in Boston.

ANA MARÍA SHUA is the author of four books of micro fiction in Spanish. Some of those stories are included in *Quick Fix: Sudden Fiction* (2008), translated by Rhonda Dahl Buchanan. A second book of stories in English, *Microfictions*, translated by Steven Stewart, was published by Bison Books (University of Nebraska Press) in 2009. Shua graduated with an advanced degree from the University of Buenos Aires, then lived in exile in Paris during the military dictatorship before returning to Argentina. Her more than fifty volumes include novels, collections of larger stories for adults and for children, poetry, essays, and film scripts; her novel *Los amores de Laurita* was made into a movie. She has been translated into many languages, has won many national and international awards, and is often invited to lecture at universities and micro fiction conferences in Europe, the United States, and Latin America.

NICOMEDES SUÁREZ ARAÚZ was born in the Amazonian Bolivian town of Santa Ana in 1946. A poet, fiction writer, essayist, and visual artist, he has published, under his name, eleven books, including six of poetry, and, using heteronyms, has published more than five dozen volumes. In 1977, he was awarded Bolivia's national Premio Edición Franz Tamayo for his poetry volume *Caballo al anochecer* (*Horse at Nightfall*). In 1973, he formulated the celebrated *Amnesis*, an Amazonian-inspired aesthetics based on amnesia as a structural metaphor for the creation of artistic works. Two of his poetry books have been published in English translation:

El poema América (*The America Poem*, translated by Willis Barnstone), and *Recetario Amazónico* (*Edible Amazonia*, translated by S. F. Brown). His work has been included in many anthologies in Spanish, English, Portuguese, French, Italian, and German. He is professor emeritus and director of the Center for Amazonian Literature and Culture at Smith College, Massachusetts. He lives in Santa Cruz, Bolivia, with his beloved wife, Kristine.

CARMEN TAFOLLA has authored more than fifteen books, including short fiction, poetry, children's books, nonfiction, and screenplays. In 1999, she received the Art of Peace Award for work that contributes to peace, justice, and human understanding, and she has been recognized by the National Association for Chicano Studies for "giving voice to the peoples and cultures of this land." Her short-story collection, *The Holy Tortilla and a Pot of Beans*, won the 2009 Tomás Rivera Book Award, and her children's book *What Can You DO with a Rebozo?* was named an ALA Notable Book, a Pura Belpre Honor Book, and a Junior Library Guild Selection. Her children's biography of Latina civil rights leader Emma Tenayuca was a *Críticas* magazine Best Children's Book of 2008.

LUIS ALBERTO URREA was born in Tijuana, Mexico, to a Mexican father and an American mother. His first book, *Across the Wire*, was a *New York Times* Notable Book and winner of the Christopher Award. He won an American Book Award for his memoir, *Nobody's Son: Notes from an American Life*; and his short-story collection, *Six Kinds of Sky*, received a Book of the Year award from *ForeWord* magazine. His nonfiction book *The Devil's Highway* won the 2004 Lannan Literary Award and was a finalist for the Pulitzer Prize and the Pacific Rim Kiriyama Prize. His historical novel, *The Hummingbird's Daughter*, won the Pacific Rim Kiriyama Prize

ABOUT THE AUTHORS

for fiction. He lives with his family in Naperville, Illinois, where he is a professor of creative writing at the University of Illinois at Chicago.

LUISA VALENZUELA was born and now lives in Buenos Aires, Argentina. She has lived in Paris and Barcelona and spent ten years in Manhattan (1979–1989), where she was writer in residence at Columbia University and later at NYU's Writing Division. She is a frequent traveler to Mexico, where she is published by Fondo de Cultura Economica, among other houses. Many of her books have been translated into English: the short-story collections *Open Door, The Censors, Strange Things Happen Here, Other Weapons,* and *Symmetries,* and the novels *Clara, He Who Searches, The Lizard's Tail, Black Novel (with Argentines),* and *Bedside Manners.* Among her most recent books are *La travesía* (a novel), *Peligrosas palabras* and *Escritura y secreto* (essays), *BREVS: Microrrelatos completos hasta hoy* (micro stories), and *Los deseos oscuros y los otros, cuadernos de New York* and *Acerca de Dios (o aleja)* (memoirs). In 2008 two new collections of short stories appeared in Spain, *Tres por cinco* and *Juegos de villanos.* She has just completed a new novel, *El mañana.*

MARISELLA VEIGA was born in Havana, Cuba. She went into exile in the United States with her family in 1960, and grew up in St. Paul and Miami. She received a B.A. in English from Macalester College and an M.F.A. in poetry from Bowling Green State University. Her writing has appeared in numerous magazines, newspapers, and literary anthologies. She won The Pushcart Prize XX, Special Mention in Short Fiction; the Canute A. Brodhurst Prize for Best Short Story in *The Caribbean Writer;* and the Evelyn LaPierre Award for Journalism. She is a nationally syndicated col-

319

umnist with Hispanic Link News Service. She released a spoken word CD, *Square Watermelons: Ten Essays on Living with Two Cultures*. She lives with her husband in St. Augustine, Florida.

SOCORRO VENEGAS was born in San Luis Potosí, Mexico, in 1972. She is the author of the story collections *La risa de las azucenas* (1997), *La muerte más blanca* (2000), and *Todas las islas* (2002). Her first novel, *La noche será negra y blanca*, won the 2004 Carlos Fuentes Premio Nacional de Novela Ópera Prima and was published in 2009. English translations of her stories have appeared in *Coal City Review*, *Concho River Review*, the *Listening Eye*, the *Modern Review*, *New Madrid*, and elsewhere.

ALMA LUZ VILLANUEVA grew up in San Francisco's Mission District with her mother and her Yaqui grandmother. Her published works, which have been widely anthologized, include six books of poetry, three novels, and a collection of short stories. Among her many awards is an American Book Award for her novel *Ultraviolet Sky*. A faculty member in the M.F.A. low-residency creative writing program at Antioch University Los Angeles, she lives in San Miguel de Allende, Mexico, and travels to give readings and workshops.

HELENA MARÍA VIRAMONTES is the author of the collection *The Moths and Other Stories* and the novels *Their Dogs Came with Them* and *Under the Feet of Jesus*, which was a New Voices Quality Paperback Book and Discover Great New Writers finalist. She has edited anthologies of Chicana essays and criticism, and her own work has been widely anthologized. She received the John Dos Passos Prize for Literature in 1996 and has taught at the Breadloaf and Writers at Work conferences. She is a professor at Cornell University.

ABOUT THE TRANSLATORS

CHRIS ANDREWS was born in Newcastle, Australia, in 1962. He teaches in the School of Languages and Linguistics at the University of Melbourne. In 2005, his translation of Roberto Bolaño's *Distant Star* won the Vallé-Inclan Prize.

CEDRIC BELFRAGE was born in London in 1904. During the 1920s and 1930s, he worked in London and Hollywood as a film critic, journalist, press agent, and editor. He was a cofounder of the *National Guardian* (which later became the *Guardian*). In 1955, after he appeared before the House Un-American Activities Committee, the U.S. government deported him to England. He traveled to Cuba and throughout South America before settling in Mexico, where he died in 1990. The author of over a dozen books, he is also noted as a translator of the Uruguayan author Eduardo Galeano. His translation of Galeano's trilogy, *Memory of Fire*, won a citation from PEN in 1988 and an American Book Award from the Before Columbus Foundation in 1989.

PAUL BOWLES (1910–1999) was born in New York but traveled widely and lived most of his life in Morocco. His first success was as a composer, but he later turned to writing. His best-known work is his novel *The Sheltering Sky*. A two-volume set of his work was added to the prestigious Library of America in 2002. Authors whose work he translated include Jorge Luis Borges and Jean-Paul Sartre, in addition to many Moroccan writers.

LINDA BRITT is a professor of Spanish at the University of Maine at Farmington. Her publications include two collections of translated short fiction and numerous critical articles. She is also a playwright whose most recent work, *Mrs. Smith Goes to Washington*, a one-woman show on the life of Senator Margaret Chase Smith, has been touring schools.

RHONDA DAHL BUCHANAN is a professor of Spanish and director of Latin American and Latino Studies at the University of Louisville. She has published articles on contemporary Latin American writers and edited a book of critical essays, *El río de los sueños: Aproximaciones críticas a la obra de Ana María Shua*. Authors whose works she has translated include Alberto Ruy-Sánchez, Perla Suez, and Ana María Shua.

LELAND H. CHAMBERS has translated eight books, including Julieta Campos's *The Fear of Losing Eurydice*, which was a finalist for the PEN Center West's Translation of the Year Award for 1994; and Juan Tovar's *Creature of a Day*, which won the 2000–2001 Eugene M. Kayden Translation Award. He coedited, with Enrique Jaramillo Levi, the anthology *Contemporary Short Stories from Central America*. His translations of short fiction have been published in numerous literary magazines and anthologies. He is an emeritus professor of English and Comparative Literature at the University of Denver.

JOSÉ CHAVES has an M.F.A. from the University of Oregon and writes poems, short fiction, and nonfiction. His work has been published in the *Atlantic Review, Jeopardy, Danforth Review, Buzzwords, Café Irreal, Rattle, Highbeams, Recursive Angel, Alsop Review, helicoptero, Brevity Twelve, CrossConnect, Vestal Review,* and *Exquisite Corpse.* He edited *The Book of Brevity,* translations of Latin American flash fiction, and is finishing a memoir in progress, "The Contract of Love."

MARGARET JULL COSTA has been a translator of Spanish and Portuguese since 1987. Her numerous awards and prizes include the Portuguese Translation Prize in 1992 for her version of *The Book of Disquiet,* by Fernando Pessoa; the translator's portion of the 1997 International IMPAC Dublin Literary Award for Javier Marías's *A Heart So White;* the 2000 Weidenfeld Translation Prize for José Saramago's *All the Names;* the 2006 Premio Valle-Inclán for Javier Marías's *Your Face Tomorrow 1: Fever and Spear;* and in 2008 the PEN/Book-of-the-Month Award and the Oxford Weidenfeld Prize for her translation of Eça de Queiroz's masterpiece *The Maias.*

PATRICIA DUBRAVA has translated and published work by the Mexican poet Elsa Cross in a variety of journals, including *Tameme* and the White Pine anthology *These Are Not Sweet Girls: Poetry by Latin American Women.* Her translation of Rafael Courtoisie's short-story collection *El mar rojo (The Red Sea)* was published in 2004. Chapters from her translation of Courtoisie's novel *Caras extrañas (Strange Faces)* have appeared in *Two Lines* (2007), *Turnrow* (2008), and *Rhino* (Spring 2009). Dubrava has published two collections of poems, *Choosing the Moon* and *Holding the Light,* and teaches creative writing at Denver School of the Arts.

COLA FRANZEN is the translator of fifteen books of fiction, poetry, and criticism by, among others, Alicia Borinsky and Saúl Yurkievich (both born in Argentina), Juan Cameron (Chile), and Antonio José Ponte (Cuba). She lives in Cambridge, Massachusetts.

AMY SCHILDHOUSE GREENBERG has published more than one hundred stories, essays, interviews, and translations in magazines, newspapers, and anthologies in the United States and Mexico. She has lived in New York, Paris, and Mexico City, and since the 1990s has taught in the Artists-in-the-Schools program and for the Ohio Arts Council.

EDITH GROSSMAN was born in Philadelphia in 1936 and now lives in New York. She is noted for her translations of fiction by major Latin American authors, including Carlos Fuentes, Gabriel García Márquez, Jaime Manrique, Mayra Montero, Augusto Monterroso, Alvaro Mutis, Julián Ríos, and Mario Vargas Llosa. Her translation of Cervantes's *Don Quixote*, published in 2003, received wide critical acclaim. In 2006 she was awarded the PEN Ralph Manheim Medal for her body of work.

SEAN HIGGINS was born in New York in 1961. He received a B.A. in Latin American Studies from the University of California-Santa Cruz and an M.F.A. in Writing from the University of San Francisco. His translations of works by Latin American writers, including Cristina Peri Rossi, Arturo Arias, and Poli Délano, have been widely published in magazines and anthologies.

PSICHE HUGHES has published translations of works by Carmen Boullosa and Cristina Peri Rossi. She is the coauthor of the *Dictionary of Borges*.

ANDREW HURLEY has published translations of novels, short stories, essays, and poems, including the works of Cuban writers

Heberto Pedilla and Reinaldo Arenas. He is retired from the faculty of the University of Puerto Rico.

TOSHIYA KAMEI is the translator of *The Curse of Eve and Other Stories* (2008), by Mexican writer Liliana Blum. Other translations have appeared in the *Fairy Tale Review, Metamorphoses, Nimrod,* and *Words Without Borders,* and the anthology *The Global Game* (2008), among other publications.

CHRISTOPHER LELAND was born in Tulsa, Oklahoma, in 1951. A noted translator of stories by Luisa Valenzuela, he is also the author of five novels and three works of nonfiction, including *The Last Happy Men: The Generation of 1922, Fiction, and the Argentine Reality.* He is a professor in the English department at Wayne State University in Detroit.

ALBERTO MANGUEL was born in Buenos Aires in 1948 and became a Canadian citizen in 1985. He has lived in Israel, Argentina, Italy, and England, and now makes his home in France. He is an anthologist and translator, and contributes regularly to newspapers and magazines throughout the world. He is the author of five novels, including *Todos los hombres son mentirosos* and *News from a Foreign Country Came,* which won the McKitterick Prize (UK) and the Writers' Union of Canada Award for Fiction, and *Stevenson Under the Palm Trees,* as well as several works of nonfiction.

KIRK NESSET is the author of two books of short stories, *Paradise Road* (2007) and *Mr. Agreeable* (2009), as well as a nonfiction study, *The Stories of Raymond Carver.* His books of poems and translations, *St. X* and *Alphabet of the World,* are forthcoming. His awards include the Pushcart Prize and, in 2007, the Drue Heinz

Literature Prize. His stories, poems, and translations have appeared in the *Paris Review, American Poetry Review, Ploughshares, Southern Review, Kenyon Review, Gettysburg Review, Iowa Review, Agni, Sun, Prairie Schooner,* and elsewhere. He teaches creative writing and literature at Allegheny College.

LIZABETH PARAVISINI-GEBERT is the author of a number of books, among them *Phyllis Shand Allfrey: A Caribbean Life, Jamaica Kincaid: A Critical Companion, Creole Religions of the Caribbean,* with Margarite Fernández Olmos, and *Literatures of the Caribbean.* Her articles and literary translations have appeared in the *Journal of West Indian Literature, Callaloo, Jean Rhys Review, Journal of Caribbean Literature, Obsidian,* and *Revista Mexicana del Caribe,* among others. Since 1991 she has been a professor at Vassar.

MARGARET SAYERS PEDEN, professor emeritus of Spanish at the University of Missouri, has translated more than forty books by, among others, Laura Esquivel, Carlos Fuentes, Pablo Neruda, Octavio Paz, and Mario Vargas Llosa. Among her numerous awards and honors are the Gregory Kolovakas Award from PEN and fellowships from the National Endowment for the Arts and the National Endowment for the Humanities. In 1998, the Guadalajara International Book Fair, the American Literary Translators Association, and the University of Guadalajara recognized her for distinguished service to the arts.

ALASTAIR REID, born in Galloway, Scotland, in 1926, has lived in Spain, Switzerland, Greece, Morocco, Latin America, and the United States. A poet, essayist, film director, and translator of Latin American writers, he has published over forty books and served as a traveling correspondent for the *New Yorker* magazine.

SANDRA REYES is the prize-winning translator of the poems of Chilean poet Nicanor Parra and editor of *One More Stripe to the Tiger: A Selection of Contemporary Chilean Poetry and Fiction* and *Oblivion and Stone: A Selection of Contemporary Bolivian Poetry and Fiction*.

MARK SCHAFER has translated the prose and poetry of Eduardo Galeano, Jesús Gardea, Gloria Gervitz, David Huerta, Virgilio Piñera, Antonio José Ponte, and Alberto Ruy Sánchez, among others. He is also a widely exhibited visual artist. He lives in the Boston area.

KATHERINE SILVER is a translator, editor, teacher, and writer who has lived for long periods in Chile. She is the author of *Chile: A Traveler's Literary Companion* and has translated the works of Elena Poniatowska, José Emilio Pacheco, and Antonio Skármeta, including Skármeta's *Ardiente Paciencia (Burning Patience)*, which inspired the Academy-Award-winning film *Il Postino*, about Pablo Neruda.

DANIEL TUNNARD has a diploma in translation from the Institute of Linguistics, London. A writer and translator based in Buenos Aires, he is currently taking all the buses in Buenos Aires and writing a book about it. Read excerpts at danieltunnard.blogspot.com.

DAVID UNGER, born in Guatemala, is the author of the novel *Life in the Damn Tropics* and has translated eight novels and poetry collections from the Spanish, including Silvia Molina's *The Love You Promised Me*, which was short-listed for the IMPAC Prize. He is director of the Publishing Certificate Program at City College of New York and teaches translation in the Graduate Writing Program.

ABOUT THE EDITORS

RAY GONZALEZ is one of America's foremost authors, editors, and scholars of Latino literature. He is the author of three books that include flash or short-short fiction, *The Ghost of John Wayne, Circling the Tortilla Dragon,* and *The Religion of Hands,* and more than a dozen books of poetry and essays. His work has won numerous honors, such as the PEN/Josephine Miles Book Award, the Carr P. Collins/Texas Institute of Letters Award for Best Book of Nonfiction, and the Lifetime Achievement Award in Literature from the Border Regional Library Association. His writing has often been included in *Best American Poetry* and *Pushcart Prize: Best of the Small Presses.* He is the editor of twelve anthologies, is the founder of the journal *LUNA,* and has been poetry editor of the *Bloomsbury Review* for more than twenty-five years. He is a professor of English in the M.F.A. Creative Writing Program at the University of Minnesota in Minneapolis.

ROBERT SHAPARD has edited Norton's *Sudden Fiction* series and *Flash Fiction Forward*; with Josip Novakovich, *Stories in the Stepmother Tongue,* stories by writers who emigrated to the United States; and a number of literary magazines, among them *Manoa: A Pacific Journal of International Writing,* which he cofounded with Frank Stewart. He has taught literature and fiction writing at several universities, spending more than twenty years at the University of Hawaii, where he directed the writing program. As a fiction writer he has won awards from the National Endowment for the Arts and the Council of Literary Magazines and Presses; in 2005 his chapbook *Motel and Other Stories* won the Predator Press national competition in the short-short story.

JAMES THOMAS founded the Writers at Work conference in Park City, Utah. He has taught fiction writing at Bowling Green State University, the University of Utah, Baylor University, Wright State University, and Antioch University; among his many editing credits are the Norton *Flash Fiction*, *Sudden Fiction*, and *Best of the West* book series; and the literary magazine *Quarterly West*, which he founded. He is author of *Pictures, Moving*, a collection of stories, and has received two National Endowment for the Arts Fellowships, a Wallace Stegner Fellowship from Stanford University, and a James Michener Fellowship from the University of Iowa.

ACKNOWLEDGMENTS

Alarcón, Daniel: "The Visitor" from *War By Candlelight*. Copyright © 2005 by Daniel Alarcón. Reprinted by permission of HarperCollins Publishers.

Allende, Isabel: "Our Secret" from *The Stories of Eva Luna* by Isabel Allende, translated from the Spanish by Margaret Sayers Peden. Copyright © 1989 by Isabel Allende. English translation copyright © 1991 by Macmillan Publishing Company. All rights reserved. Reprinted with the permission of Scribner, a division of Simon & Schuster, Inc.

Alvarez, Lisa: "Cielito Lindo." Reprinted with the permission of the author.

Anaya, Rudolfo: "The Native Lawyer" from *Serfina's Stories*. Copyright © 2004 by Rudolfo Anaya. Published by University of New Mexico Press. By permission of Susan Bergholz Literary Services, New York, NY, and Lamy, NM. All rights reserved.

Arzola, Jorge Luis: "Essential Things," translated by Margaret Jull Costa. Appeared in *Grand Street* 71 (online 2003) and *New Sudden Fiction* 2007. Reprinted with the permission of the author and translator.

Benavidez, Jr., Fernando: "Montezuma My Revolver" from *Pindeldyboz*. Reprinted with the permission of the author.

Benedetti, Mario: "The Expression," translated by José Chaves from *The Café Irreal*, no. 9. Reprinted with the permission of the translator. "La expresión" copyright © Mario Benedetti Estate c/o Guillermo Schavelzon & Asociados, Agencia Literaria, info@schavelzon.com.

Bolaño, Roberto: "Phone Calls" from *Last Evenings on Earth* by Roberto Bolaño. Copyright © 2002 by Editorial Anagrama, translation

Cofer, Judith Ortíz: "Volar" from *The Latin Deli: Prose and Poetry.* Copyright © 1993 by Judith Ortiz Cofer. First published as a Norton paperback 1995. All rights reserved. Originally published by the University of Georgia Press.

Contreras, Hilma: "Hair," translated by Lizabeth Paravisini-Gebert, from *Green Cane and Juicy Flotsam: Short Stories by Caribbean Women,* edited by Carmen C. Esteves and Lizabeth Paravisini-Gebert. Copyright © 1991 by Rutgers, the State University. Reprinted by permission of Rutgers University Press.

Courtoisie, Rafael: "The Scribe" from *The Red Sea*, translated by Patricia Dubrava. Reprinted by permission of the author and translator.

Denevi, Marco: "The Lord of the Flies," translated by José Chaves, from *The Café Irreal*. Reprinted by permission of the translator. "El dios de las moscas" from *Falsificaciones* by Marco Denevi, Buenos Aires, Corregidor, 2005.

Díaz, Junot: "Alma." First published in *The New Yorker* and reprinted by permission of Junot Díaz and Aragi Inc.

Estrada, Josefina: "The Extravagant Behavior of the Naked Woman," translated by Margaret Jull Costa, from *Storm: New Writing from Mexico*. Reprinted with the permission of the translator.

Farias, Antonio: "Red Serpent Ceviche" from *Latino Bloom: An Anthology of U.S. Latino Literature*. Reprinted with the permission of the author.

Galeano, Eduardo: "Chronicle of the City of Havana," from *The Book of Embraces* by Eduardo Galeano, translated by Cedric Belfrage with Mark Schafer. Copyright © 1989 by Eduardo Galeano. English translation copyright © 1991 by Cedric Belfrage. Used by permission of the author and W. W. Norton & Company.

García Márquez, Gabriel: "Light Is Like Water" from *Strange Pilgrims: Twelve Stories*, translated by Edith Grossman. Copyright © 1993 by Gabriel García Márquez. Used by permission of Alfred A. Knopf, a division of Random House, Inc.

Gilb, Dagoberto: "Shout" from *Woodcuts of Women*. Copyright © 2001 by Dagoberto Gilb. Used by permission of Grove/Atlantic, Inc.

Gutierrez, Stephen D.: "Clownpants Molina" from *Latinos in Lotusland*, edited by Daniel A. Olivas, 2008, Bilingual Press/Editorial Bilingüe, Arizona State University, Tempe, Arizona.

Herrera, Juan Felipe: "How to Live with a Feminista and (Still) Be a Macho: Notes Unabridged" from *Muy Macho*. Reprinted with the permission of the author.

Jaramillo Levi, Enrique: "The Book without Covers" from *Duplications and Other Stories*, translated by Leland H. Chambers. Reprinted by the permission of Latin American Literary Review Press.

Lavín Cerda, Hernán: "The Eternal Dog," translated by José Chaves from *The Café Irreal*, no. 9. Reprinted with the permission of the author and translator.

Leis, Raúl: "Señor Noboa," translated by Leland H. Chambers, from *Contemporary Short Stories from Central America*, edited by Enrique Jaramillo Levi and Leland H. Chambers, pp. 236–37. Copyright © 1994. By permission of the University of Texas Press.

Lopez, Robert: "Asunder" from *New England Review* (2005). Reprinted with the permission of the author.

Martinez, Juan: "Customer Service at the Karaoke Don Quixote" first appeared in *McSweeney's* (December 7, 2000). Reprinted with the permission of the author.

Mastretta, Ángeles: "Aunt Chila" from *The Women with Big Eyes*, by Ángeles Mastretta, translated by Amy Schildhouse Greenberg. Copyright © 2003 by Ángeles Mastretta. Used by permission of Riverhead Books, an imprint of Penguin Group (USA) Inc.

Medina, Pablo: "Zapata" from *Exiled Memories: A Cuban Childhood*, by Pablo Medina. Copyright © 1990 by The University of Texas Press. Reprinted by permission of the publisher, Persea Books, Inc., New York.

Méndez, Lupe: "What Should Run in the Mind of Caballeros." Reprinted with the permission of the author.

Monterroso, Augusto: "The Eclipse" from *Complete Works & Other Stories*, by Augusto Monterroso, translated by Edith Grossman. Copyright © Augusto Monterroso. Permission to reprint the translation granted by the translator.

Muñoz, Manuel: "The Wooden Boat" and "Astilla" from *Zigzagger*, by Manuel Muñoz. Published by Northwestern University Press, 2003, Evanston, IL.

Naranjo, Carmen: "When New Flowers Bloomed," translated by Linda Britt, from *When New Flowers Bloomed: Short Stories by Women Writ-*

ers from Costa Rica and Panama, edited by Enrique Jaramillo Levi. Reprinted by the permission of Latin American Literary Review Press.

Olivas, Daniel A.: "La Guaca" from *Devil Talk*, by Daniel A. Olivas. Published by Bilingual Press/Editorial Bilingüe, Arizona State University, Tempe, AZ, 2004.

Ortega, Julio: "Migrations," first published in *The Art of Reading and Other Stories* (Wings Press, San Antonio, 2006). Used by permission.

Pacheco, José Emilio: "The Captive," translated by Katherine Silver, from *Battles in the Desert and Other Stories*. Copyright © 1981 by Ediciones Era, S.A., copyright © 1987 by Katherine Silver. Reprinted by permission of New Directions Publishing Corp.

Padilla, Ignacio: "Chronicles of the Second Plague" from *Antipodes*, by Ignacio Padilla, translated by Alastair Reid. Translation copyright © 2004 by Alastair Reid. Reprinted by permission of Farrar, Straus and Giroux, LLC.

Paz Soldán, Edmundo: "Counterfeit," translated by Kirk Nesset. Reprinted with the permission of the author and translator.

Peri Rossi, Cristina: "The Uprooted," translated by Sean Higgins, from *New World/New Words: Recent Writing from the Americas*. Reprinted with the permission of the author and translator.

Piñera, Virgilio: "Insomnia," translated by Alberto Manguel, from *Black Water: The Book of Fantastic Literature*. Copyright © Alberto Manguel c/o Guillermo Schavelzon & Asociados, Agencia Literaria, info@schavelzon .com. Permission to reprint granted by Agencia Literaria Latinoamericana.

Pizarnik, Alejandra: "Devotion," translated by José Chaves, from *The Café Irreal*, no. 9. Reprinted with the permission of Dr. Fabián Nesis and the translator.

Ponce, Pedro: "Victim" from *Double Room: A Journal of Prose Poetry and Flash Fiction*. Reprinted with the permission of the author.

Ponte, Antonio José: "In the Cold of the Malecón" from *In the Cold of the Malecón*. Copyright © 2000 by Antonio José Ponte. Translation copyright © 2000 by Cola Franzen and Dick Cluster. Reprinted by permission of City Lights Books.

Ramírez, Sergio: "The Centerfielder," translated by David Unger, from *The Picador Book of Latin American Stories*. Reprinted with the permission of the author and translator.

Rey Rosa, Rodrigo: "The Proof" from *Dust on Her Tongue*, by Rodrigo Rey Rosa, translated by Paul Bowles. Copyright © 1992 by Rodrigo Rey Rosa. Reprinted by permission of City Lights Books.

Reyna, Louis: "The Hitchhiker" from *Palabra: A Magazine of Chicano & Latino Literary Art*, no. 3 (Fall/Winter 2007–2008). Reprinted with the permission of the author.

Ríos, Alberto: "The Back of My Own Head in a Crowd" from *World Literature Today* (July–September 2003), pp. 61–62. Reprinted with the permission of the author.

Rivera, Tomás: "Eva and Daniel" from *Tomás Rivera: The Complete Works*, by Tomás Rivera. Copyright © 1965 Arte Publico Press–University of Houston. Reprinted with permission from the publisher.

Rodríguez, Alicita: "Imagining Bisbee" from *New Stories from the Southwest*. Reprinted with the permission of the author.

Saenz, Andrea: "Everyone's Abuelo Can't Have Ridden with Pancho Villa" from *Mississippi Review* (Spring 2006). Reprinted with the permission of the author.

Shua, Ana María: "Cannibals and Explorers," "Respect for Genres," and "Theologian" from *Quick Fix: udden Stories*, translated by Rhonda Dahl Buchanan. Translation copyright © 2008. Reprinted with the permission of White Pine Press, www.whitepine.org.

Suárez Araúz, Nicomedes: "Manuelito," translated by Sandra Reyes, from *Oblivion and Stone: A Selection of Contemporary Bolivian Poetry and Fiction*, edited by Sandra Reyes. Translation copyright © 1988 by Sandra Reyes. Reprinted with the permission of the author and the University of Arkansas Press, www.uapress.com.

Tafolla, Carmen: "Tía" from *The Holy Tortilla and a Pot of Beans: A Feast of Short Fiction* (Wings Press, San Antonio, 2008). Used by permission.

Urrea, Luís Alberto: "The White Girl" from *Latinos in Lotusland*, edited by Daniel A. Olivas, Bilingual Press/Editorial Bilingüe, Arizona State University, Tempe, AZ, 2008.

Valenzuela, Luisa: "Cat's Eye," translated by Christopher Leland, from *Open Door: Stories by Luisa Valenzuela*. Reprinted with the permission of the author and translator.

Veiga, Marisella: "Fresh Fruit" from *Latina: Women's Voices from the*

Borderlands, edited by Lillian Castillo-Speed. Reprinted with the permission of the author.

Venegas, Socorro: "Johnny Depp," translated by Toshiya Kamei. Reprinted with the permission of the author and translator.

Villanueva, Alma Luz: "People of the Dog" from *Weeping Woman: La Llorona and Other Stories*, by Alma Luz Villanueva. Bilingual Press/ Editorial Bilingüe, Arizona State University, Tempe, AZ, 1994.

Viramontes, Helena María: "Miss Clairol," first published in *Chicana Creativity & Criticism: New Frontiers in American Literature* (University of New Mexico Press, 1996). Copyright © 1996 by Helena María Viramontes. By permission of Stuart Bernstein Representation for Artists, New York. All rights reserved.